Comment
"Poppy in p

I loved this novel! It was all just so realistic and I loved that, and was heartbroken for Poppy. Once I started reading it, I genuinely did not want to stop. It's the sort of book that just carries you along with it and you feel like you are in the story and want to help/fight for Poppy. It's such an important story and one that will stay with me for a long, long time.

Katherine O'Herlihy, School Librarian

Poppy is so strong and brave and I loved the way her best friend helped her. I hope I could be a best friend like that.

Chloe age 15

I liked this book because although it is sad in places, it's really exciting. I like to think I could help any of my friends who were abused, like Kavya helped Poppy.

Jessica age 13

I would have loved to have read this book when I was younger, I would have realised that I wasn't alone.

Nic, a survivor of child sexual abuse

Sue's novel is engaging and gripping whilst also being informative about trauma. The more we are talking about abuse the more hope there is of change.

Jenny, a survivor of abuse

Sue does a brilliant job of showing us the world through Poppy's eyes. She takes a difficult subject and handles it with sensitivity, but never holds back on the far-reaching consequences of abuse.

Vicki Flippance

This is a sensitive and convincing portrait of a young girl navigating many challenges – including abuse from her stepfather. Although it is heavy subject matter, the story is told with empathy and insight. Poppy is an engaging young narrator, and the characters in her world come alive on the page.

Dorothy Dyer

Despite the horrendous challenges she is facing, Poppy is just like any other teenager. She cares deeply about her best friend and wonders whether the new boy fancies her. Sue really brings Poppy's world to life and has us all rooting for her by the end of the very first page.

Victoria Goode.

Other books

Some of the other books written by Sue Atkinson

Climbing out of depression, Lion Publishing

Building self-esteem, Lion Publishing

Pathways through depression, Lion Publishing

First steps out of depression, Lion Publishing

Supermaths, Hodder and Stoughton

Seven dizzy dragons, Cambridge University press

Breaking the chains of abuse, Lion Publishing

Struggling to forgive: moving on from trauma, Monarch

POPPY IN PIECES

Poppy in pieces

SUE ATKINSON

J Hogan (Times review

SVP

Dedication

This book is dedicated to all the people who have been abused. Remember, it was never ever your fault. All the shame belongs to the person who abused you.

About childline

If you have faced any kind of bullying or abuse, **Childline** is open 24 hours a day, 7 days a week. They say 'We're here for all young people.

0800 1111, calls are free in the UK.

You can talk to Childline confidentially about any worry or problem you have, or go online https://www.childline.org.uk/

and search our message boards to get feedback from other young people.'

Foreword

Notes to readers

A note from Dame Esther Rantzen who is the founder of Childline.

Dear Readers,

In this book you will find the story of Poppy, a young person who survives very tough times, and it also shows the support that Childline provides to all the young people who reach out for help or guidance.

Poppy tells her own story, and it reveals the strength we can unexpectedly find within ourselves to refuse to let suffering overwhelm us. It proves that, even if yesterday was painful, tomorrow can bring us hope and happiness.

Everyone's journey is unique, but many others would like to stand alongside you to provide support and guidance if you need it and reach out for help. At Childline we understand how difficult life can be, and how many challenges young people can face. If you, too, have endured difficult challenges, like Poppy, I hope this book will remind you of your own strength and resilience. And that you are not alone.

I send you my very best wishes,

Dame Esther Rantzen, Founder of Childline

A note from Sir Peter who is Chief Executive Officer of NSPCC.

Shockingly, 7 children in a classroom experience abuse before they turn 18. "Poppy in Pieces" tells the story of one young person, and highlights how vital it is that children and young people know that there are people who they can talk to, who will listen and understand.

Childline provides a safe space for children and young people to turn to, about anything big or small, 24 hours a day, 365 days a year. With the right help, children can get the protection they need to keep them safe and the support they need so that abuse doesn't shape their future.

Sir Peter Wanless

ISBN 9781916552029

First Printing, 2024

Chapter 1

Who am I?

Who am I? GCSE English holiday homework.

August 30th

I am no one.
You took me from myself
severed me with your sword
slicing me into pieces
that slipped away from me.

Barbie dolls and Lego
glittery strappy shoes
and party dresses
rainbows and sleepovers
lost in the shadows
my guts torn out
leaving me empty.

But each time you come for me
each time you invade me
my hatred grows
and one day
I will kill you.

But I'll go to prison if I kill him. So I won't.

Of course I won't! I'm not crazy. Or stupid.

Anyway, I can't give this to Mrs Campbell. She'd send me to School Shrink, a dusty woman who roams the corridors, smiling, sucking me in through her clenched teeth.

I put my secret diary down on the bed and hug my knees. This time next year I'll be starting sixth form, with Kavya. But only if I get good enough GCSE grades.

I'm never good enough.

I hold Angus, my teddy, to my face and wriggle to get more comfortable, shifting my pillow behind me, my shoulders scraping along the posters beside my bed. I still care about global warming. Of course I do. But the posters I put up years ago are old and torn. Kavya and I were on a mission to save the planet.

What did I know back then? Before I turned thirteen.

I still want to save the planet, but I can't even save myself at the moment.

I stare at my Monet poppy picture on the wall opposite my bed. I long to go into it. Lose myself in the field of bright red flowers. Leave this world and go into my own world where I am safe.

But I must finish the poem.

Who am I?

My mind is blank, so I text Kavya.

Poppy: Done English homework yet? xx
Kavya: Just doing it. Meet at park later?
Poppy: Can't mum out at work xx
Kavya: Ok. Hugs xx

It was a brilliant idea of Kavya's to put photos all over my mirror so that I don't have to look at myself. I focus onto the picture of little me clutching Gran's red sari, her face so full of peace and her long black hair in a plait that reaches to her waist. And I love the one of Kavya and me at the end of a 10k Race for Life, grinning because we ran the whole way in our pink Cancer Research vests. Kav fighting back tears because, despite all the treatment, her Mum had just died. Kav was so brave that day.

There's lots I could change in my bedroom, but I don't. I like my pink walls and duvet cover that I've had since Dad was with us. And the torn edges of the posters fit somehow. Mum wants me to upgrade it all. No way can I face that amount of change.

If I did change my room it would have to be white.

Virgin white.

Spotless.

August 31st tomorrow. My fifteenth birthday. I hate my birthdays.

Two years since the chaos in my life all started.

Must try to finish my English coursework today because I've still got all that physics to do. I pick up my secret diary and purple pen.

Who am I? Version 2

I am big sister
doggy ball thrower
poo picker-upper
breakfast maker
dutiful daughter
runner through fields
best friend hugger
laugher at jokes

babysitter
nappy changer
baby bather
robot maker
chocolate cake eater
unexploded grenade
pin puller.

If I take out the last two lines that'll do, and I can type it out on my laptop later. Mrs Campbell always says she likes my poems but everyone else thinks they're rubbish. Not Kavya, of course. But Mia says they're hopeless because they don't rhyme.

But I don't like rhyme. It's too tight.

Too dried up.

Too much what people expect. So not me at all. Except that I try to get top grades in everything.

Plan A. Get to uni with Kavya. But I'm getting too many 5 and 6 grades. That's not good enough. I've got to get more 8s and 9s if I'm going to get into uni.

I'm not good enough.

Chapter 2

Birthday girl

August 31st and my birthday. Kavya did our paper round for me this morning even though it was my turn to do it.

I do physics homework all morning then, after lunch, I pull my curtains to block out the summer heat and lie on my bed and stare at my poppy picture. I'm dreading the rest of the day because Mum's going out to work again tonight. I try to focus on my Miranda lines for the audition for parts in *The Tempest*. Five days before school starts.

But I can't focus on anything except the chaos in my head.

Life didn't used to be like this. I used to be good. Not any-more. Now secrets and lies eat up my insides. I thought if I were a kind person and worked hard, I'd get to uni and have an ordinary life...or maybe even an exceptional one. Be an engineer or a volcanologist or whatever and have friends. Go out to films and eat pizza and stuff like that.

Somehow that's not happening.

But I have Kavya. I shut my eyes, pretending I'm beside my best friend. If everything works out, we'll escape from home and go to the same uni together.

I lift my *Tempest* script again. Try to memorise my lines. I know I'm a good actor. I act every day just to survive. Not only will I be a brilliant Miranda in the play, I'll get an 8 or a 9 grade for English Lit next summer because I'll know the play so well.

It would be fab to get at least one 9 grade. Fancy me getting an old A star! I hope Mum would be impressed.

'Poppy! Come and help with the cake!'

Better go down straight away. Mum agreed to make me a chocolate cake, but it feels as if she's against me. Because of all my lying I suppose. So I must go into dutiful-daughter-and-kitchen-helper mode.

The bald stairs are hideous now Carl, stepfather from hell, has thrown away the carpet. The shiny varnished surface is slippery, and I must learn to get down them silently. It could save my life.

Or Zara's. Or JoJo's.

The third stair down squeaks on the left. So does the fifth one. And the ninth if you tread on the middle. And the last one is best avoided all together.

Biscuit sees me and skids on the hall floor, leaping up at me, her tongue licking my hand. 'Hello lovely girl,' I say as I kiss her head, burying my face in her white fur. She's my lifesaver.

'Come on, Poppy,' Mum says. 'Never mind your dog. I haven't got all day. I'm working tonight.' She sweeps her long black hair away from her eyes, her fingers making a chocolate smudge on her cheek.

'What shall I do?' Mum's pouring the chocolate mix into two tins.

I must keep her happy.

'Get going on the washing up,' Mum says, 'and put these eggshells in the food bin – and find the birthday candles. I think they're in that last drawer.' She points to the corner of the new kitchen. Everything is in different places since the old kitchen was ripped out.

I hate the new stark white cupboards and black granite work surface. It feels too cold and harsh.

I start clearing up and take a deep breath and risk asking again.

'Mum, please can I text Kavya and invite her to tea?'

'How many times do I have to say – no!'

'But it's my birthday and she's my best friend…'

'I just want it to be family. Surely you can understand that?'

We used to be a family. Before Dad left.

'I don't know why you can't be friends with a nice girl like Mia,' Mum says.

I say nothing. Nice girl isn't quite how I'd describe Mia these days.

'You're spending your birthday tea with your family,' Mum says. 'The people who love you the most.'

There's nothing I can say to that but I'm realising that Mum keeps dominating my life. And I need to tread carefully because Mia's mum and my mum have been friends since Mia and I were friends in primary school.

So many walking-on-eggs moments.

Mum puts the two cake tins in the new oven – shiny white of course. She sets the timer. 'Get them out when it rings. I'm going up to change.'

Once she's gone, I lick the bowl and wooden spoon like I used to when I was little. When Mum and I made cakes together with Zara, when we were still with Dad. I finish the washing up, dry everything, put it all away, hoping I'm putting things in the right place. Then I wipe all the surfaces so Mum will smile at me and say something kind.

But she doesn't come down again so I get the cakes out and tip them onto a cooling rack, wash the cake tins, then go back to my room. Time to do some more physics. I slog at it for an hour, glad I've got the study guide Mr Stevens recommended. Mostly physics makes no sense at all.

Forces. These are an invisible mystery.

Like feelings, full of catastrophic energy that push you around.

Then it's all too much and I want to cut myself, but I lie on my bed and space out instead. I focus again onto my Monet picture of the poppy field Dad bought me. I'm not me anymore. I'm in my picture, running through the poppy field, free, being little Amilee, laughing with the other children.

It's where I am safe.

Where I lose time...where I'm free to be someone else.

I stay in the poppy field, happy, playing.

'Poppy! Come down! Time for cake.' Mum will have done chocolate icing with fifteen pink candles. I want to stay safe inside my poppy picture, but I drag myself back to the present.

I can hear JoJo is back from our childminder next door and he and Zara are laughing.

I must pretend to be happy.

I practise getting down the stairs silently – stand on the shiny floor in the hall by the phone just for a moment while Biscuit leaps up at me and I cuddle her.

I know Carl is in the kitchen – probably doing his I'm-a-good-daddy thing with JoJo.

I take a deep breath, but his voice invades my head.

Even if you tell someone, they won't believe you.

'Poppy! Poppy!' JoJo bounces in his highchair and bangs his spoon on the black granite breakfast bar. I grin at my little brother.

'Hello beautiful boy.' I walk through the kitchen and kiss his ginger curls.

Carl brushes past me. Too close.

Feeling dazed I try to take a deep breath, but his voice still rattles around my head.

You will do as I say, when I say.

He and Mum have already started on a bottle of red wine.

Mum is lighting the candles. She smiles at me, and I smile back, and she leads the singing. 'Happy birthday to you...' Everyone sings like we're a normal happy family.

I sit on one of the new unstable bar stools and blow out the candles.

'Make a wish,' says Carl. So I do, feeling the bar stool wobble under me. Wondering if he might guess what I wish for. His small bald patch, that he tries to hide, catches the light from the ridiculous candelabra he had put up above the breakfast bar.

Mum takes one of the biggest knives from the new knife block. 'You cut it,' she says, so I grab the knife handle and stab the cake in the middle.

My heart thunders in my ears as the thought of being stabbed in the back cuts through me. I put the knife down.

'Please...Mum...you cut the rest.'

'Goodness me. What's got into you these days?' she says. She slugs some wine. 'You can't even cut slices of cake? Honestly, girl, pull yourself together.' She drains her glass and Carl reaches across the breakfast bar and pours her some more.

I do some deep breathing. Try to stop my hands trembling. I sit on the stool next to Zara, feeling it wobble. I don't dare look her in the face because I must hide so much from her.

'This is from me,' Zara says. She slides her gift across the black granite. I open the package carefully.

'Salted caramel fudge,' I say. 'My favourite. Thank you.' I hug her. She'll have to stop plaiting her hair like that now she's twelve. She looks like an eight-year-old kid. But actually that might be a good thing in this house.

'This is from your mum and me,' says Carl. He's smiling at me.

Trying to be a normal stepdad.

It's a card with money inside.

'A hundred pounds,' says Mum, all sparkly eyed. 'Carl is so kind to us.'

'Thank you so much,' I say, doing my I'm-grateful look.

Mum hands us all cake. JoJo squeals and picks up his slice and shoves it into his mouth with both hands. Most of it sticks to his face. Zara laughs and looks at me. We smile at each other, and I take a picture of our little brother on my phone.

I must keep Zara close.

'I know you'll spend the money sensibly,' says Carl. He reaches forward and taps the money with his sausage-fingers hand.

'Of course,' I say, smiling at him.

He smiles back, his sausage hand still on my money.

It'll go into my get-to-uni-and-get-out-of-South-London-for-good fund that he doesn't know anything about.

I wish Mum had let Kavya come for tea and cake.

'Once my shed is all sorted, we must get on with the robot, Poppy.' I look up at Carl. My words catch in my throat. I choke on my cake.

'I reckon we have a good chance at winning Robot Wars next year,' he says. 'You, me, Steve. A winning team. On TV as well.'

I try to say something, but my throat has shut.

'Poppy!' says Mum.

'Yes,' I manage to get out. 'Winning team. That's great, Carl.'

The cake is sickly sweet, and I take a swig of water.

'I have to get ready for work,' says Mum. She's already wearing her green top and trousers ready for a night shift at the vets. 'JoJo's had his tea, so he just needs a bath.'

'Of course,' I say. I know I can't voice my fear about how much of JoJo's care is done by others. Not Mum.

'And there's a casserole in the oven that'll be ready at six.'

'Yes, Mum.' It won't be one of Gran's recipes. Mum's stopped making me my favourite meals.

'I need to sign off with the men building my shed,' says Carl going out of the patio doors into the garden. His shed is enormous, and the men have taken days to build it. We had to get rid of our trampoline so the shed would fit in the garden. I miss bouncing on it after school with Zara, laughing together, JoJo begging for a turn so we lift him up and he loves it.

Loved it.

I bath JoJo and put him in his cot. Zara starts his music mobile, and he shoves his thumb in his mouth and shuts his eyes.

I envy his ability to fall asleep.

Zara chatters as we eat Mum's casserole. Her gym club has a display coming up. Carl nods as if he's interested.

'I can do a cartwheel on the beam now,' she says.

'You're amazing,' I say.

Zara and I load the dishwasher. My hands tremble.

Carl takes his wine through to the lounge and watches the seven o'clock news and I creep upstairs. I listen for him, knowing he's waiting till Zara is in her room.

I hug Angus my teddy and go into my poppy picture to try to feel safe.

Then I hear Carl come up the stairs.

I shudder.

Feel sick.

I'm not safe anywhere because I know he's coming for me.

Chapter 3

Haircut

I had a long shower last night to wash the awfulness away, so in the morning I'm out quickly to do the paper round. At last it's raining so I'm being washed clean again...and I love it. Hopefully that's the end of the summer scorching heat and the world feels fresh as I cycle around the streets. I dread the three minutes it takes to deliver to the two houses on Ashbury Road. I always feel I'm being watched. I can't handle this, so I cycle at top speed and shove the papers through the letter boxes. Then I'm gone.

Hopefully the Ashbury Road Gang don't even know who I am or where I live. My heart skips a beat at the thought of them coming to the playground in the park. When they do, Kavya and I shoot off quickly.

We keep a low profile, but I hate it that we all have to live with the fear of being stabbed. Kavya says I'm just being paranoid.

Often Carl is up when I get home but today, he isn't. No one is. So I lie on my bed where I can see all the photos covering my mirror. I look at Dad playing cricket in the park with me and Grandpa. I used to feel free back then but now it feels as if everyone is trying to control me. I feel under my pillow and hold onto the silk of Gran's favourite red sari that Mum let me keep. I miss Gran so much. If she hadn't died, she'd have helped me with Carl.

I need a plan.

But my brain is empty, so I sit up and take the band out of my ponytail and brush my hair. I've only ever had it trimmed because Kavya's Aunty Anjali said trimming it makes hair stronger and I suppose I wanted long black hair down to my waist like Gran had. It's an Indian thing, Gran used to say.

I look at my photo of Gran and Grandpa on the beach, the day he forgot to take a sun hat so he tied a handkerchief on his ginger hair, but he still got burnt on his face. He was such a funny and kind man.

I keep brushing, then the most stupendous, brilliant and amazing plan hits me.

Get my hair cut.

Short. Really short. Mega short!

It's not some cosmic law that women have long hair.

Mum would be mad at me and go on about my crowning glory, but I want to be me. Not an extension of her. And I don't want to conform, like it's a thing at school that long hair is in. Some people turn up with a different hair style every day, but Mia and her gang usually go for the long straight style – up in a ponytail when school demands that. Mia says that long straight is the best style, so her cronies tend to do as she does.

I don't think they dare say or do anything different.

I text Kavya.

Poppy: Have brilliant plan. Meet 10 am today at yours? xx

Kavya: What plan? xx

Poppy: Tell you when I see you xx

Kavya: Ok. 10am xx

I hear Mum come in from her night shift and come upstairs for a shower. I go down to make porridge for everyone with raisins and chopped apple. I hear JoJo wake, so I change him and put him in his highchair.

'Narna. Narna,' he shouts so I chop a banana into his porridge, loving the time being alone with him before anyone else comes down.

Then Carl is there, making coffee. 'Great porridge,' he says, 'thanks, Poppy.' He eats, gets his keys, and he's gone so I can breathe properly.

Mum comes down in her dressing gown. She's weary from her night shift so I make her black coffee and she sits on one of the wobbly bar stools and stares at her phone.

'You OK if I take Biscuit out?' I whisper to Zara.

'Yes. Course.'

We both look at Mum.

'I'll be fine,' Zara whispers. 'I can manage JoJo.'

I have time to do our usual route of twice round the lake in the country park and Biscuit does her favourite thing, chasing the squirrels in the patches of woodland.

When I get back, Zara has already taken JoJo next door to Mrs Bernstein, his minder, and Mum's asleep on the sofa.

When I leave to meet Kavya, Biscuit wants to come too. 'Later,' I say to her, but she still whines and looks sad.

I wish I could talk dog so I could explain.

Kavya's waiting by her front door that's between her aunty's salon, The Magical Hair Cut, and The Big Breakfast Café where Reggie and Kavya both work.

'What's this brilliant plan then,' says Kavya, as we both wave to Aunty Anjali in her salon.

We walk down the High Street towards the tram stop, the traffic so noisy I have to shout. 'What if we get our hair cut. Really short. Today.'

'What? Are you crazy? Aunty will go mental?'

'I'm fed up conforming Kav. Let's do it. I feel as if I'm being ordered around all the time. Do this. Do that. I want to do something for me that says I'm me.' I sense her hesitation. 'But you don't have to do it too.'

'We can't get it done at Aunty's salon,' she says. She'd ring your mum – and Aunty would tell me I'd regret it.'

'And will you regret it?' We stop and face each other.

'Nah. You're right,' says Kavya grinning at me. She takes hold of both my hands and spins me around, narrowly missing other people on the pavement. 'You're a genius, Poppy. That is exactly what we need to do. Be us.' She flings her arm around my shoulders. 'In three years we'll be off to uni anyway, then no one can tell us what to do.'

'Let's go into Croydon,' I say. 'There's that place in South End that says you don't need an appointment. I've got birthday money, so I'll pay.'

We're both giggling as we reach the tram stop, and I know I'm right about my hair. I have to be me.

The salon in Croydon has gaps so we get our cuts straight away. I love my cheeky pixie style and Kavya looks fabulous – like Mum's favourite newsreader, Naga someone. The hairdresser gives us cash for our long hair so we end up not having to pay anything.

Of course Mum goes ballistic when I get in.

'Your crowning glory! Gone!' she says. 'How could you do that? It looks hideous.' She pours herself some more wine. It's not even lunch time. 'Did Kavya's aunty do it?'

'No. We went to Croydon.'

'How dare you be so underhand like this,' she says. 'I know it was Kavya put you up to it. That girl!'

Please, God, don't let her take my phone off me. 'No, Mum, it was my idea, I just – '

'Go to your room. I don't want to look at you.'

I call Biscuit to come with me.

'Leave your dog here. I don't like her in your bedroom.'

Zara is at the top of the stairs listening. 'Poppy,' she whispers. 'It looks great. But why the hell did you do it? You knew it would make Mum angry.'

'She'll recover,' I whisper.

'Why can't you just be normal for once? Stop annoying her!'

I'm realising that Zara is angry.

'I'm not deliberately making her mad,' I say.

'Yes you are. Duh! Haircut. Why do you ruin everything?' she says. 'We have to keep Mum in a good mood.' Zara looks frightened and I hadn't expected that.

'I know that. Good mood. Mum.' I say, wishing somehow that I could make everything OK for Zara.

'She'll be mad at you for ages,' she says.

'S'pose so. But I'm old enough to choose how I have my hair.'

'Get in your room, Poppy!' Mum yells from the kitchen. Zara turns immediately and goes into her bedroom.

I sit at my desk, wondering if Mum might ground me, and I get the last of my holiday homework done. I slog at it. Check it all carefully. I must get 8s or 9s in everything so that I can escape.

Chapter 4

Mia and the Bitch Brigade

A text comes from Kavya.

Kavya: You ok? Finish caf shift 2pm Meet at playground? xx

Poppy: Don't know if I'm grounded xx

Kavya: Ok. 2pm if you can xx

Poppy: Ok xx

I heard Mum and Zara have lunch earlier, but Mum didn't call me down to join them – which was ok by me. But now my stomach is rumbling so I creep downstairs, hoping I can get a sandwich without Mum seeing me. I can hear her snoring in the lounge, an empty wine glass on the coffee table beside her. So I can't be grounded. And she hasn't taken my phone either, so I got away with the whole hair thing.

Just.

I make a cheese and marmite sandwich and pack snacks and drink in my backpack and leave home quickly. I have time to walk Biscuit round the country park before I meet Kavya. I eat my sandwich and enjoy the dampness in the air as Biscuit races in circles with a Jack Russell.

We walk past the drystone wall at the end of the churchyard, past the enormous yew tree that spreads its branches low over the grass. My hiding place where I disappear when things get too bad.

I wonder for the millionth time if today is the day I tell Kavya about Carl. I try to keep his voice out of my head, but it feels impossible.

No one will believe you.

Your mother will throw you out if you say a word.

I shudder. I know it's true that Mum won't believe me after all the lying I did. I was all over the place when I was bunking off school after Carl first started on me.

My thirteenth birthday. I try to swallow but can't and my inside surges with panic. I bend down and cuddle Biscuit until I feel calmer.

I reach the playground. There are only a few small children in the sandpit, with parents on the picnic benches nearby. I'm relieved no one from school is here. No one to shout at me. None of Reggie's annoying comments. No one to put me down. Tell me I'm worthless.

I know that already.

I tie Biscuit up to the fence. She hates it and whines, but I want to go on a swing and no dogs are allowed inside the playground. I'm keeping that doggy rule but ignoring the sign that says the play equipment is for under fifteens only. Now I'm fifteen and one day, I'm a rule breaker.

I don't think of myself as a rule breaker. But I suppose I was wrong to get my hair cut without asking Mum. But I'm not even a tiny bit sorry. I reach up and feel how short it is, loving the breeze on my neck and the sense of lightness inside me. I'm glad I did it, despite Mum's rage.

I push myself forward and back on the swing and space out. I'm with Dad and he's pushing me on the swings near our old house. The playground there was bigger with a better climbing frame and Dad was always laughing when he took me there, wearing his white cricket hat and being my perfect daddy.

Before Carl.

Biscuit barks and I snap back into the present. Check Biscuit's safe. I mustn't space out like that because someone could steal her.

I don't think I could live without her.

Mia and the Bitch Brigade are walking through the playground gate, silver cans of drink in their hands. Probably gin and tonic from the shop on the High Street. There's no gaggle of boys following them. Not since Jack dumped Mia – again.

Mia is tanned from her weeks in Spain and her eyes focus onto me. It's as if we have some weird magnetism between us, fatally being drawn to each other through hatred. Her courtiers are behind her, Isobel looking bronze and stunning after her time in Florida. Presumably they've come to celebrate Mia's sixteenth birthday today. I will never get used to the fact that she's a year older than me but we're in the same academic year.

In unison Mia's gang flick their long fair hair back. All of them with perfect make up, strappy tops and designer jeans.

Everything I'm not.

Oh God, why did you make the popular kids so mean? It's so odd that Mia seems to only want the world to see her as cool and powerful and as if she's not bothered about schoolwork. But she effortlessly gets more 7s and 8s than me and when we were friends in primary school, she was always the clever one. That annoys the hell out of me.

I hold my breath as the Bitch Brigade approach.

Mia grips onto the frame of the swing and towers over me, shifting her designer handbag further onto her shoulder. She has even more unbelievably expensive handbags than Mum has. 'Your hair looks ridiculous,' she says. 'And since Miranda would have long hair, it's clear that I'll get that part. Not you. So don't bother coming to the audition.'

She takes another swig of her drink. The courtiers do the same.

Clones.

I don't know what to say.

'Anyway,' Mia says, 'your skin is too dark. Miranda was European.' She inspects her purple nails.

I keep my face neutral but inside me I'm a mess of boiling mud. I tell myself that I'm proud that Gran was Indian.

'Happy birthday,' I say, keeping my voice steady. I glance up at her blue eyes, her face so stunning, yet also angular and fierce. 'Sweet sixteen, eh? I hope your party's good.'

Mia doesn't even smile. She just looks grim and annoyed.

I fake-beam at the courtiers, who don't smile back. They look ready for action – except Scarlet who's hanging back as always.

I mustn't show any fear. But blood is pounding in my ears.

'My party will be perfect,' Mia says as she swings around the pole she's holding. 'I don't invite nerds.' She flicks her hair back again and shifts her bag further onto her other shoulder.

'Parties aren't my thing,' I say. Mia and her parties are in a different world from mine.

'Nor is the audition your thing,' she says, 'and you wouldn't want anyone to get hurt, now would you?' Her voice is intrusive and dry, like a desert sandstorm that blows dirt into every part of your being.

'Meaning?' I say, trying to hide my trembling hands.

'The Nerd will find out. Won't she girls?'

The courtiers move around me, and I can't stop a sharp intake of breath as Flora and Isobel dagger-stare at me.

Mia studies her nails again, holding her hand out near my face.

The nails are pointed.

The courtiers smirk, then giggle behind their hands. Scarlet looks terrified. It's time she left Mia's gang.

Thoughts are crashing around my brain.

I need to escape.

I stand up. Mia and I are face to face. She has a hungry look that makes my knees feel weak.

What might she do? She grabs my arm and digs her nails into my flesh. I stare at her, not even flinching.

'Good afternoon, comrades.'

It's Reggie.

Mia lets go of me. Her gang spin around and I'm uncertain about whether the situation has just got better or a whole lot worse.

But Kavya is just behind Reggie, my stomach unclenches and I sit back down on the swing. Kav brushes past the Bitch Brigade and sits on the swing next to mine, runs her hand through her short black hair and then reaches out and holds my hand.

Reggie hovers. I watch him out of the corner of my eye. His gang is nothing like as violent as the Ashbury Road Gang, but Reggie and his gang are unpredictable. My fear of being stabbed in the back makes me tremble.

'I expect you were just leaving, Mia, weren't you?' says Kavya, her dark brown eyes huge and her get-lost-Mia face that she does so well making me want to laugh.

'It's the Lezzie,' Mia smirks at Kavya, 'whose hair is even more stupid.'

'Go away, Mia. You're boring everybody.' Kavya manages a huge yawn, then grins at me.

'I think Mia was encouraging Poppy to do her best at the audition to be Miranda,' Reggie says, touching his quiff. 'Weren't you Mia?' His face mocking as he grins at her.

'Losers,' Mia says, but a moment of uncertainty flashes across her face and I'm sure there's a fleeting look of fear. She turns and walks away, the courtiers following to their usual place to sit on the roundabout where they giggle and swig booze. Probably Mia knows she can't dominate Reggie like she does the rest of us. She almost certainly knows that his unpredictability means it's best to be cautious around him.

'You OK Poppy?'

'Yes, thanks Reggie,' I say.

Although I'm not.

I don't always understand Reggie but he and Kavya are friends so I try my best to keep in with him.

'I can beat them up if you want,' he says.

I grin back at him. He's such a thug. 'Appreciate the offer, Reggie, but no. Thanks, though.'

'Ok, see ya at the audition. I'm planning on being Stephano, the drunken gang leader.' He touches his quiff again and swaggers over to the climbing frame. Some of his gang are already there, beer cans open, laughing, getting glares from the parents.

'See?' says Kavya. 'Reggie looks out for you.'

She often tries to convince me of this.

'Mum's mad as hell at me about our hair,' I say as we continue to swing together. 'She says I've lost my crowning glory.'

There's a silence. We look at each other and then we're both laughing.

'Aunty said your mum rang her and complained but Aunty denied knowing anything about our plan.'

'Which is true,' I said. 'Anyway, I think at fifteen we are allowed to say how we want our hair.'

I stop swinging and dig into my backpack. 'Salted caramel fudge. Birthday present from Zara.' I unwrap it and we stand facing each other, eating.

'This is amazing,' she says, and she flings her arms around me. 'You ok about Mia?'

'Course.' But I'm not. Why is life so overwhelming?

'Let's get out of here,' I say. 'Let's go to the den and have a party for two. I've got Haribo sours, salt and vinegar crisps, and two water bottles filled with Ribena.' I reach out and hold her hand. 'Sorry Mum wouldn't let you come to tea yesterday.'

'I know I'm not her favourite,' Kavya says. 'Let's go and do all your Miranda speeches, word perfect.'

Biscuit leaps on me as I untie her, and we head for the den. We turn off the path by a clump of hawthorn trees and clamber into a fallen ancient oak tree. It must have been struck by lightning at some point because the inside of the trunk is black.

Somehow Carl is in my head.

It was all your fault.

For the millionth time I wonder if I could tell Kavya about Carl.

'Kav, I...well...I...'

'What?'

I try to swallow but my throat is too dry to let words out.

'What is it Poppy?'

'Oh...nothing.' Maybe it's all too heavy for her to bear.

I'm such a bad person.

'It is something. You can tell me.'

'Well...you see...'

But if I tell I'll pollute her with the awfulness. I might lose my best friend and I'd never have this pure space with Kavya ever again.

I try to calm my breathing.

'Show me the photo you took of JoJo eating the cake,' Kavya says, her arms around my shoulder.

I'm so hopeless.

'Course,' I say. 'He's talking so much more these days.' I show her JoJo's chocolate covered face on my phone.

Then I'm crying and Kavya has hold of me.

Tell her.

Tell her.

Don't you dare say a word.

Chapter 5

New boy Harry

It's Thursday after school and it's the auditions in ten minutes. I sneak down the noisy corridor towards the school hall, keeping a look out for the Bitch Brigade. Will Mia do an up-front attack or something more subtle to stop me going to the auditions?

Whatever she does I'll be ready. I've just got to get through the next couple of hours and get to be Miranda. Miss Singh said people could audition who don't usually come to Drama Club so someone brilliant could turn up and get Miranda. But it's probably between me and Mia. She likes to think she's better than me. But I'm better than her.

At least I used to be.

Before.

I tuck myself into a corner between lockers. Most people are streaming out of the main door, heading home.

No sign of the Bitch Brigade so I scurry to the next corner.

Being Miranda is the only way to survive this term. Being someone else and escaping from having to be me.

I keep thinking about new boy Harry. He sat down next to me in registration. OK, it was the only free seat, but as he sat down he smiled at me, all lopsided and gorgeous.

Thinking of him now makes my back tingle. He's so perfect with his white-boy floppy brown hair, green eyes and cute freckles.

I think he might come to the audition because I overheard him chatting to Mia.

Of course, she's got her talons into him already.

'Loser!' Mia comes from nowhere and barges into me. I stagger. Drop my bag. Reach out to steady myself on the wall.

'Go home,' Mia hisses in my ear. 'Or else.'

She kicks my backpack. Pens and pencils spew out.

Then she marches towards the hall, leaving the Bitch Brigade surrounding me.

'Go home,' says Flora, breathing minty breath over me. Her eyes are cold so I look away.

Isobel punches me in the back. 'Home. Now.'

Scarlet stays silent. It's time she let herself be who she really is.

I stare at my feet, motionless, until they leave.

I shove things back in my backpack.

It would be easier to go home. But I march down the corridor and pull open the hall door. A barrage of sound hits me with more than fifty people laughing and chatting, waiting for the auditions.

I slink in focusing on the September sun streaming through the huge open windows, making light patterns on the floor. I hear Mia's voice and see her heading for me.

What can I do?

Kavya, Jack and William are putting out the blue plastic chairs so I rush towards them, throw my arms around Kavya, breathe in her sweet lemony smell.

'Mia knows you'll be Miranda, not her,' Kavya whispers in my ear, 'so she's probably mad as hell.'

I sit and pull out my *Tempest* script from my bag.

'You don't need that!' says Kavya.

'Security blanket,' I say, risking a glance at the Bitch Brigade. Mia is leaning on the wall near the windows, designer bag hanging off her shoulders. The huge navy blue curtains billowing beside her.

She glances at me just for a moment. I attempt a glare back.

'Come on, girl,' says Kavya, bending down to hug me. 'I believe in you.'

I wish I believed in me.

No one will believe you.

Kavya moves off to help Jack and William with the chairs and I squeeze my eyes tight to shut the Carl monster out of my head.

You started it, you slut.

Images crash into my head, like some awful horror movie with scorpions crawling over my skin. Pain like a carving knife invades me, cutting me off from who I was.

Asking for it.

I'm gasping for breath.

If you say a word, it will destroy this family.

I try to find my way back to the present.

I'm in the school hall and the monster isn't here.

I focus onto Reggie and his gang fooling around on the stage. Crabbe and Goyle flinging their arms wide, shouting, brandishing imaginary swords. They've been Crabbe and Goyle ever since we read Harry Potter in English in Year 7 and the names have stuck.

Reggie's the ring master, staggering as if he's drunk. He's winding his gang up and they're laughing, worshipping him. He reaches up to touch his impossible brown quiff that he's had since primary school. Rumour has it he steals clear PVA glue from the art room to keep it in place. My wish to touch it grows daily.

I know I'm weird.

Kavya comes and sits next to me. She leans into me and whispers. 'New Harry's just arrived and he's at the back of the hall on the tiered seating. Alone.'

My face heats up, and I daren't turn around.

'It's OK to like him you know,' she says. She grasps my hand and looks distant. She never used to worry about not fancying boys but since Queen Bee Mia noticed, the taunts from the Bitch Brigade have been hard to ignore, calling us lezzies just because we're best friends. Not that Kavya cares. I'm so glad for her when she says, 'proud to be gay,' right back at the Bitch Brigade.

'But what if you fall in love,' I've asked her a few times.

'We still do plan A and go to uni in the same town,' she says whenever we talk about it, and then we hug. I think if she falls in love, somehow, she'd still include me and I love her for that.

We watch Mia and the courtiers amble to the back of the hall.

'Uh oh,' says Kavya, taking my arm. 'Mia's talking to Harry.'

I feel heavy. Kavya squeezes my hand.

The noise in the hall fades as Miss Singh walks in, her tiny slim figure so delicate, her jet black hair drawn back around her soft face and dark eyes. She's wearing her turquoise blouse again and her dragonfly brooch. She looks nervous and I smile at her.

Reggie's gang leap off the stage, still shouting and laughing.

'Health and safety everyone – we'll always, and only, use the steps each side of the stage to get on and off, please,' Miss Singh says in her clear voice. She told us once that she played Ophelia on stage in the West End. Wish I'd seen that.

Reggie grins and salutes her, still staggering. Could he actually be drunk?

I hope Miss Singh auditions the female parts first. I want to go home and curl up under my duvet and sink into my poppy picture.

'Right,' she calls out above the chatter, 'let's find our male stars first.' She wants the boys gone. Can't blame her but a shudder runs through my body. I need to endure at least another hour.

'Girls, remember I said you can audition for male parts as well if you want,' Miss Singh sits on a plastic chair and puts her clip board on her lap.

'Can boys be up for female parts too?' Reggie shouts, Crabbe and Goyle doubling up as if it's the joke of the century.

'Of course,' says Miss Singh.

'I really fancy being Miranda,' Reggie says. 'As long as I can have a stunning dress. But I guess I'd rather be Stephano. I've been practising being drunk all summer.' He touches his quiff again and we all laugh.

We know we must keep Reggie sweet.

Harry ambles forward to the chairs. Please don't sit too near me. Please sit right next to me. He sits down three rows in front of me. He had the chance to sit next to me, but he didn't.

Of course he didn't.

Is Harry sensitive? Does he write poetry? Or does he carry a knife like the Ashbury Road Gang? Which gang will drag him in? Probably Reggie's.

Mia follows Harry and she sits next to him. Harry smiles at her – he's gorgeous.

Mia's chatting to him and I know I could never do that. She's too far in front for me to hear what she's saying. I need to get away from them, so I grab my bag and move right to the back of the hall.

I space out, imagining me on the stage as Miranda...Mum hugging me because I've been so brilliant...

...Then I'm running a cross country race, winning by miles...

Must stay in the present.

I focus onto Enzo dancing on the stage with a few young Year 7 boys and girls. Enzo does amazing balletic moves as always. The Year 7 kids must know they don't stand a chance to be Ariel the Spirit up against him.

'Come forward all those wanting to try for the part of Ferdinand,' Miss Singh says.

Harry stands up, holding a script and walks onto the stage with four others. The thought of Harry playing opposite me, falling in love with me as Miranda, sends shivers through my body and I have to space out with Dad on the boat...

...One day he'll come and rescue me...

The Bitch Brigade keep turning and looking at me. Even at this distance I can see their eyes blazing hate as they sweep back their impossibly blonde hair and slither towards me.

My brain says 'escape,' but...

I stand up. Lock eyes with Mia.

She tosses her hair over her shoulder. 'So, Crater Face,' she hisses, 'I'm going to be Miranda. Not you.' She pushes her face right up to mine. 'So you need to leave right now.' She stabs me in the chest with a pointed nail.

I take a step back, but the courtiers surround me.

'Leave right now,' Mia says.

I sling my backpack onto my shoulder, then dodge between Isobel and Flora and run to where Miss Singh is sitting. I slide onto a plastic chair next but one to her.

She looks up from her clipboard and smiles.

I know the Bitch Brigade will give me hell this term, but I don't care.

Defying Mia feels good.

Harry and some others get off the stage, get their bags and leave. He doesn't even glance at me.

But what if Mia gets Miranda?

She'll get Harry.

My body heats up with shame at the memory of Nightmare Nativity play back in Year 3. Mia won the starring role that time. I intend to win this time. But I shouldn't have done what I did.

Xavier's doing his audition. It's obvious he'll be the star of the play and get the main part of Prospero. He's striding across the stage, banging the stick he brought with him. Man of magic. Miranda's father.

He'll get into drama college definitely, but Mum won't even let me apply. She says, 'get a proper job,' so I'll work hard, be an engineer. Acting will have to fit in around my brilliant career building robots. Or I'll be a volcanologist, working out when eruptions are going to happen.

'Those who want to try for Miranda up next,' says Miss Singh, so I get up.

Xavier marches down the stairs off the stage, still leaning on his stick, no emotion on his face when he's not playing a part, but his dark eyes intense as always. He freaks me out with the look, the silence, the refusal to engage.

'You know Shakespeare intended the play to be an allegory about God controlling the world, don't you?' he says as I pass him. 'And I'm God, so watch it.'

Xavier spoke to me.

And people call me weird!

Mia is just behind me as we climb onto the stage.

I must get Miranda because I can't cope being me.

Chapter 6

Lies

I jolt awake, the image of Carl in my head, his face red, his mouth open and yelling.

You'll never be good enough.

I do the deep breathing that School Shrink taught us all in Year 7. In for five, out for nine. It's tough to do that, but I want Carl out of my head.

Sleep wouldn't come last night because I kept thinking I could have done the audition better.

Should have done better.

I don't know how to face this term if I messed up and don't get Miranda. Especially if Mia gets the part. It would become a long slow drag until the performances in December.

Maybe Miss Singh will put up the list of who's got which part today?

It's Kavya's morning to do the paper round and my heart skips a beat at her having to go into Ashbury Road Gang territory.

Mum's driving me crazy with her over-the-top questioning. She's so suspicious of me, but I don't know why. Unless she knows what Carl's doing to me.

I shut that thought out and prop up my head with my hands so I can see my photos covering my mirror. I love that one of me standing next to Gran at Mum and Carl's wedding. I'm wearing a lilac bridesmaid dress and I'm holding onto Gran's new golden sari. I miss Gran so much. She'd have helped me with Carl.

My special countdown calendar to Zara's birthday is next to my mirror. She's thirteen on 31st December. One hundred and ten days to go.

I tell myself I could get rid of Carl by her birthday. You have to have aims in life Miss Singh told us in religious studies. So, it's my aim to make Carl leave.

But I don't have the slightest clue how to do that, so I drift off with Dad, down the river, him rowing, laughing, both of us so happy.

'Poppy, get up,' Mum calls. 'Come on darling. You don't want to be late.'

She'll have made me porridge, so I'd better get up.

Soon.

I hear Zara come upstairs and go into the bathroom. She'll be doing her deep cleansing routine that Mum taught us.

'Look after your skin,' Mum had said. 'That's the way not to be left an old maid,' and other old-fashioned stuff like that. I gave up the routine because showering at night is enough. More than that is obsessive.

Like me when I take long showers to wash the monster off my body. But it can't be healthy that my twelve-year-old sister is neurotic about getting blackheads.

My phone says I must get up in three minutes to give me time to walk to school.

'Poppy! Come on!'

I crawl out of bed and inspect the scars on my arm. I promise myself no more cutting.

I tell myself that every morning. But the craft knife I stole from Carl's tool kit is hidden under my bed. And I intend to keep it there.

I scoop up my pile of clothes from the floor and dress quickly.

'Poppy!'

'Coming!' I grab my school backpack and get down the stairs, practising again to do it silently.

I know the CCTV camera above the stairs is filming me. So is the one on the hall ceiling. Carl clearly has a secret plan to control and spy on us. I complained about this but Mum went crazy and threatened me with no pocket money for a month.

So I shut up about it. She goes over the top if I'm negative about Carl.

Biscuit leaps on me as I go into the kitchen, and I kneel down and cuddle her.

'Morning, Poppy.' Carl's sitting at the breakfast bar. He swigs his coffee.

'Morning,' I mutter.

'Poppy!' JoJo shrieks at me and bounces dangerously in his highchair. I kiss his ginger curls.

'I don't understand why you're so late getting up some mornings,' Mum says.

What can I possibly say to that?

I don't belong here.

She puts a bowl of porridge on the breakfast bar, and I sit on one of the new bar stools.

'Thanks, Mum.'

I loathe these kitchen stools. I never know when they're going to unbalance me.

Carl crunches his toast and I shudder. I glance at him and he's watching me.

You were asking for it.

I can't survive this term if I can't be Miranda. It's agony having to wait to find out.

I reach out for Dad's hand. He's rowing me down the river, and...

'Earth to Poppy.'

'What?'

'You're in a dream again, Poppy. Honestly. I don't know what's wrong with you.' Mum glares at me. 'So do you mean it's OK for me to go?' she says to Carl.

'Of course. Book yourself into that clinic,' he says to Mum. 'You get whatever – facelift – anything. Go for a couple of nights and I'll manage the kids. I'll pay so just get whatever you want done.'

'Thanks,' says Mum. 'You're so good to us all.'

'But you're gorgeous just the way you are,' Carl says. Mum grins. He looks at me for a moment and my insides burn.

He puts his plate by the sink. 'And in a few weeks Steve and I might go on another long golfing weekend to Spain.'

'That sounds good,' Mum says, but I'm sure I see a moment of anxiety on her face. Carl and his work partner, Steve, have only just come back from Spain.

Zara comes back into the kitchen, immaculate, hair in a neat ponytail.

'Look at you,' Carl says. He puts his arm around her. 'Just a few months from being a teenager.'

I freeze.

Carl's smiling at Zara and she's smiling back.

She's so innocent.

I can't swallow the porridge in my mouth, so I quietly spit it out.

'See you all as usual about six thirty,' he says. 'Maybe tonight you could help me with the robot again, Poppy?'

I wobble on the unstable stool and feel maggots crawling up to my throat.

'Poppy?' he says. His blue eyes pierce into me and my stomach lurches.

Mum glares at me but I can't get any words out.

'Well,' Carl says, 'have a good day anyway, Poppy.'

'Bye-bye, JoJo,' Carl says, waving.

'Dada,' JoJo squeals, banging his spoon.

Mum and Carl kiss and I hear him walk down the new solid wood hall floor and pick up his keys from the little table. What's different now is that we don't hear the roar as his Porsche starts up because he bought a new one, bright red, and it's electric. I was impressed he chose to make that change away from petrol. Sleazy Steve, of course, bought a new petrol one. They both made loads of money at their firm with some special robot that sold all over the world.

'Brush your hair,' Mum says, handing me the brush from the drawer. 'Look at you!'

I love my new impish style – I brush for a few seconds to stop it sticking up.

I love it sticking up, but Mum goes crazy. She's still furious with me about the haircut.

Zara goes to do her flute practice in the lounge, and I kiss JoJo's curls, loving the softness of them on my lips and his damp baby smell. But there's porridge in his hair and his spoon jabs into my blazer.

'Careful, you little terror!' I wipe my sleeve with the dish cloth, loving his wide grin.

'Poppy!' he yells, bouncing in his chair, his bowl bumping up and down.

'See you tonight gorgeous boy,' I say. I shove a piece of toast into my mouth and try to get out of the door before the Daily Inquisition.

'Why don't you wait for your sister?' Mum says.

'Mum, we've got totally different friends. We're different people. Different...ideas.'

'You could walk with her to school, surely?'

I don't quite know how to tell Mum that Zara doesn't want to be with School Nerd and Social Outcast.

Maybe if I'm Miranda that might change?

'Got something I must do before school, at school,' I lie. I hear Gran's voice telling me that all the lying will come back to bite me one day. 'Anyway, Zara's been at high school for a year now. She doesn't need me.'

I shoulder my backpack and leave.

'Brush your teeth,' Mum shouts, but I ignore her.

I must keep Zara close.

Nearly a teenager.

It's a lie that she doesn't need me.

She does.

Chapter 7

Parts for The Tempest

I waited anxiously all week then, yesterday, Miss Singh told us that the parts for *The Tempest* would be on the Drama Club notice board in the morning. I have a bad night, Mia's face in my head and I keep waking up. If Mia gets Miranda, she'll be impossible all term.

Carl is up early today and is managing breakfast, so I cuddle Biscuit then leave home and walk the long way through the country park to calm myself. Mia will just have to learn to live with it if I'm Miranda and she isn't.

I kick up the autumn leaves, remembering how much I used to love doing that with Zara when we were younger.

Before.

Before my life went into meltdown.

I walk around the country park until it's time for school. The entrance hall is busy as I walk through the main doors. I feel dizzy and have to steady myself and walk slowly.

The Year 7s who tried for the part of Ariel the Spirit are playing a chasing game, dodging around the jungle of huge pot plants that appeared last time the school inspectors came.

The Year 7 kids smile at me. The fact that I'm Social Outcast doesn't seem to have reached them.

Yet.

Enzo and Noah come through the main door, and they join the group clustered around the Drama Club notice board.

Miss Singh walks down the stairs from the staff room. She's so stunning in her rainbow skirt and her red top.

I walk next to her, and we trade smiles.

'Well done, Poppy,' she whispers.

My heart leaps. Does she mean I'm Miranda?

The crowd part to let Miss Singh reach the notice board and she pins up the list. 'Rehearsals after school tomorrow, everyone.' And she's gone.

I hardly dare look at the list, so hover behind the group and see Reggie and Kavya come through the main door, walking together towards me. Reggie pats his quiff. I don't understand their friendship. They're definitely not going out. I think they're close just because they live next door to each other, but it's the only thing that Kavya clams up about.

I wish she wouldn't.

She smiles and runs towards me, her arms outstretched, and we hug.

'Well?' she whispers in my ear.

'Haven't seen the list yet.' But I know I'm grinning.

'Shall I shove to the front and read it?' she says.

'I'll do that,' says Reggie and he barges to the front with Crabbe and Goyle. 'Ladies and gentlemen,' Reggie says, 'I'm Stephano. Of course. Gang leader supreme.'

Mia and the Bitch Brigade come towards us down the corridor.

'Ooh, Mia,' Reggie calls to her, his voice high pitched and snarky, 'You're a Spirit, but, wow! Wait for it! Poppy is Miranda and Mia is her understudy. Hah! I can't see that working!'

I daren't look at Mia.

'I'm the geek's understudy!' She's angry.

'That's not fair,' says Isobel.

'I'm better than her.' Mia flicks her hair over her shoulder, and they move into a little huddle. I can sense their rage.

Reggie looks at me and does a thumbs up and for a moment he smiles.

'See? Reggie's pleased,' says Kavya.

'Wasn't it weird that he fancied being Miranda?' I say.

'Don't go there,' Kavya replies, her voice sharp and insistent.

I'm Miranda. Miss Singh chose me. I love you, Miss Singh.

'Who's Caliban?' Kavya calls to Reggie.

'I am,' says Noah, 'because inside me is a monster trying to get out.' His steel grey eyes looking me up and down.

Breathe. Someone had to play the monster. Better that it's Noah on the edge of Reggie's gang and not Crabbe or Goyle. They've been whispering and laughing at me ever since Miss Singh told us Caliban tried to rape Miranda before the opening scene of the play.

It almost made me wonder if I really wanted to be Miranda. I look at my feet and wish I still had my long hair so I could hide behind it.

You're nothing. Useless. Hopeless.

I'm never going to get Carl's voice out of my head.

'Oh, Noah, you'll make a great Caliban,' Kavya says. 'Plenty of make-up...or I'll make you a mask...ugly as hell.' Noah pulls a face at me, running his tongue around his mouth. He's disgusting. My tummy leaps and I look away, blinking back tears.

Mia pushes through the crowd and reads the cast list. Then she edges towards me, a different designer handbag hanging off her shoulder today, the courtiers surrounding her.

'Congratulations Poppy, I'm sure you'll be brilliant,' Mia says loudly, then she puts her face right up to mine.

'Stupid slut,' she hisses. 'Just because the bitch drama teacher made you Miranda, doesn't mean you'll end up doing all the performances, or – come to think about it – any of them.'

'Grow up, Mia,' Kavya says. 'Why must you always behave like a spoilt eight-year-old? Oh, I know – because you are one.'

'Drop dead, Lezzie,' Mia spits back.

Then she stops abruptly. 'Harry!' she says. 'Well done. You're Ferdinand.' She walks towards Harry and takes his arm. He sweeps his hair from his forehead, searching out the cast notice.

Harry is Ferdinand.

Bubbles run down my spine.

Rehearsing with him.

'Harry, you'll find me so much easier to work with than Poppy,' Mia says, smirking at me. 'I'm, shall we say, more flexible. More in the real world. Less of a nerd, to put it politely.'

Kavya squeezes my hand.

Harry's face shows nothing, and he glances at me. But then there's a twitch of his lips. He raises his eyebrows.

At me.

I put my hand on the wall to steady myself.

Harry and I have to fall in love in front of everyone. On the stage.

Oh God.

Nightmare.

Delicious.

Hideous.

Wonderful.

'We'll get to rehearse together,' says Mia, still clinging on to Harry. She looks at me, her face telling me Harry is hers.

I walk away, Kavya following.

'See you later,' I say, words firing out of me like bullets. I stride down the corridor to registration, my head spinning, Kavya trying to keep up with me.

I know Harry will like Mia better with her shampoo advert hair and big boobs.

'You're Miranda, so don't let her intimidate you.' Kavya hugs me and I melt into her.'You said all summer you wanted that part, and you did it!'

'I also said I'd stand up to Mia. Like I used to be able to.'

Before.

It was easy to feel brave and determined as we sat on the swings at the park back in August. But now a sense of unease settles in my bones. But I'm not going to get dragged into Mia's bitchy games.

Mr Robins is already in our tutor room and Reggie comes in, doing his drunken Stephano-the-gang-leader act, people around him laughing and cheering.

'This drunkenness is from experience then, is it, Reggie?' Mr Robins is smiling and running his hand through his neat black beard, his painting apron spattered with multicolour blobs of paint and the red brown stain of clay.

'Yes. It's beer. Beer and me are great friends,' says Reggie, staggering, his laugh infectious. Enzo and Noah around him, laughing and clapping. Crabbe and Goyle on guard.

'Well done, Poppy,' Mr Robins says. I smile back at him.

'And Harry,' says Mr Robins, as Harry glides through the door, Mia still hanging on with her talons showing. 'Well done. Great start to your new school.'

'Harry, mate,' says Reggie shoving Mia out of the way. 'Come and sit with us at lunch.'

I hold my breath. I don't want Harry to join Reggie's gang, but I don't want him in Mia's grip either.

Everyone watches Harry.

'Got to catch up with work lunch time,' he says. 'Who'd move house for Year 11 eh? Exams in eight months...as my parents tell me...every day.' And he slides into the chair next to me. He smells of laundry detergent and springtime, and my heart races.

'OK everyone. Settle down.' Mr Robins moves to his desk.

Reggie mutters.

Crabbe and Goyle frown.

Mia stalks to the back row with the courtiers.

Harry's at his desk one side of me. Kavya on the other.

I make no attempt to hide the grin on my face.

I glance up at Mr. Robins and he's grinning too.

Chapter 8

Miranda!

'I got Miranda.' I dump my bag on the kitchen floor. I still find the new white kitchen tiles disconcertingly shiny and cold. Biscuit skids on them as she greets me, her claws clacking, her tongue out, licking me, and her tail wagging. I go and get the floor cloth before Mum tells me off for Biscuit's muddy pawprints by her dog flap.

I said it was stupid to have a white floor, but no one listened to me.

'What?' says Mum. She's sitting at the black breakfast bar watching her iPad, sipping her tea – some concoction with turmeric and cinnamon, meant to do something miraculous.

There's an empty wine glass too.

'Miranda, Mum. I got the part of Miranda...you know...what I rehearsed all summer.'

'Did you?' she says and takes another swig of her tea. 'Oh, yes. Oh darling, how wonderful. But I don't want you spending too much time on that. Work comes first.'

I know that. But I must be Miranda too. I feel myself heat up at the thought of rehearsing with Harry.

I bend down and snuggle my face into Biscuit's fur.

'Mia's my understudy.' I swallow. I dare not say anything negative about Mia. Our mums being friends – which is a nightmare.

'Mia? Lovely looking girl. Great skin. Cheek bones to die for.' She pats her own cheeks.

'The play is on in December. You'll come, won't you?'

'Oh. Um...Course I will. Now, I'm on late shift tonight. Hope that dratted squally cat we had in on Monday's gone home. Yowled all night. Casserole's in the oven. Should be ready at six thirty.' She gets up and runs her hand along the length of the stark white range cooker. 'Carl's so good to us, isn't he? New everything. He always said he'd make a million. But you must be more grateful, Poppy. He gives me a hard time when you behave so badly.'

I didn't know that. My knees feel weak, and I take hold of the breakfast bar. 'Sorry...so sorry, Mum, I'll try to be grateful.'

Carl gives Mum a hard time because of me? I struggle to breathe. In for five. Out for nine. I sink into being Miranda, free on my island.

'Give JoJo his tea at five. Cheesy pasta. Bath at six.'

I snap back into the present. 'Mum! I have homework.'

'I know darling, but I have to get to work. You think it's easy being a veterinary nurse? Surely you can do a few things to support me after all I do for you?'

If she didn't frown at me so much, she wouldn't need to spend so much on Botox to fill in all the lines on her face.

'I know, Mum. Course I'll feed JoJo.'

'Don't let him have any more little oranges,' she says, tipping the rest of her tea in the sink. 'And make sure you put one of the bigger nappies on for the night.'

'Yes, Mum.'

'Carl and Steve are in the garden painting the shed.'

I try to swallow but I panic because I can't – how will I cope with Steve's leery glares?

'Carl says he's almost perfected the robot. And he'll be in later after he's finished sorting his stuff in the shed.'

I bend down to Biscuit again and breathe in her doggy smell. That makes me feel safe.

'So, keep Carl in a good mood tonight, my girl. None of your rudeness. OK?'

Rudeness!

'I mean it, Poppy. Please keep him in a good mood.' It's hard to read Mum's face but I think she's a bit frightened of Carl. I hate him for giving Mum a hard time.

I wish I could tell Mum about him. But I just can't.

She won't believe you, because you're a liar.

I know it was all my fault. I feel so dirty. And even if Mum did believe me and she told Carl to leave, how would we manage just on Mum's part-time salary?

I don't even want to think about it.

'Poppy!' says JoJo, pushing open the kitchen door and brandishing a red truck. His plump face smeared with chocolate.

'Give me a hug, beautiful boy.' I sweep him into my arms. He smashes his truck on my head and giggles. 'Hey!'

'We've been playing fire engines,' says Zara, striding over to the cupboards. 'I'm thirsty.'

Could I tell Mum about Carl?

I'll tell her you led me on and she'll believe me.

'D'you want some?' Zara holds up the bottle of blackcurrant squash.

'Yes, please.' I flick a switch in my brain to shut Carl's voice out.

But it doesn't work.

Focus on the squash. Focus on the squash.

I know I should give up sugary drinks because of gargantuan spots that erupt like volcanoes on my face. Zara always makes the blackcurrant far too strong but I both want the sugar but hate it at the same time.

I watch Zara, knowing I feel jealous of her poise. Her confidence. But I suppose I was like that when I was twelve. It's good that her boobs haven't started growing yet so she still looks like a little girl.

Mum leaves.

Could I tell Mum one day? I'd need to catch her in a good mood.

Don't you dare say a word or I'll do something your family will never recover from. And it will all be your fault.

I get my *Tempest* script out and sit at the breakfast bar. Zara and JoJo are watching Peppa Pig on the television in the lounge. Zara's so good with him.

Must learn my speeches so I never make a mistake. Miss Singh will like that.

'U will b rubbish as Miranda' flashes up on my phone from someone called Sexygirl. Could be Mia. Could be Isobel, or Flora.

I can't focus on Miranda's words.

It's the three of us alone with Carl in the house again tonight. Hopefully he'll be in a good mood if the robot building is going well. I used to enjoy helping him.

Before.

I hope he won't come for me tonight.

My whole body surges and it feels as if my heart will burst out of my chest. I try to calm my breathing.

I stretch my hand along the kitchen counter to the vicious square corner. I tried pointing out that these will be exactly at JoJo's head height in a few months time. I flinch, remembering Mum's venom.

'Don't say a single word,' she hissed. 'We must be grateful to Carl.'

I freeze again at the memory.

I must be grateful to Carl.

Chapter 9

Who is Miranda?

Miss Singh calls me over to her at the end of a rehearsal in the hall. Everyone else is grabbing their bags and going home and I wonder what I've done wrong. I weave through the lines of blue plastic chairs towards her. I want her to like me.

'Poppy, I just wanted to ask you about the speech in Act 1 Scene 2 that starts: *Abhorred slave* – this one.' She points it out on her script. 'It's just after Prospero's lines where we learn Caliban tried to rape Miranda.'

'Yes, Miss. I've learned that speech.'

'Do you have a moment just to talk about it?'

'Yes. OK.' I'm wondering where this is going.

'It's difficult to talk about rape, I know,' she says, and I feel my insides freeze.

'We just need to think through how Miranda might respond to Caliban's attempted rape, so are you really OK just to talk about it?'

'I'm fine about talking about it,' I say. Though I'm not, and I feel as if my knees might give way.

'Lots of Shakespeare is open to different interpretations,' she says, 'and what I want you to think about is whether you want to play Miranda as fierce and determined – so she would be able to say that quite aggressive speech? Or is she much more of a child? Some scholars think the speech should really belong to her father, Prospero.'

'Oh,' I say. 'But I thought it was my speech – telling Caliban off.'

'Yes,' she says. 'It could be yours. It depends how you want to play Miranda. Is she strong and mature? Or is she still a little girl? Does that make sense?'

'Er...yes.'

'Are you OK, Poppy?' She's staring at me, her eyes kind and caring. 'Have I upset you?'

I snatch in a breath. 'No.'

'Let's both sit down for a moment.'

I sit facing her.

'Are you upset?' she says, reaching a hand out and resting it on my arm just for a moment, 'because you've already learned the speech?'

'No. I'm not upset at all.' What is she seeing in me? I try to make my face blank. Unreadable. I know I'm good at acting as if I'm not upset.

'OK. So, Poppy, can you take a couple of days to get more into Miranda's head? Come and find me if you want to talk about it again. Think – is Miranda still a child that may not even have understood what Caliban was trying to do to her? Or is she bold and forthright and would be able to tell Caliban off in that speech? Think about it and we'll meet up with Xavier in a couple of days. It was Xavier who raised this issue with me.'

So Xavier fancied doing one of my speeches. That's actually what is going on.

'Thanks, Miss,' I say, though I'm not sure why I'm thanking her. We both get up and I shoulder my backpack and walk out of the hall. She is the nicest teacher in the universe.

Xavier manages to look unbothered by anything, but he clearly wants to be the big star of the play. I suppose like lots of the boys, he's confident. And that speech is a good one because you have to say it with passion. You can visualise the applause and your Oscar as you say it.

I think about what Miss Singh said but I don't know what to decide. How am I going to play Miranda? I don't know. How am I going to play you? Are you strong? Or feeble like me?

Why is life always so difficult? Please God, why is everything about being alive so complicated?

Two days later, school has just finished, and I make my way to Miss Singh's religious studies room where she asked me to meet with her and Xavier. The air in the classroom is hot and stifling, and there's a lingering smell of bodies making it hard to breathe.

I stand where the sun is streaming in through the window, still wondering what I'm going to say to her. Xavier follows me into the room. His face is hard. Distant. He says nothing so I turn away from him. I can never make small talk.

Miss Singh walks in, smiling at us. 'Thank you both for coming. Poppy, I hope you've had enough time to think about it all.' She looks at me, a hesitant smile on her lips.

My mind is in chaos, and I can't get any words out. She's going to think I'm stupid.

'Um...'

'OK, Poppy. Don't worry. I'll tell you what I've been looking at on the web. As I said before, scholars think that it should actually be Prospero's speech, not Miranda's, but –'

'That's what I think.' Xavier is staring at me with his usual intense expression. 'So I think I should say that speech.'

I knew he'd say that. He wants to be a mega star and get all the applause. I look at the back wall of the classroom. There's a huge display on blue paper with *The Tempest* written in the middle and 'Caliban' to one side with lots of pictures of monsters, probably done by the Year 7s.

'Poppy?' Miss Singh is looking worried. I must pull myself together and decide.

'Do you want Miranda to be strong and defiant?' she says. 'So you want to say the speech? Or are you going to play her as an innocent fifteen-year-old somewhat overprotected child who's cherished and sheltered by her father? So you'd play her as someone who wouldn't be capable of saying that to Caliban.'

I don't know what to say.

'Poppy?' Miss Singh expects me to speak.

'Er...I don't know...I learned the speech...er...'

'I think I should say it,' says Xavier. 'Miranda's just a child – a simpering female. No way she'd tell the monster off for trying to rape her. So best if –'

'I don't know,' I say. Blood rushes through my ears making a buzzing noise in my head.

'It's how you want to play her, Poppy,' says Miss Singh.

'I...I don't know.' I need to get out of here.

'Then I should say it,' Xavier says, shouldering his backpack and looking as if he's had enough of both of us.

'It's up to Poppy, Xavier. She's Miranda. She's getting inside Miranda's head...what do you think, Poppy? Do you need a bit more time to think about it?'

I want to stand up for myself. For Miranda. I used to be determined and strong, but now there's a pool of sadness inside me and I'm drowning in it and unable to make decisions...with Xavier towering over me and his brick-wall face...how could I even think that I could stand up to Caliban...fight him off as he lies on top of me?'

'I think Miranda's a bit feeble really,' I say, 'she's just a child...her dad would tell Caliban off. Her dad would protect her –'

'So the speech is mine,' Xavier says, turning to leave.

'Xavier, wait,' Miss Singh holds up her hand. 'Let's just check...Poppy? Is that what you want?' What I want is to space out and just be allowed to be Miranda because that's better than being awful me. I'd thought she was strong, but maybe I haven't understood her at all.

'She's...she's a feeble...weak fifteen-year-old...pathetic...in pieces...She wouldn't say anything. She'd be too frightened.'

Chapter 10

Look into his eyes

The hall is hot again today despite the windows being open. Reggie's on the stage with his gang, fooling around, pretending to be drunk like they are in the play. They're passing around the bottle of wine they use for their scenes, and I can't help laughing at them. Do they actually have wine in that bottle?

What's Miss Singh going to say?

Mia and the other Spirits are in a huddle. She sees me. Gives me the death-ray look.

I know why I deserve this venom.

I'm such a bad person.

I wish I could take back what I did in primary school. But I can't.

Tristram the choreographer comes in and leads the Spirits off to the basketball court to practise their dances.

I sit on the seats at the back of the hall. Kavya's painting the backdrop in the art room and without her I'm letting myself be Miranda and feel her freedom.

Harry is sitting with Jack and William, who play the baddies in the play. Those two have been friends since we were all at primary school together and that's a good group for Harry to join. They were two of the three kings in Nightmare Nativity play in Year 3.

The memory of it makes me quiver.

Mia and me at each other's throats.

I must stop looking at Harry.

Xavier ambles into the hall. He seems not to mind being on his own. Even in primary school he'd just stand alone in the playground. He was Joseph in Nightmare Nativity play. Of course. I envy him his ability not to care about alone-ness. Although maybe he does care. How does anyone know what another person might be thinking?

He's an amazing Prospero, star of the play. He's mad as hell though, that he has a girl understudy. He keeps muttering that as Prospero he's God, and God is a man not a woman. No wonder people think he's a bit mental.

Miss Singh comes into the hall, smiling as always, and even Reggie hushes as she takes charge. He hides the bottle of wine in the wings.

'Xavier and Noah,' she says, 'You first. Act 1 Scene 2 from where Caliban comes in. I want to hear you do the *Abhorred slave* speech, Prospero.'

I'm not really sure why I was so feeble and let Xavier have my speech, but I go up the steps and wait in the wings. Prospero marches around the stage, banging his staff on the floor, every bit a confident alpha male. He's bossing the monster Caliban around. Using his power to control.

'Hag-seed, hence!

Fetch us in fuel and be quick.'

Noah does the clumsy monster so well. They're both so good. Much better than I'll ever be.

I do the relaxation exercises Miss Singh taught us, clenching every muscle tight then relaxing...I shut my eyes...being Miranda on her island.

But I don't have to play Miranda as this simpering female. I could always tell Miss Singh that I've changed my mind and I want to say the assertive speech about the monster trying to rape me.

But Xavier has just done it better than I could.

I say my lines then I drift off with Miranda, breathing her in, and taking charge of my life – ignoring Caliban the monster.

'Prospero, Caliban and Miranda, you're wonderful!' Miss Singh calls. 'You've all worked hard.' Xavier and Noah grin at each other. 'Poppy and Harry! The log-carrying scene, please. Poppy, remember you love this man! Show us that total adoration!'

My knees feel weak. The stairs onto the stage feel like I'm climbing Mount Everest.

Harry does his wood-carrying thing, his neck muscles bulging. Kavya offered to make him lighter wood with chicken wire and papier mâché but he said he wanted to keep it as real as possible.

This is where we fall in love, and I feel sweat in my arm pits. I hope I don't smell.

Focus.

I move out from the wings, say my lines to him where I offer to carry the logs for him. But, of course, I'm playing Miranda as a feeble woman and there is no way Harry, as Ferdinand, is going to let me help carry the logs.

'No precious creature,' Harry says, and I can't look him in the face.

Having Harry this close to me is overwhelming. His face is glistening in the heat.

'Look at Ferdinand, Miranda!' Miss Singh calls, her voice full of laughter.

I look at Harry and he does his lopsided smile and raises his beautiful brown eyebrows. I want to kiss them.

Who would have thought that eyebrows could be so delicious?

art is galloping, and I'm not Miranda any more. I burst ughing, so does Harry.

'Really you two,' says Miss Singh. She's laughing, so is everyone in the hall. I feel the heat creep up my body.

Reggie yells 'Come on you young lovers!' He grins at me, almost friendly.

I blush. Good thing Mia's not seeing this. She'd go on about it for ever.

'OK, Ferdinand and Miranda,' says Miss Singh walking towards Harry and me. She looks up at us on the stage. 'You are both good actors and you know you can do better than this. Take a break. Sit at the back of the hall and get to know each other.'

'Waayhey!' yells Reggie, doing a weird dance and waving his arms around. Rumour is he takes tranquilisers. They clearly aren't working.

'OK, Reggie,' says Miss Singh as I slink off the stage, 'Let's have you and Trinculo up here for your murderous-gang scene. Poppy, Harry, practise looking into each other's eyes. Get into character! I know twelve weeks sounds a lot, but it'll be December before we know it.'

Although Miss Singh is smiling, I sense the annoyance in her voice. I can't let her down.

'Come on,' whispers Harry and I follow him to the seats at the back of the hall.

We sit close to each other.

My skin is zinging. Don't let me faint. I try to think of something intelligent and interesting to say.

'Miranda's a bit pathetic to be honest,' I blurt out. 'Love at first sight and all that. I don't usually struggle...really like being someone else...I'm usually better than this...I mean...I prefer to be someone else than being me.'

'Then let's do what Miss Singh says. Look at me.'

His green eyes have blue flecks. Perfect.

I have to look away. To distract myself I get my phone out of my blazer pocket and stare at it.

'I'm having extra lessons on Saturday mornings to catch up,' Harry says. 'Moving house for Year 11 stinks. But I hear you do that free 5k parkrun sometimes.'

I want to know how he knows that.

'Maybe one Saturday I could run with you?' He raises one eyebrow.

'Yes,' escapes out of my mouth, all enthusiastic and stupid. Sweat is pouring down my back. 'That would be great.'

'So what if I do parkrun one Saturday then we go to the swings and hang out?'

'OK,' I say. I just about manage not to swoon right there and collapse on the floor.

'And you go to that running club Tuesday night at the track?' His hand is so close to mine.

'Mmmm.' How does he know all this?

'I hear you take your dog to club nights.'

He's been spying on me.

'I might join running club,' he says. 'Mum has to let me out one night a week. Come on, practise looking at me again,' he says, 'we've got to get this scene right.'

I look. And gulp. I stare at my phone again. Maybe Harry will ask me for my number.

He doesn't.

Come to think of it I've never seen him with a phone.

When Miss Singh calls us back I feel more comfortable with Harry close to me, but the Bitch Brigade are back from learning their dances with the choreographer, and Mia is glaring at me. I feel her eyes burn into me. She hates me.

But Harry is meeting me one Saturday to do parkrun.

He's not meeting her.

And Tuesday running club maybe. I don't go every week – not when Mum's working because I have to guard Zara.

Chapter 11

Let's go to Manchester

Mum's already drinking when I get back from school. She's sitting at the breakfast bar, already dressed for work, and looking intently at her phone. She doesn't even look up.

There's a glass of red wine beside her. It's booze every day now. I tried talking to her about drinking then driving, but she just yelled at me.

I bend down and cuddle Biscuit, loving her warm doggy smell.

'JoJo's in bed,' Mum says, 'and a meal's in the oven. Carl'll be back for six thirty.' Her face is vague.

'OK. I've got loads of homework,' I say, 'so I'll get started on it.'

I go upstairs and knock on Zara's bedroom door. 'Hiya. You OK?'

She's working at her desk, looking pale, so I move towards her.

'I'm OK,' she says, her brow furrowed.

I put an arm around her, see she's drawing a map of the Pacific ring of fire and the tectonic plates of the world. 'Oooh, my favourite thing,' I say. 'Do you realise that those tectonic plates are still moving? We're moving. Right now.'

'You're such a nerd.' She almost smiles.

'If I become a volcanologist I'll be able to work out when a volcano is about to explode.'

Silence.

'Are you actually OK? Or are you just saying it?'

She still doesn't say anything, so I squeeze her shoulders.

'I just want to do my homework.'

'OK.' As I go through the door she whispers, 'Mum put JoJo in bed before half past five tonight. That's so early. Then she went on her phone. It's as if...she doesn't want us around.'

'Oh...' I wait in the doorway, and whisper back, 'But you get on with Mum OK, don't you?'

'S'pose so.'

'I expect she's tired. Work...and she likes to be on her phone with her friends.' I wish I hadn't said that last bit. I think Zara's right and Mum would rather talk to her friends than us. My knees go weak. I'm worried that Zara's worried. I should have picked that up before now.

'You know I'm there for you, don't you?' I say.

She looks up at me, twisting one of her plaits around her fingers. I see it on her face. No. She doesn't know I'm there for her. But I don't know how to make that better. 'You're my little sister and I will always look after you.'

My heart is hurting.

She sort of smiles. But says nothing, so I go to my bedroom.

There are only ninety-seven days before Zara is thirteen.

Ninety-six days to get rid of Carl.

But my brain can't even start to think how to do that.

The hideous thought rushes through me that he might not wait till her birthday, like he did for me. He could start on her any time.

I bury myself in my chemistry homework. But I'm breathing fast like I've just sprinted round the country park.

Later, Carl calls us down for our meal. He's chatty tonight telling us how a big toy shop in central London has bought one of his robots, 'and they're selling internationally as well. Work hard girls, and you get loads of money like me and Steve.'

This is his mantra.

Biscuit's sitting by my feet, looking up at me, her big brown eyes saying, 'Feed me.'

Zara's doing her best to keep the conversation going with Carl, wittering on about her gymnastics. 'I'm the best in my group on the beam,' she says.

'That's splendid,' says Carl, sounding almost as if he means it.

Maybe he does mean it.

He keeps glancing at me, but I'm ignoring him and being strong Miranda.

'Oh, Poppy,' he says, all casual. 'I've bought four tickets for the Robot Wars final in Manchester. You. Me. Steve, and I thought you'd like to bring your friend Kavya along.'

My mouth goes dry. I stop chewing.

'What about me?' says Zara.

'I've booked two nights in a posh hotel,' he says. 'Saturday and Sunday nights, start of October half-term week, so I know you're free. I thought you'd like to see who's overall winner this year. My money's on Explosion – impenetrable outer layer and a deadly axe. Crashes down onto opponents, knocking them dead. It's going to be on telly as well.'

I drop some of my chicken on the floor for Biscuit.

I have no words. I feel my face go hot and blood drums in my ears. I hold onto Dad. When will he come and rescue me?

'What do you say?' Carl shovels another forkful of stew into his mouth. 'Cool, eh?'

'It's a treat, Poppy.' Zara's staring at me like I'm an idiot not to jump at the idea.

'Come on, Poppy.' Carl slugs some wine. 'You'll enjoy it. And with loads of spending money for you and Kavya you'll have a ball.'

'I'd like to go,' Zara says, hurt in her voice. She flashes me a fierce look.

I see Carl's mouth move, but the din in my head is too loud to make much sense. I hang onto Dad as the words float past me.

Carl and Sleazy Steve.

Me and Kavya.

Carl grabs my wrist. 'Look at me! It'll be fun. Answer me!'

I still have no words, just thoughts banging around my head, clashing into each other, making chaos.

'I'd love to go,' says Zara, giving me her I-can't-believe-you're-doing-this look. I can't explain why she must never come with Carl and me for these outings.

I take a deep breath and mutter something. Lies of course. About being busy. Chemistry tests straight after half-term. Got to get good grades to get into uni.

I can hear Gran's voice saying the lying will come back to haunt me. But Gran would want me to be safe. God, is it OK to lie sometimes? So Carl won't get me?

I load the dishwasher, Carl lurking pretending to be busy, but actually he's waiting for Zara to go to bed.

I want to take Biscuit to the country park, but I can't leave Zara.

I know what Carl wants and I start to feel sick. I go to my room and try to focus on the chemistry homework.

Chlorine. A deadly gas.

I knew he'd come for me. He wedges my desk under my door handle so that no one can interrupt.

'You want this, I know you do,' he says. 'You're just a dirty slut.'

I take deep breaths.

Feel myself freeze.

There's nothing I can do.

I hold down the molten magma bubbling up inside me.

He injects me every few months, and today is one of those days. As he leans towards my thigh, I wonder what it would be like to take a kitchen knife and stab him?

Don't be crazy. Don't think like that. I switch my brain to how relieved and happy I should be that I won't have his baby.

I suppose that should make me feel relieved and happy but it doesn't. I cut off from everything. Squash the rage down inside me till I feel blank.

Must feel nothing.

I go out of my body and into my Monet poppy picture on the wall opposite my bed. I'm Claude Monet's little girl and I'm called Amelie. He's a kind dad. I live with him in the house in the distance and I'm happy, running through the field of poppies with my brothers and sisters.

I'm free.

Afterwards, Carl leaves my desk chair in the middle of my room.

Leaving me.

Vacant.

I don't know how long I lie on my bed. An hour. Two. Maybe three. The house is completely dark and silent when I get in the shower to wash it all away. Then it's hard to get to sleep because I feel I'm disappearing. As if I'm just a gauzy afterthought that can't be seen, not worthy of being part of the human race.

I'm in my alternative world of sunshine again, running through the golden field of grasses and poppies...

... But no one knows I'm there and the woman and the little children in the picture move around me, unaware I'm screaming for help.

In the morning Mum has a go at me. 'Come on darling, you'd love to go to Manchester, wouldn't you? Two nights in a posh hotel! Spending money! Come on!'

I don't meet her eyes. Try not to engage with her. Keep feeding JoJo his cereal.

But I could tell her everything.

Right now.

No one will believe you.

'Why don't you go, Mum? Luxury weekend with Carl.' My voice is taught and quiet.

Zara's face lights up. 'And me. Please.'

'Yes. Take Zara. I'll look after JoJo.' I shove another spoonful into his mouth. 'You know I can do that. And Kavya can come round and help me.'

'Kavya.' Mum frowns. 'You spend too much time with that girl.'

'But we can look after JoJo, you get a weekend away.'

'But Carl especially wants you to go, darling.' Mum makes herself a coffee in the new machine. 'I think he's upset you're so reluctant to help him these days building the robot. He's trying to get you back into it.'

'No. I won't go.'

'We must be grateful to Carl,' Mum says. 'He does so much for us.'

I try to read her face. I'm sure she's afraid, but she turns and starts emptying the dishwasher.

I don't know what to say, so I scoop up the rest of JoJo's cereal, shove it in his mouth, kiss his curls, grab my backpack and head out the door.

I've got to stop thinking vaguely about how to prove to Mum what Carl's doing. I must be more focused. There's so little time.

What kind of plan would Alex Rider think of? Or James Bond? Or Jason Bourne? Or even Miss Marple?

I have to come up with a brilliant plan.

But I'm just feeling like I'm feeble Miranda with an empty brain.

Chapter 12

Chopping

For the next few days Mum keeps having a go at me about going with Carl and Steve to Manchester. We're preparing the evening meal together and she goes on and on about it.

'But you love Robot Wars,' she says. 'And Carl wants you to go so much.'

If only you knew.

Is this the moment to tell her what Carl does? My heart begins to hammer in my chest. Come on. Tell her. Be brave.

You're a slut. Asking for it.

'You're upsetting Carl,' she says. 'He's angry with you. And with me.' She slugs some red wine as she stirs the onions in the pan.

That Carl is angry with her because of me makes shivers run down my spine. Do I have to protect my mother as well as my sister?

And what about JoJo? This is a new thought and my hands tremble, so I have to stop chopping, frightened I'll cut myself.

I hate knives.

'Please, Mum. I'm desperate not to go. Please don't make me.'

'Poppy! We must do what Carl says!'

'Mum!'

'Get those carrots and peppers chopped.'

I focus on the vegetables.

'Yes! We must do what he says. You have no idea how awful it is for me when you disobey him.'

I can tell from Mum's voice that she's close to tears although she keeps facing away from me.

'Are you ready for the veg?' I'm not sure what else to say.

'Yes. And I'm ready for you to behave.'

I tip everything on my chopping board into the pan. Mum grabs the board from me and scrapes it aggressively. Her rapid movements make me step back. My head is in chaos, and I don't know how to stop that. I try being Miranda and breathe her in.

Mum rips the lid off a tin of tomatoes with a violence that makes me gasp. I hate it when Mum's like this. I know she'd be angry like this if I told her about Carl. That's why I'm never going to tell her.

I'm gasping for air, and I know what I have to do.

'OK, I'll go to Manchester.' I try to slow my breathing.

'I should think so. Lots of girls would love to have a father who takes them on luxury weekends. Two hundred pounds to spend! And for Kavya. That's the bit I'm less keen on but Carl insists you'll want your friend with you. And that's so kind of him.'

'Yes,' I say. Meaning no, because I have no intention whatsoever of going to Manchester. It's still weeks away so I'll make a plan.

Kavya and I will disappear.

We can do that.

Chapter 13

Running club

Tuesday. Running club tonight. I must tell Kavya about Manchester.

We're sitting in the hall watching the Spirits do their dances on the stage. They're good and I can't help admiring the Bitch Brigade as they weave and float around each other. Mia always was brilliant at ballet.

'Hiya.'

Harry sits next to me.

'Oh...er...' Try to stay calm.

'I've looked up how to join running club,' he says, 'and I'm allowed to come twice before I pay anything.'

'Right,' I say, my body rigid. He's too close to me. I try to swallow.

'So I'll try to come tonight if I can. Mum might not let me.' He pushes his hair out of his eyes. 'She's being a bit of a nightmare.'

'I totally get that,' I say.

'Well done, Spirits.' Miss Singh claps and the girls on the stage smile. Mia looks at me, sitting next to Harry.

'Your dance is brilliant,' Miss Singh says and Mia smirks at me as she comes down the steps from the stage.

I look away.

'Poppy and Xavier,' Miss Singh says. 'Let's go over that bit in Act 1 again where Miranda sleeps.'

I get up and Mia heads straight for Harry and sits where I've been sitting.

'Meet me at the swings tonight,' she says to him, looking at me. Making sure I heard her.

I don't hear Harry's reply.

He's coming to running club. With me.

Isn't he?

But I know Harry won't be interested in me in the long term. He just chats because we're together so much at rehearsals.

That evening I finish my English essay on the themes of forgiveness and justice in *The Tempest* and print it off. I don't know why Prospero was quite such a pushover at the end of the play. I don't think I'd have forgiven Antonio and the King quite so easily after what they did.

Revenge seems more appropriate.

As I wait for my ancient printer to grind out the pages, I look at the photos above my desk. Gran with Zara and me at London Zoo. I miss Gran's kindness. I never understood why Mum called her a nightmare mother. Gran was always kind to me, and Zara.

I love that photo of Grandpa standing next to Gran on the pier at Brighton, a knotted handkerchief on his head because he's losing his ginger hair, and he forgot his hat. His nose is bright red. I'm glad it was JoJo who inherited Grandpa's gingeryness. Bea in our year gets horrible teasing because of her red hair.

It's not only me Mia targets.

A message flashes up on my phone.

Kavya: meet 7.30 at swings b 4 club x
Poppy: OK x

My printer stops and I slam my lap-top shut, unsure why my heart is racing.

Maybe it's that Harry might come to running club tonight? Maybe it's that I must tell Kavya about Manchester? For my plan to work she needs to lie to her aunty, saying we'll go with Carl and Steve but actually we'll be disappearing. I know Kavya won't want to lie.

So I'm caught in a trap.

Oh God. Why is my life so awful? Are you there, God?

And if Kavya wants to know why we can't go with Carl and Steve, I might have to tell her what Carl does to me.

How on earth do I do that without putting too much pressure on her? My body freezes as I try to come up with a form of words that I could say.

What if I lose my best friend through this? What if I end up telling her and then she'll have the pain as well, and every time I'm with her we'll both be thinking about Carl and not about our friendship.

Because to tell her will kill our friendship.

I try to shut that thought out of my head, but it stays there, spinning, shouting at me.

I could lose Kavya.

I'm such a terrible person.

What if Kavya says why didn't I scream when he did it? Why didn't I push him off? Why didn't I tell Mum?

I don't know.

I should have screamed.

But I froze.

I'm aware that I'm doing that weird breathing, as if I've just run a 5k race and I'm out of breath and my heart is racing.

Why didn't I just shove Carl off?

I focus onto my poppy picture. Let myself go into the field and play in the long grass with the other children.

I hear Zara playing her flute in her room and I'm back being Poppy Stewart, school weirdo. I need to get out of my room right now, so I change into leggings and my white long-sleeved running shirt and put my phone in my running belt.

Mum's shift doesn't start till nine so I've got a bit of time to chat at the end of running club before I must be back home.

I must protect Zara.

What about JoJo? That thought is too hideous.

Biscuit jumps down from my bed and scratches the door, looks at me with her big brown eyes and does her pleading whine that means 'walkies right now.'

I creep downstairs, only treading on the bits that don't creak, but Biscuit's claws clack on the bare polished wood. Carl and Mum are glued to some loud game show on the television.

A camera on the ceiling watches me.

There's a TV burst of applause and laughter and Biscuit and I make a dash for it down the last few steps. I pull on my trainers – elastic laces are brilliant – click Biscuit onto her lead and grab a key. 'Done my homework,' I say. And I'm gone. Out the front gate and running down the road towards the country park.

We turn the corner by the churchyard then cross the tram tracks and run across the wooden bridge over the stream. I let Biscuit off her lead, and she sniffs and wees.

I consider running down the right-hand path to the swings but I'm not ready to face Reggie and his gang. They're likely to be there on a running club night, all beered-up and throwing out taunts. And what if the Ashbury Road Gang are challenging Reggie's gang again and a fight breaks out? I hate the thought that people come into the park carrying knives. Reggie says that Wolf, the Ashbury Road leader always carries a knife.

Reggie.

And Kavya. What is it with those two? I feel shut out of their closeness.

Reggie's just so weird. I don't like the way he dominates people. It's obvious he's trying to pull Harry into his gang. I want Harry to be free, though, and not tainted by Reggie.

But I'm not God, organising people's lives.

Still half an hour before I need to meet Kavya.

And maybe Harry. Unless he's meeting Mia.

Carl's face burns into my mind. So I do step-ups on a tree stump to try to block him out. I zone out as I step up and down, walking with Dad over the island to where the puffins nest...feeling safe with him....

My legs start to hurt.

Dad *will* come and rescue me.

Exhausted I sit on the tree stump, scratching Biscuit behind her ears. That first memory of her, the day after my thirteenth birthday. 'Happy belated birthday,' Carl said. A tiny scrap of white fluff sitting in the crook of his arm, her little brown eyes peering out at me. She was trembling.

He put her in my arms and immediately she started licking my hands, bouncing up towards my face. We looked into each other's eyes.

It was love at first sight.

I thought Biscuit was a sorry gift from Carl. I thought he meant, *'Sorry. I won't do that again.'*

I shiver at my naivety back then, all full of excitement at being a teenager, taking Kavya to a film, then the pizza restaurant with Carl's money but just Kavya's older cousin, Darcy looking after us. The waiter bringing a cake with a firework candle on it, everyone singing and clapping, and my face burning up.

Time to meet Kavya. And Harry – hopefully. So I head to the swings.

Kavya's standing by the fence, laughing, and Reggie and his gang are on the climbing frame. No sign of Mia or Harry.

'Hi lover-girl,' Reggie calls to me. Crabbe and Goyle laugh. He seems obsessed about Harry and me on stage. 'Kissy-kissy-kissy,' he shouts.

I ignore him.

'He only means to be friendly,' mutters Kavya. She grins at me and hugs me. I love her lemony smell as she holds onto me. Love her arms around me. She knows the Reggie/me relationship is hopeless.

We leave the swings and jog down the lane towards the sports arena. The usual people are there, chatting, laughing, jogging. We smile back but keep to ourselves.

I tie Biscuit up to a wooden post by the spectator stand where I can keep an eye on her, and we jog slowly around the track to warm up. I keep looking around to see if Harry is there. But I can't see him.

'I don't think he's here,' Kavya says. We both burst out laughing and I grab her hand and squeeze it, a warm fizz running down my spine. Mum tells me how crazy I am to want to go to uni in the same city as Kavya, but I can't imagine being separated from her. Ever.

But inside my soul is crying. Harry's with Mia.

Chris the coach gets us doing some exercises, his voice calm but forceful, expecting a hundred percent effort every time.

We're sprinting two hundred metres around the track, walking two hundred. But soon I'm exhausted. Kavya is still going, so I drop out, my heart beating too fast.

I want Harry to be here.

I take Biscuit to the drinking fountain. Shouldn't have done quite so many step-ups. And no sign of Harry. Is he with Mia at the swings?

I try to swallow but can't.

Mia. And Harry.

Kavya comes for a drink. I know it's my moment to tell her my plan for Manchester.

'Kav...I...well, you see –'

'Poppy!' It's Harry running towards us. 'Can't stop...' he says. His face is flushed, and he looks upset. 'Just wanted you to know...Mum's angry...took my phone...sorry...er...sorry...gotta go.'

He runs off.

'He wanted to be with you,' Kavya says all dreamy-eyed. We both giggle like little kids.

Mum will go out soon for her night shift at the vets so I must get home for Zara. I can't face telling Kavya about Manchester.

Chapter 14

Parkrun

I wake early. It's Saturday. And Harry might come to parkrun.
Unless he's now hooked up with Mia.

I keep putting off talking to Kavya about Manchester so much it's become this big grey blockage, sitting on my chest, stopping me talking. But I'm going to do it today. Mum and Carl might get suspicious because Kavya's aunty hasn't rung them to confirm. Must find a way to tell Kavya without any detail about Carl.

My throat tightens.

How can I do that?

If she found out about Carl, it will be too much of a burden for her.

I'll tell people that you started it.

Asking for it.

I look at my phone. More posts, probably from Mia or her mates.

Gorgeousgirl: Crater Face is hopeless as Miranda.

Gorgeousgirl: Crater Face needs to go.

I tell myself I'm not going to let myself get upset.

But I am. I've been awake two minutes and already I've got herd-of-elephants-in-my-tummy feelings.

I hear JoJo singing, so I go and lift him out of his cot, enjoying his first smile of the day, kissing his curls – feeling glad again that I have such a sweet baby brother.

I mustn't let Mia's posts get to me.

But I know deep inside me that I'm a worthless person and I deserve to be treated like this.

Biscuit greets us in the kitchen as if we've been away for a year, then she clatters out of her dog flap into the garden. I notice the lights are on in the shed, so Carl is up already. I hate it when he's up early because I feel he invades my happy space.

I make porridge and try to get most of JoJo's into his mouth before he sprays it around the room.

Biscuit comes back in, and I give her some of her food which she gobbles in five seconds.

'Greedy gannet.' She wags her tail at me.

I love my dog.

I picture myself with Harry at parkrun this morning.

Breathe.

It's still only seven o'clock so I play with JoJo and his fire engine. I put on the TV and half watch it. The cartoon characters survive traumatic injuries, then get up and life goes on.

Zara joins us, bringing her bowl of porridge into the lounge.

'OK for gymnastics?' I say.

She nods. 'Coach says I could get gold at the next competition.'

'You're a star,' I hug her – feeling proud.

I have to keep a good relationship with her.

Mum'll be up late. Hungover.

I have to keep pretending all is well.

'Nee naw!' JoJo yells, crashing his fire engine into my knees.

'Ouch!' But I'm laughing. Some pain is bearable.

Carl comes in from his shed and brings his breakfast into the lounge too.

'Great porridge, Poppy,' he says, sitting on the sofa. No one would know, just looking at him, as he chats with JoJo.

We look like a normal happy family, children's TV blaring.

Nobody watching it.

Nobody watching us.

We're far too normal.

Once Mum's up I make her coffee then leave the house. Biscuit barks her high-pitched yelp of outrage that I've left her behind.

Today will be our usual family safe Saturday. I smile to myself. Mum takes Zara to gymnastics and JoJo to the crèche at the arts centre. Mum does her yoga, then coffee with her mates.

My phone beeps. Not another Mia nasty.

Kavya: Have to do extra shift at caf. Illness. Can't make ParkR. xxxx

I jog into the country park. It won't matter Kavya can't make parkrun. Maybe it's better just me and Harry.

He probably won't come. Who am I kidding that he wants to be with me?

Get real, girl. He'll be more interested in Mia and her big boobs.

I shiver. The wind from the north is arctic cold.

He's there. I see him at the back of the crowd of runners, jogging on the spot.

He sees me and moves towards me. Smiling. Brushing his floppy hair away from his face. I feel the blush creeping up my body. No. Please don't let me go bright red.

'Hi,' he says. His body trim and fit in his black shorts and blue rugby shirt.

I try to say hi but there's a lump in my throat the size of Mount Everest. I cough and splutter. More proof that there is no good God. I try again to speak but all that comes out is a mousy squeak.

'Come on,' he says as the runners start to move off. I set my watch to record my time and run next to Harry.

'I've never run five kilometres before,' he says, 'so take it gently. I'd die of shame if I can't get round.'

I go at what I hope is a good pace for him. Oh God. Please make this go well. I'll be good. I'll stop lying. I'll do anything. Just make this go well.

'What is it with you and Reggie?' he says.

'Oh. Um...He's really good friends with Kavya...and she's my best friend...so sometimes it's a bit awkward. Don't think he likes me very much.'

'He offered me protection,' Harry says. 'From Wolf and the Ashbury Road Gang. But I've no idea who they are.'

'Keep it that way,' I say. 'They all go to Ashbury Academy...rumour is they carry knives...want us to live in fear of them...and I do.'

'Jack and his mates give me the lowdown on who to avoid at school and all that.'

'Jack's much nicer now he's stopped going out with Mia.' It probably wasn't wise of me to mention Mia.

Harry pulls ahead of me, and I catch him up. He's laughing and he pulls ahead again. So I catch him up again.

'I thought you were worried you might not make it to the end,' I say.

'You're going too slowly for me,' he says.

'Right,' I say. 'Let's do something about that,' and I go into near sprint mode. There's just one more loop of the park so I know I can keep up that pace. He's keeping up with me – I'm glad about that but we stop chatting and focus just on the run.

We get to the end together and I let him go into the finishing funnel ahead of me and I'm relaxed and enjoying being with him. 'We were just over twenty-three minutes,' I say, looking at my watch. 'Not quite my fastest but pretty good.'

I get my phone out. He might ask me for my number.

But he doesn't. Perhaps his mum still has his phone?

'Better go,' he says, putting his jacket on.

I'd hoped we could hang out at the swings.

'Maths tutor,' he says. 'I asked him to come an hour later this week but Mum's mad at me for doing that – don't know if I can do this again.'

'Why did you move for Year 11?'

'Dad's job. Promotion he couldn't turn down. My parents are throwing money at me catching up. Nightmare private tutors. If I don't pass everything brilliantly in the summer, I'm dead.'

'That must be tough,' I say.

Then he's gone and I'm standing on the wet grass, shivering in the cold wind, my trainers soggy. I pull my jacket on.

I could go to the café to see Kavya, get a hot chocolate, tell her my plan for Manchester. It's still a few weeks away but I must tell her.

The elephants in my tummy are back.

Come on! Just tell her!

I finger the angry zit on my forehead.

I deserve to be called Crater Face.

Mia's right. No one is going to fancy me.

I can't go home – Carl will be lying in wait for me. Mum won't be home from her yoga class till after twelve. It's annoying Kavya's working – we usually hang out after parkrun.

I could go to the café – sneak home and get Biscuit first. I could be so quick that Carl is caught off guard. Defeat the CCTV.

Defy Carl.

Wow! That feels good, even if it is a risk.

I'm back to elephants-in-my-tummy mode as I run through the country park and up our road then up the front path. I look through the letter box to try to see Carl. He isn't in the lounge because the TV isn't on.

If he's in his shed, he will have seen me at the front door on the CCTV.

I have about thirty seconds.

It's crazy but I take a chance.

My hand shakes. Can't get the key in the lock.

Ten seconds gone.

I rush in. Biscuit clatters in her dog flap.

I see Carl out of the patio doors coming out of his shed. He's seen me in the kitchen. My heart is pounding as he strides towards me.

I'm running back down the hall. 'Biscuit!' She follows me. I grab her lead. Slam the front door and we're sprinting down the road. I'm gasping for breath and wait till we're in the country park before I put Biscuit on her lead.

I hide in the first clump of dense bushes, crouching down, not caring about the thorns, waiting to see if Carl has followed us.

But he hasn't.

Of course he hasn't.

I'm losing it.

We head for the café and I sit at a table outside with the smokers. Reggie sees me and comes out, his quiff stiff and tall. I still long to touch it.

'What?' he says.

'Hot chocolate, please,' I say. I give him what I hope is my best you-are-my-mate smile.

He sniffs, pats his quiff, and walks back into the café. I know he'll tell Kavya to serve me, and I can quickly tell her about Manchester. I go over the words in my head. Try some deep breathing to calm myself.

In a few minutes Kavya appears with my steaming mug, marshmallows floating. Something hidden in her other hand.

'Did Harry come?' she says. 'How was it?'

'OK,' I say. 'He's fast. But not as fast as me.' We both giggle.

She hugs me and bends down to give Biscuit a sausage.

Come on. Say it. 'Carl wants to take both of us to Manchester for the Robot Wars final. Half term.'

'Brilliant.'

'Not so brilliant actually. He wants Steve, his work partner to come as well.'

She looks at me. 'So?'

She doesn't get it. She's so naïve. But maybe that's good? She won't guess what Carl does.

'This is the plan,' I say. 'We'll say we'll go but we actually won't. We'll disappear.'

'But why –' she says.

'I need you to get Aunty to phone Mum and say you will come.'

'Why isn't it –?'

No. No. No. Don't ask me questions. 'When do you get off your shift?'

'Two,' she says.

'Meet me at the swings then? I'll explain.'

'OK. Must go now or I'll get told off.'

She goes into the café, and I sip my hot chocolate.

Parkrun went well.

And I've escaped Carl.

A good safe Saturday. So far.

But this afternoon I have to find a way to tell Kavya a bit more about disappearing instead of going on the train with Carl. Hopefully I can do that and still keep what Carl does a secret.

If you dare tell anyone I'll kill you.

Chapter 15

Telling Kavya

That afternoon I tell Mum I've got an extra training session at running club so she'll let me out. It's a lie of course.

Gran wouldn't like that.

I run with Biscuit through the country park, but I feel tense, blood hissing through my ears, and I can't breathe properly.

I have to do this.

Kavya is already at the playground, leaning on the fence watching Reggie and his gang on the roundabout. They're smoking and swigging beer out of cans getting louder and louder. Then Reggie sees me and starts a shouting conversation with me and I'm burning up because all his gang are looking at me. 'Have you seen your Miranda dress yet, Poppy?' he yells at me.

I don't know what to say. I'm on guard as Miranda because there is always danger with Caliban the monster roaming around.

'You must know if you've seen it, girl,' Reggie is persistent so I know I must reply.

'Not seen it yet,' I yell back at him.

'Can't wait to see you in it,' he yells back. 'Maybe I can try it on?'

His minions collapse in laughter.

'Can we go to the den, Kav?' I say. 'I need some peace.'

'Great idea,' Kavya says. 'Reggie's building up to a manic episode, so we're best out of it.' She holds my hand, and we swing our arms high like we used to when we'd just met in Year 7.

'I'm hoping you're going to give me more detail about this disappearing instead of going to Robot Wars,' she says.

'Yeah. Highly private, though' I say, 'so I'll tell you...when I'm sure we won't be overheard.'

Kavya looks around. 'There's no one here, Poppy!'

'I know,' I snap back at her. 'Sorry. Didn't mean that. I just want to be private.'

'OK,' she says and puts her arm over my shoulder. 'I'm ready to listen to anything you want to tell me.'

My throat chest tightens, and I try to take a deep breath. But I can't and start to panic. Could I tell her everything? No. Just tell her the minimum.

We walk down the narrow road between the sports arena and the country park. We've had a dry and sunny few days and I'm praying no one else will be at the den.

We turn off the path by a clump of hawthorn trees and walk behind bramble bushes, then clamber into the fallen tree trunk of the ancient oak tree. I usually love being here because I feel safe.

But today it's different.

I sit with my arms around my knees. Kavya puts one arm around me.

'Tell me,' she says. 'Is it that stuff about Manchester and Robot Wars?'

'Yes. As I said, Carl wants to take you, me and Steve his work partner. Remember Carl and I used to watch it every week on TV.'

'Yes...that thing where the robots end up in pieces and they fight to the death?'

'Exactly. We definitely shouldn't go.'

'Why? I'm up for it.'

Stay calm. Just say the words you planned.

'We need to pretend we're going. But not actually go.'

'That doesn't make much sense, Poppy. Anyway, half-term isn't for a few weeks yet.'

'I know...just...I mean...get Aunty Anjali to agree to let you go. Tell her to ring Mum and say thank you very much – and all that gush. Tell Aunty we're leaving early first Saturday of October half-term. Back on the Monday morning. Carl will buy everything, train tickets, hotel rooms. And he says he'll give us spending money.'

'This gets better...so why don't you –?'

'It's complicated.'

Tell her. Everything.

Tell her!

I'm shaking all over.

Kavya hugs me but my whole body is in panic mode.

'Breathe,' she says. 'Come on, do that breathing School Shrink taught us. In for five, out for nine.'

I try to calm myself.

'What on earth is going on Poppy?' she says, her arms still around me and her hot breath on my neck.

'I've said enough. Just get Aunty to agree and ring Mum to say you can go.'

'OK...but –'

'Not a word to anyone that we're not actually going.'

'OK...but –'

'Don't ask me to say anymore!' I'm louder than I mean to be.

'Poppy...I must know why. Come on. You can tell me...Please.'

'I can't. Tell Aunty the minimum. Get her to do the phone call. That should keep Mum and Carl happy.'

Kavya hugs me again. I love the warmth of her skin on my skin, but I'm crying, deep sobs, and she holds me and strokes my hair.

If I did tell Kavya everything about Carl, what could she do? Nothing.

And it'll be too much for her to handle. And what if she says why didn't you just push him off?

Why didn't I?

I'm such a bad person.

Everything feels heavy. Images flood through my mind, Carl shouting. Mum angry. The pressure of Carl on my body. Struggling to breathe.

Who can I really trust?

Don't you dare say a word or I'll kill you.

'What's actually going on, Poppy?'

Words form in my mind that I never thought I could say out loud. They're surging up wanting to be said. Can I trust her?

What if I ruin our friendship?

I'm trembling. And then I feel something open up inside me. A sense of lightness. This is my best friend here beside me.

Tell her.

Don't you dare say a word. It's our secret.

I start breathing again. 'Don't ever tell anyone this,' I whisper. 'Promise.'

'Promise,' she whispers back in my ear, her warm breath against my cheek. The fresh smell of her body comforting me.

I take a deep breath. The din in my head so loud I hardly hear my voice above it.

'Carl makes me have sex with him.'

I feel Kavya jolt.

They'll know you're lying.

Biscuit shifts at my feet. I hear myself moan. My head spins with a panic of tumbling words surging through me. Carl's voice screaming at me.

I'll make your life hell if you breathe a single word.

'Poppy,' she whispers. Then she's silent. I feel her shoulders rise and fall against me.

'Oh, God, you don't believe me!'

No one will believe you after the lies you've told.

'Poppy, of course I believe you!' She cups my head in her hands and turns my face towards her. She wipes away my tears with her thumbs, but I can't stop crying.

'It's true,' I say. 'True. But he said no one would believe me.' I slide down out of the tree and sit by Biscuit on the dead leaves, my face on my knees, gripping my arms around my legs.

No one will believe you.

'I've known for ages there was something wrong,' she says, crouching down beside me on the ground.

Panic. I can't now un-say the words.

...I'm floating with Dad in the boat on the river, his lazy rowing calming me as we drift through leafy willow trees, the sun glinting through the branches...Small birds jump from branch to branch, keeping in touch with each other with soft trilling contact calls...

'Poppy. Poppy. Don't space out. You have to tell School Shrink. It's child abuse. You're underage. He's broken the law.'

'Like that'll bother him,' I say with more venom than I expected.

'When did it start?'

'My thirteenth birthday. Mum took Zara to gymnastics in the morning. Left Carl and me alone.'

'You mean the afternoon we went to that film...then a meal?'

'Yes.'

'I thought you were being a bit odd that evening...thought it was cos of your birthday...Why don't you tell your mum?'

She will never believe you. She'll know you're lying. She'll send you away.

'She'll just say I'm lying.'

'Miss Singh. Tell Miss Singh. She's so amazing in religious studies. She'd understand. You know she will.'

'Kavya, I can't tell anyone. I only told you because of Manchester. Carl and Steve. You and me. Buying us. Get it?'

'Oh,' she says.

Silence.

Maybe she gets it now.

'I see what you mean,' she says. 'You're right. We definitely shouldn't go. So if you feel you can't tell anyone, do you want me to say something to someone about it?' Kavya says. 'What about Aunty? She's so cool with everything and she'd know what to do.'

'No! Promise you won't! Unfamiliar feelings are surging through me. Kavya's Aunty Anjali is great, but we can't tell anyone.

'OK. My lips are sealed,' she says.

My body's trembling. 'It's all my fault, what Carl does.' My throat tightens. It doesn't want the words to leave my mouth.

'Oh, Poppy. How can it be your fault?' She puts her arms around me.

'I let him do it,' I say. 'I let him.' I hide my face in my arms as shame clamps around my heart.

'Come on, Poppy. Tell me – what's the big plan about Manchester?'

I take a deep breath. 'We say we'll go. Pack a bag the night before the train leaves. Look all enthusiastic about who all the finalist robots are. But then on the Saturday morning, early, we just disappear. Disappear off the face off the earth.'

'Wow! Some plan, Poppy!'

Carl's face fills my mind.

I gasp for air. Then I'm crying again, pathetic, hopeless weeping engulfs me.

Biscuit nuzzles me but I'm gripping my knees too tightly to stroke her. I reach out for Dad in my head, but my brain is full of hazy images screaming at me that I'm a terrible person.

I feel in pieces.

I think I've just ruined the most special friendship I've ever had.

I gasp for air again, as if I want to stay alive and go on breathing.

Chapter 16

Reasons

The next day I decide I must sit in my bedroom and catch up on homework, but I can't concentrate. I'm worried that I've put too much onto Kavya and she might not want me for a friend anymore. I'm hoping she'll keep her promise not to tell anyone. But what if she doesn't? Then my phone rings and it's her. I'm almost embarrassed to talk to her.

'Can you come round, Poppy,' she says. 'I want to show you some stuff I've been looking at online. I've found something perfect for you.'

'Oh,' I say but dreading what she's planning to do. She sounds like she usually does – so maybe she still wants to be friends with me?

'I've got marshmallows,' she says. 'I'll make hot chocolate.'

I almost want to ask her if she's kept her promise not to tell, but instead I say, 'I'll be there in ten.'

Mum says it's OK to take Biscuit with me and I take the quick route to Kavya's, up to the High Street. Kavya wouldn't have invited me round unless she was OK about me dumping stuff on her. But I'm worried about what she's found online.

Biscuit's jumpy with all the traffic, but she cheers up as we pass The Big Breakfast Café. She can smell the sausages and pulls towards the door, sniffing around the feet of the smokers sitting outside, looking for morsels.

Next door is Anjali's hair salon, The Magical Haircut. That's a lie. Nothing magical about a haircut, although my short hair makes me feel free, so maybe that's a kind of magic. And Mum will eventually stop telling me off about it. The salon is shut on Sundays, so I knock on the door to the upstairs flat.

Kavya answers the door, and we go up the stairs and Kayva's aunty is smiling down at me. 'Poppy,' says Anjali, 'how lovely to see you.' She smiles at me, and I always feel accepted by her. 'Stay for lunch if you can, Poppy,' she says.

I can tell Kavya is desperate to tell me something. I can't help being nervous in case she thinks she's found some easy solution for being stuck with a sex-mad stepfather. But Kavya's chatty and friendly and she makes us both hot chocolate and takes the cookie jar with her into her bedroom.

I sit on her bed as usual and feel myself relax. I love this room. The walls are painted pale blue and covered with posters about saving the planet. Up to date ones, not like my curling ancient ones.

'Listen.' She shuffles up on the bed next to me and Biscuit. 'Remember when we went out and watched the London Marathon last year?'

'Mmmm.'

'We saw Pantosaurus...remember?'

'What?'

'The runner dressed as a green dinosaur...raising money for Childline.'

'I'm not following you.'

'You know...what's in your pants is private...didn't you get a presentation at primary school?'

'What...?'

'I was about ten when we had a school assembly about it. Then we did it in PHSE. Remember? You were there.'

'What are you saying?' I'm aware my hand is trembling and I'm trying not to spill my drink.

Kavya puts her hot chocolate on her bedside table and looks at something on her phone.

'I've been looking online,' she says. 'I know you feel you can't tell anyone...what Carl does...I sort of understand that...'

'Total nightmare. Police.'

'But I'm so angry at Carl...what he's done to you...he's broken the law –'

'I can't tell anyone. I just can't.'

'But that's where Childline comes in. It's not just the 0800 phone line. There's other stuff too. Look.' She shows me her phone. 'There's all kinds of info. Look at this message board. Just what you need. You could tell them what Carl does. Wouldn't that be the simplest thing to do?'

My whole body lurches. I don't want to look at her phone. As if it were that simple. Just tell?

'I can't.' I feel myself sink into the mess of it all again. I put my drink on her desk and curl into a ball with my arms around my legs, my face on my knees as if I want to hide.

'It makes no sense Poppy, not to tell anyone. Why can't you?'

'You want a list of reasons?' I say. I don't mean to sound so angry. No one understands. I stroke Biscuit who's snuggled in beside me.

'You have a list?' She puts a hand on my knee and for a moment I shrink back. 'Do you want to tell me?'

Don't you dare tell. You hear me? Don't you dare.

'OK. I made a list about a year ago...in my private diary Gran gave me. There were maybe seven reasons. I can't remember...there's no particular order...first...Carl told me not to tell anyone, so it feels unsafe to have told you.'

'Oh, Poppy.' She leans into my neck and hugs me. 'I'm so glad you told me.'

I'll kill you if you utter just one word about it. It's our secret.

'He said he'd kill me if I told.'

'But he won't do that! Course he won't.'

'You think?' I say knowing I'm being a sarky bitch.

'He won't kill you!'

'You don't know him,' I say.

No one will believe you. They'll believe me.

'There's no point in telling anyway because he said no one would believe me.'

'I believe you...so he's wrong, Poppy. Listen to me. He's wrong.'

You're nothing more than a barefaced liar.

'Look at me, Poppy,' Kavya says, taking my face in her hands and turning it, 'I think you must try to tell your mum.'

'No!'

'What have you got to lose?' Kavya says.

'My life.'

'How many times do I have to tell you? He won't kill you!' Kavya holds me and pulls me towards her.

'But I've lied so much – when I bunked off school all those times when I was thirteen. Mum will never believe me.'

It's all your fault. You know what you did. You started it. Little whore.

'Anyway,' I say, 'this must be about reason number four, I deserved it. It was my fault.' I hide my face on my knees again, shame seeping through my body.

'How can it be your fault?' Kavya's rubbing my back so tenderly I want to weep for a year.

I swallow. 'I want him to be gone. I feel hugely guilty that twice I've gone out of the house when Zara's been at home with him. I feel such a bad person for leaving her.'

'You're not a bad person!' says Kavya.

'But he might start on her. She's nearly thirteen. Ninety-two more days before her birthday.'

'And you're counting them? Oh Poppy! It's your mum who should be looking out for her daughter, not you.'

'But...I must protect my little sister.' Guilt races through me making my chest tighten and I struggle to breathe in.

If you tell your mother, she'll send you to a children's home because she'll believe me

'And...well...fifth...I don't fight him off. I let him do it. And I know you'll think I'm a terrible person for doing that.'

'Oh, Poppy.' Kavya's leaning towards me and hugging me. 'Course I don't think that.' My body gives in and I'm crying with her holding me.

Then I pull away from her. 'I need to go now.'

'But you could stay and have lunch with us.' She jumps up. 'Come on. Let's go online to Childline...'

'I can't...but thanks...you know...trying to help. And thanks for not saying I could just have pushed him off...I was worried you'd say that...as if it was that easy.'

'Oh, Poppy, I know it must be so difficult...'

'Of course it's difficult! Sorry...don't mean to be so shouty. This must be about reason six and it's really important. Even if I could come up with a plan to get rid of Carl, how would we manage just on Mum's salary? She'd blame me if Carl left...it would be all my fault.'

'Oh Poppy, let me hug you.'

'Mum would choose Carl over me any day. I know she would. And Zara would blame me...and JoJo would miss his dad.'

I get up and Biscuit leaps up too and I clip on her lead.

'Listen, Poppy, no one will know it's you if you contact Childline. Whatever you say, it can't get back to Carl.'

I'm so weary. Why is everything such a struggle? Come on God. Do something.

'I need to go home,' I say. Kavya's face is sad, and she hugs me, but guilt is numbing all my senses and I feel dead inside.

I walk the long way through the park to go home, Biscuit trailing behind me trying to sniff every autumn leaf.

You like it, Poppy. You know you do.

And, reason number seven, what no one must ever know is that sometimes I like the sexual feelings with Carl. I'm a bad person. I'm hating what he's doing but liking the feelings – and that does my head in.

And, my secret last reason...I can't tell anyone about me kissing him that day.

Asking for it.

Chapter 17

Costume

It's my turn to do the paper round the next day and I rush along Ashbury Road at top speed. I still worry that things could be a bit awkward with Kavya now after what I've told her about Carl and my reasons for keeping silent. I decide the only thing to do is to meet up with her as soon as possible so that I can convince myself that she still wants to be friends with me. I text her once I'm home.

Poppy: will call 4 u xx
Kavya: Great. xx

'Sort of wish I hadn't told you,' I say as she pulls her front door shut and we walk to school down the High Street. 'I was selfish, landing so much of my stuff on you. I'm so sorry.'

'No...I'm glad you told me...I just feel...you know...a bit awkward.'

'I know what you mean,' I say. 'I feel a bit weird too. But we're OK, aren't we? Us two?'

'Course we are,' she says. She grins one of her fabulous grins at me and I know we're OK. Still friends.

'And I promise I won't say a word to anyone,' she says. 'So don't worry.'

'You're such a good friend,' I say. I reach out and put an arm around her shoulder.

'Best friends for ever,' she says, and we laugh. 'I'm still up for Plan A if you are?'

'You bet.'

'Three more years and we can get you away from here,' she says. 'Get you somewhere safe.'

That sounds good. Maybe it'll be OK I told her because she's being her normal self.

In registration Harry still sits next to me and each morning I wonder how he will be towards me.

'Great run, Saturday,' he says, quietly, as he slides into his chair. I grin at him, but Mia and the cronies walk through the door and do their look-at-me-I'm-beautiful stuff, hair tossing and nail inspecting.

'Ah, girls,' says Mr Robbins getting up from his desk, 'Poppy, Mia, and all of you Spirits – please go to the textiles room straight after school today. Costume fitting with Mrs Graham. She's got some wonderful fabric and ideas for your dresses.'

'Thanks, Sir,' I say. But my stomach leaps. I might have to take my shirt off. I'll have to get Kavya to come too so I can hide behind her like I do in PE. No one must see the scabs on my arms. I don't want anyone to know I cut.

'However good the costume is,' Mia whispers to me, 'it can't make you look anything other than clumsy and ugly.'

'Is that the best you can come up with,' I say back. I watch the Bitch Brigade strut to the back of the class. I'm trembling. What if someone sees my scars and tells Mum?

I creep into the textiles room after school, my body tense. Kavya couldn't come with me because there was a crisis with the scenery – the boat for the opening scene when the tempest is raging needed urgent attention. I couldn't beg her to come because I told her I'd stopped cutting ages ago. So if I have to get undressed I'm on my own. Maybe I can hold my arms close to my body?

The smell of lavender and sewing machine oil is quite comforting in some strange way, but my body is in panic mode. I keep doing deep breathing. I move across to a table with different coloured bundles of fabric and two sewing machines, put my backpack on the floor and prop myself up against tall cupboards.

With my back to something I feel safer.

Please don't let there be a confrontation with Mia.

I'd probably be out for revenge too. Just like she is.

My phone pings again.

'Ugly slut.'

I don't know who sent this. But it's Snapchat so it will just disappear.

I'm obsessing about the Bitch Brigade. I try to clear them from my head. But can't. They will hound me every day between now and the performances in December.

How can I endure all those weeks of taunts and put-downs?

Life wasn't too bad when we were in Year 3. Until the Nightmare Nativity play – as Mum called it, when Mia got the part of Mary. I wanted to be Mary. I know what I did was wrong. But she was wrong too. I didn't mean to rip baby Jesus's head off. It was an accident. Mia kept crowing that she was Mary and I wasn't, and I just exploded and grabbed the doll. If Mia hadn't yanked it back, the doll would have stayed in one piece. Mia was beside herself with fury that I'd done that to her rosebud-lipped white doll. Mum had to buy Mia a new doll and it wet its nappy.

I wanted a doll like that, and I cried for a week until Mum's new boyfriend, Carl, bought me one. He was my hero back then.

In the end we did the nativity play with my black doll, who was more like baby Jesus than Mia's doll with fair curly hair and shutty blue eyes.

I tried explaining this to our Year 3 teacher, but she relegated me from the Inn Keeper's Wife – whose words were, 'Yes, dear' – to the part of a silent Third Weasel.

I've felt like a silent third weasel ever since, but meeting Kavya on the first day of high school changed everything.

I hear Mia's laughter in the corridor, and my heart beats faster. The Bitch Brigade march through the door of the textile room, confidence spilling from them, Mia at the front, sharing some joke. Probably about me.

She looks at her phone. Glances over at me. Smirks. Then that hostile look she gets like she wants to destroy me completely.

They dump their bags on a table, and in unison they release their long hair from their school regulation tied up hair, ponytails, running hands through their hair, head tossing and chatting. Scarlet gives me an uneasy look. It's clear she's not happy being part of the gang, but maybe she doesn't know how to escape?

Mia turns to me again and mouths, 'Crater Face'.

I look away and try to ignore her but find myself fingering the volcanic spot on my chin.

My breathing goes crazy. I try in for five, long slow breathing out for nine. When we were all in Year 7 and School Shrink was teaching us this mindfulness and breathing stuff, it all seemed such crap – so irrelevant.

Now it's the deep breathing that saves me. No wonder they call me weirdo and geek. Because I am.

A few other girls who play Spirits and dancers slouch into the room and stand in small groups, whispering behind their hands. Mrs. Graham walks in, wearing her usual floaty clothes that hide her extra weight, pale blue and a matching scarf hanging down in front.

'Mia and Poppy, both here. Excellent. This way girls, let's try on what I've made for you.'

I try to relax and unclench my fists.

'Moss green,' says Mrs. Graham holding up some fabric from the table. 'Perfect for life on an island. I've stitched the shoulder and side seams so if you both try it on, I'll make sure your bras don't show. Behind the screen please Poppy, and take your shirt off. You too Mia. Shut the classroom door please, Scarlett.'

I stare at the dress. 'It doesn't have sleeves,' My voice is croaky, my body trembling.

'I thought sleeveless would be best,' says Mrs. Graham. 'Lovely flowing fabric. Come along, both of you, shirts off.'

I go behind the screen with Mia and struggle out of my shirt, trying to hold my arms against my body. My brain is screaming at me 'sleeveless, sleeveless,' and I feel myself disintegrate into pieces.

No one must see my cuts.

Mrs. Graham slips the dress over my head. I have to put my arms up to get it on. I know she's seen my scabs from the look on her face.

Mia is staring. Her shirt half off. She sees them too.

Mrs. Graham's eyes are kind. 'Oh Poppy,' she whispers. I relax a bit, her lavender smell somehow soothing me for a moment. But I can't stop my tears. Mrs Graham hands me a tissue.

She might not tell anyone. I clench my jaws to stop myself crying. My secret's out.

For a few moments there's a tense silence.

'OK now?' Mrs Graham says.

I nod. But it's a lie.

There's a chance she might not tell anyone. But who am I kidding? Of course she'll tell. Probably School Shrink – and I'll be summoned.

'Then let's do the fitting.' Mrs. Graham straightens the dress. 'Arms up. Hold it there while I put some pins in the arm hole.'

Mia looks from my arms to my face. I'm sure she knows how I got the scabs, and I can't tell if she's shocked or mocking me. I look away. Now she's got even more ammunition to fire at me. More things to send around Insta to make me look stupid.

I'm desperate that Harry doesn't find out I cut. And Mum!

'There we go,' says Mrs. Graham. 'Careful of the pins now. And this is the sash that we'll just tie around you, so the dress will do for you and Mia. Look in the mirror.'

I don't look in mirrors unless I have to, but I risk a glance.

'It's going to look perfect. On both of you.' Mrs. Graham is behind me, smiling at me, holding the sash around my waist. 'You're both such pretty girls.'

I hear Mia snort.

I hate how I look. My nose, my eyes, my mouth, my body. All of it is hideous.

'I don't want to share a dress,' says Mia. 'It's unhygienic. And I'm much bigger than Poppy.'

She means her boobs.

'There's not much difference in your sizes,' says Mrs Graham, 'and I made the dress this style so it would fit you both.'

Mia scowls and gives me one of her stares as if I'm some inferior life form.

But maybe I am.

'Let's slip the dress off over your head,' says Mrs. Graham. 'I'll have to see if I can make another dress, Mia. If I have time and enough fabric, maybe. But there's just Yolanda, Olivia and me doing costumes and we can't work miracles. And I'm planning to make all you Spirits and dancers wonderful dresses. You'll love them. Plenty of fabric in flowing skirts. Lots of colours.' She indicates to the multi-coloured pile on the table.

As I struggle out of the dress, a pin pricks me. I don't care. It's nothing like the agony of knowing I won't be able to conceal my cutting. Mrs. Graham will almost certainly tell. There will be more people probing inside me. I just want to be left alone. I can't beg Mrs. Graham not to tell. Not with Mia here.

I get dressed without looking at anyone. If I have to wear that dress for performances, how will I hide my arms?

'Come and see me tomorrow at twelve,' Mrs Graham whispers. 'Staff room.'

I nod.

Mia's still complaining at having to have the same dress as me, and the rest of the Bitch Brigade are lurking, fingering the fabric on the table. Probably hoping for a dress that will outshine everyone else.

But I'm out of the room and down the stairs to the art block. Kavya's tried in the past to stop me cutting but she doesn't understand. No one does. And I can't explain it to anyone.

I deserve to feel pain like that.

But I know it's crazy-nerd-girl stuff.

I have to find Kavya.

I just want her arms around me, but I'll have to admit I'm still cutting myself. Not often. But I'd told Kavya I'd stopped.

Liar.

Chapter 18

Cut deeper

I climb up the stairs to the staffroom the next day at twelve and wait outside for Mrs Graham. I don't know who she would have talked to before she sees me, but I hope I can persuade her not to tell Mum I'm cutting myself.

What if Mia puts it online? Oh God, please don't let Harry find out.

I clench and unclench my fists, telling myself to stop stressing.

Next to the staffroom door is a Picasso picture of a blue woman. She's got long black hair in a kind of ponytail bun thing and she's sitting naked with her back to me, resting her head on her arms. I know how she feels.

'Who are you waiting for?' asks some woman I don't know. She's wearing a white lab coat and has dark magenta lips.

'Mrs Graham,' I manage to say although my throat is threatening to close up.

'I'll see if I can find her for you,' Magenta Lips says. She smiles – and I tell myself she's not my enemy. So I smile back.

'Thanks.' I make a mental note to get a print of the blue woman for my bedroom wall. I think we have a lot in common.

'Poppy, thanks for coming.' Mrs Graham's wearing her rose pink floaty dress and a matching scarf. I want to run away. 'There's an empty classroom just here. Follow me.'

I follow her and she shuts the door behind me.

'You might not know, but I'm the school safeguarding lead person so when I saw your scars I had to talk to Mr Robins, because he's known you since Year 7. He said he'd see you this afternoon and...er...we both think that we need to tell your mother.'

'Please don't.' My body slumps. This is a mega-disaster.

'I think we have to Poppy, and school counsellor says she'll be able to see you in a couple of days.'

'Please don't tell my mum.'

'Oh Poppy, remember, we all want to help you.'

'The thing that will help me is not telling my mum.'

Your mother won't believe a word you say. She knows you're just a compulsive liar.

'She has to know Poppy. And I had a good idea about your Miranda dress. We have some flesh-coloured tops in the costume store. What if you wear one under the dress? That'll hide your scars.'

'Oh...brilliant...thank you.'

She says a few other things but in my head I'm sitting next to the blue woman. We're both turning our back on the world, head and arms on our knees. Naked.

Mrs Graham says goodbye, I go downstairs to find Kavya. The horror of Mum finding out I'm cutting hits me, and I can't eat any lunch. I feel like the blue woman.

Exposed.

Mr Robins tells me to come to the art room at the end of school, so I take Kavya with me. I love the smell of this room, wet clay and paint. And the radio playing classical music – 'to get our creativity going,' Mr Robins told us in Year 7.

Some of the scenery for *The Tempest* is propped up against the back wall, and Mr. Robins is sitting in front of his easel.

He gets up when we go in and puts down his brushes. He's painting a storm, flashes of lightning against a dark purple-grey sky, and a dark figure standing on a cliff looking up. I think it's a painting of *The Tempest* and the person is probably Xavier being Prospero.

But it could be me.

I want to ask Mr Robins about Prospero starting and stopping storms, like God, but I don't dare, and mutter, 'Is it OK if Kavya stays?'

'If that's what you want, Poppy.' Mr. Robins wipes his hands on a cloth.

'I know about Poppy cutting.' Kavya reaches out and holds my hand. 'I want to help if I can.'

'OK,' he says. 'I know you don't want me to tell your mother, Poppy, but I think I'll have to. I won't tell her that you're seeing the school counsellor. But I can't keep this cutting to myself. I hope you can understand that.'

Yes, I understand it.

Kavya understands it.

But Mum won't understand it.

I'm reluctant to go home so Kavya walks with me and I show her the latest messages on my phone from various accounts. They're all false names but I guess most of them are Mia. Or the rest of the Bitch Brigade. Or random people who want to have a go at School Nerd and Social Outcast.

Cut deeper next time so we don't have to see your ugly face anymore.

'I think we should tell someone?' Kavya has her arms around my shoulder. 'You know...be more assertive. It's bullying.'

'But the messages will disappear anyway. And if we tell, Mia will just get a million times worse.'

'You won't though, will you?'

'Won't what?'

'Cut deeper.' She takes hold of me and turns me to face her.

'I'm not trying to kill myself.' I start to feel sick. My knees tremble.

'I want to help you to stop cutting...but I don't know how.'

'I wish I could stop. But somehow...I just do it.' I can't explain the cutting to anyone. I can't explain it to myself. However am I going to explain it to Mum?

She'll say she's ashamed of me.

I'm ashamed of me.

When I get in the lounge door is shut and I can hear cartoons on the TV and JoJo's voice. Probably Mum has told Zara to keep him in there.

The black and whiteness of the new kitchen stifles me. Mum's sitting at the breakfast bar drinking red wine. I know Mr Robins has already rung. Her face is flushed so I'm guessing she's already had too much alcohol.

'How do you do the cutting?'

'Scissors,' I lie.

'How? Where?'

'School.' She's going to know I'm lying. But I don't want her to search my room because she'd find Carl's craft knife under my bed.

'I see. And you told Mr Robins you don't know why you do it?' She drinks some wine.

'Yes. No idea why.'

I probably do know but I can't tell you. I breathe in a huge gulp of air. Mustn't throw up.

'Let me see,' she says, so I pull up my sleeve.

'How can I help you to stop doing it?'

'I...I don't know. Can I take Biscuit out now?'

'Please tell me this won't go back to how it was – when you were thirteen – Mr Robins ringing me every five minutes. I always feel so ashamed, somehow. As if he's telling me I should be doing something different.' She glugs some more wine. Looks at her phone.

It's me she's ashamed of.

'Poppy, it's not going to go back to how it was, is it?'

When I was thirteen and bunking off school, I know Mr Robins phoned her a lot.

Mum comes towards me. I take a step backwards. She puts her wine down.

My body freezes.

She hugs me. 'I'll get you some vitamin E cream to see if that'll get rid of the scars. Promise me you'll try to stop cutting.'

'I promise. Can I take Biscuit to the park?'

Mum didn't exactly tell me she's ashamed of me. I hope it won't go back to how it was two years ago. Mr Robins and I used to talk about how I felt when Mum talked about shame. He said it was probably the most important thing for me to talk about with him.

But it's hard to find words for shame because it eats up the bit of my brain that thinks straight.

It suffocates me.

Shame is who I am.

And the only words that rattle around my brain are 'I hate me.'

Chapter 19

School shrink

I'm allowed out of physics to see School Shrink, but I tell Harry I'm going to the dentist, and he says I can copy his class notes.

'And I'll explain the homework,' he says, his smile making my knees feel weak. I'll have to hide in the loo at break so I'm out of sight for a convincing amount of dentist time.

School Shrink's little room has posters all around the walls that say things like, 'I can do this. Watch me,' and there's one of a girl in school uniform saying, 'Behind every successful woman is herself.' I wonder what the boys think of that. If any boys see School Shrink. Maybe it's mostly girls who lose a grip on life?

How would I know? Harry might know. But I can't ask him.

There are two comfy chairs facing each other and a digital clock that shows the number of minutes left before I can escape. I used to have to talk to School Shrink when I was bunking off when I was thirteen.

I almost got away with that skiving. It was Mia who dropped me right in it. Getting revenge after what I did in that massive chaos during the nativity play in Year 3.

Mum was more angry than I'd ever seen her, back then when I was thirteen, telling me she was so ashamed of me seeing a shrink and she'd never believe anything I ever say to her ever again. That's why there's no point telling her about Carl.

I know I lie a lot. Helps me survive.

I got through a whole term of talking to School Shrink back then without telling her anything about what was actually upsetting me.

Carl and his dangly penis.

I never mentioned that.

And I don't intend to mention it this time either.

It's our special secret, just between the two of us. You're special to me.

I shiver.

I wanted to be special.

I glance at School Shrink. She's waiting for me to talk, but I say nothing. I love her hair. When she taught us mindfulness in Year 7, she had a big black afro, and I longed to touch it. But she's grown her hair since then and now she has lots of tight black plaits across her head and falling down her back. She has the kindest face I've ever seen, a bit like Morgan Freeman – but a woman, of course – with lots of laughter wrinkles and a soft voice.

But that doesn't mean I'm going to say anything to her, so I drift off with Dad. Please come and rescue me, Dad. We're sitting beside a lake, the sun shining, glinting through the leaves turning gold.

I suppose I should listen.

'Tell me about your family now, Poppy. You have a new little brother, don't you?'

'JoJo. He's almost two.'

'Tell me about him.'

I smile. 'He's gorgeous.'

'And your stepfather? Tell me about him.'

Breathe. I don't know what to say. But if I say nothing that'll be suspicious. 'Mum is much happier now she's re-married.' That could be a lie. But since I'm not sure it probably doesn't matter. 'And Carl has Meccano. Proper metal Meccano. Two million pieces. Everything. Motors. Gears. It's all in boxes in his enormous shed in the garden.'

'I remember you telling me about that Meccano. And you taught Kavya to make a robot and won that science fair award, didn't you?'

I nod.

'I remember you told me Carl takes you all out some weekends. How's that going?'

Just prattle about things that don't matter.

'He used to take us to places like Lego Land and Thorpe Park but now on Saturdays Zara goes to gymnastics, and Mum spends the morning at the arts centre doing yoga and drinking coffee with her mates. JoJo loves the crèche there...cars and tractors he can ride.'

'And what do you do on a Saturday?'

'Parkrun...you know...a five kilometre run...free. With Kavya... if she isn't doing a shift at the café.' I'm thinking about Harry and the way his freckles crease up when he smiles.

'Parkrun is a good way to look after your mental health,' she says.

I've said enough. My insides are bubbling up with words I can't say. If I say them, I can't unsay them. Can't catch them and stuff them back inside me.

She's looking at me. She's so kind. Gentle. I could tell her everything. I could.

Tell her about Carl! Tell her!

I'll kill you if you say a single word.

My mouth is dry, and I try to lick my lips but my tongue is rigid sandpaper.

No one will believe you. You'll ruin this family.

She's saying something. I can't hear her above the din of blood pulsing through my ears. But if I tell her, there'd be a cataclysmic explosion that would make Krakatoa look like a damp firework.

Slut.

If I tell her about Carl, it would lead to something new. Change. The big unknown.

There's a knife inside me splitting me off from me, so that I won't feel anything. Splitting me off from memories. So I won't remember.

But I do remember.

It's all my fault.

Sitting on his knee when I was twelve, watching the cricket with him. Making him popcorn in the microwave and getting cold beer out of the fridge.

Asking for it.

All my fault.

I could say that to her.

Maybe?

Best not to.

Time's almost up. She didn't ask anything about me cutting. Or maybe she did, and I wasn't listening.

She's talking again. 'I'll see you here next Tuesday at 11 am so you miss a different lesson. But Poppy, you can come and find me any time.'

Any time?

Like when Carl grabs me?

'Come to this room. If I'm with someone we'll fix a time to talk. Or catch me in the corridor.'

I smile.

She smiles back.

I think I didn't give anything away.

Lying is the way to survive.
I think.

Chapter 20

Sadness

It's my turn to do the paper round so I'm up early and Leroy, the corner shop owner, hands me the papers with his usual smile. But he's busy talking to a customer so I leave without our usual morning banter. I cycle at top speed when I'm on the Ashbury Estate and I shove the papers through the letter boxes, then I'm gone.

I keep telling myself that Wolf and his gang can't even know I exist.

My plan is always to keep out of their way. Reggie says he's not afraid of Wolf, even when he goes into the café when Reggie's working there, but I have a sneaking suspicion that secretly Reggie fears Wolf and his gang just like the rest of us.

I'm back home by seven and hear JoJo's standing up singing and jiggling the cot bars. I lift him out, change his nappy, and take him to the kitchen. I can see that Carl is up early again and is in his shed.

I make a big pot of porridge for everyone with chopped bananas and raisins. Biscuit takes up her place under JoJo's highchair waiting for food to drop.

Zara comes down and she sits next to JoJo and feeds him. She's so good with him. Love my little brother and sister so much.

Carl comes in through the patio door, his aftershave making me gag.

'Morning, Dad,' Zara says. She looks at me. I decide not to react, but I want to hug her and say it's alright. Just because I refuse to call him Dad, that doesn't mean she and I should fall out.

Carl ruffles JoJo's hair, then puts a hand on my shoulder. 'Are you looking forward to Manchester?' he says, sitting down next to me.

'Mmm. Yes. Course I am,' I lie.

I see Zara go rigid. She's angry she's not going, but I can't do anything about that.

At last Carl leaves for work and eventually Mum appears, yawning, still in her pyjamas. She had too much wine last night, so I make her coffee and she sits and drinks it silently.

I text Kavya to say I'll call for her and leave before Mum can get into Daily Inquisition mode.

Although she looks in pain.

I head up to Sandyhills High Street, telling myself I'm not going to look at my phone till I get to school. I go past the library and the leisure centre, then along past the halal butcher and Leroy's corner shop where he's loading up the stands outside on the pavement with gaudy fruit and vegetables.

'Mornin' again, Poppy. How you doing?'

'Mornin' Leroy. I'm fine.' That's yet another lie but I grin and wave. He delivers us a box of fruit and vegetables every Saturday morning and his little girl goes to JoJo's playgroup. And I babysit her sometimes with Kavya.

Leroy's cheerfulness leaves me quickly. He's so well liked by everyone, and it almost gives me the sense that I'm part of some community – Leroy's corner shop community. But the truth is that I don't belong to anything. I hardly belong to my family.

But maybe I belong with Kavya? As Miranda I belong on my island with my dad.

I'm almost at Kavya's flat when I can't resist a look at my phone. I've told myself not to, but I do anyway. There's a picture of me on Insta in my bra and knickers.

I freeze.

Then I'm breathing fast like I've just run parkrun.

I look carefully at the picture. It's taken from above. I think I'm in a cubicle in the changing rooms – so people can't see the scars on my arms. I think it's been photo-shopped to look like I'm next to a bed. Then a message comes in.

Promiscuous Poppy will have sex with anyone. Boys. Girls. She's not fussy. Join the Q.

It's posted by someone called Gorgeousgirl. Mia presumably. I stare at it. Who says 'promiscuous'? Why would anyone say such a thing? Could it be Carl? No. I'm sure he wouldn't. Does someone know about me and Carl? How can they? No. It's probably Mia. I've been waiting for her to post something about me cutting. But not this.

My body trembles. I don't want Harry to see Promiscuous Poppy – but he never seems to have a phone. I try to swallow but can't. I don't know if he does have a phone and he's on Instagram but if he isn't, probably someone will show it to him. If he sees it, he'd probably be glad to get rid of me once *The Tempest* is over.

Slut.

I make myself stop looking at my phone and put it away in my blazer pocket.

Promiscuous Poppy? However will I cope if this post goes all round school?

And it will.

The sadness is who I am. The one on the edge. The one who doesn't belong. The outsider. The rejected.

The smashed to pieces.

Worthless. Useless.

I must find time tonight to write a poem because I'm wondering if the world would miss me if Carl killed me.

Probably not.

At least it would all be over.

I glance into the café next door to Kavya's. Reggie's there serving breakfasts. No wonder he always has money.

I ring the bell to Kavya's flat above The Magical Haircut, and then she's there with her arms around me. 'Not quite ready.' She pulls me upstairs and I'm standing in their little kitchen, Kavya's aunty in her black hairdresser uniform drinking coffee.

'Poppy.' Aunty Anjali kisses my cheek. 'How are you, lovely one?'

My brain is buzzing with Promiscuous Poppy.

'Fine. I'm fine thanks.'

'Are you sure, Poppy?' Anjali says. 'You seem very tense.'

'I'm good,' I say. I'm a great actor.

Of course, not telling the whole truth is another kind of lying.

It's called deception, and though I say it myself, I am very good at it.

'Poppy?' Anjali says with her arms around me.

'Aunty!' Kavya says. 'Give Poppy a break!'

Chapter 21

Hiding

'What's going on, Poppy?' Kavya says as we go out of her door and head for school.

'You haven't looked on Insta then this morning?'

'No.'

I show Kavya Promiscuous Poppy on my phone. My hand is trembling. 'Everyone at school is going to see this. There are already over a hundred likes.'

Kavya stops walking and throws her arms around me.

'I'm only just beginning to see how mega this is,' I say as I lean into her, 'and I don't know how to handle it.' Tears sting my eyes.

'I think we should tell someone.' Kavya's face is hard and determined. 'We can't let people get away with this kind of stuff.'

'But then people will make things worse if we tell on them. It's not worth the risk.'

'Let's tell Miss Singh. She'd know what to do.'

'I'd much rather we didn't,' I say, reaching out and hugging Kavya. 'Please. The revenge could get nasty. I'll just have to ride it out. Today will be the worst. It's just...I don't want Harry to see it.'

Kavya hugs me back. 'Reggie told me Harry's mum keeps confiscating his phone. Sounds as if his mum is a spend-all-evening-doing-your-homework kind of tyrant.'

As soon as we get through the school gate people look at me, then whisper to their mates and giggle behind their hands. Boy's look me up and down smirk.

I stop. 'I can't do this, Kav. I'm going home.' I turn but right behind me is Harry. 'Oh.' We almost bump into each other.

'Poppy...so sorry...Jack showed me on his phone.' Harry is looking into my eyes.

'It's not true,' I say. 'I don't...' I look back, straight in his eyes.

'I know it's not true,' he says.

'I'm going home.' I stride back towards the street.

'Don't let them win,' Harry says, running after me.

'Exactly,' says Kavya. 'You can do this, Poppy. You're a strong woman.'

'Anyway, it's double physics,' Harry says. 'Come on. Don't make it even harder than it already is by missing another lesson.'

I do a snorty giggle, but I'm so embarrassed that Harry heard me do that. I put my hand over my mouth and nose. Harry's right. I mustn't let the bullies win.

Somehow I get myself to registration. The whole tutor group is buzzing with phones out and Mia and her cronies are giggling. I just keep looking at my feet. No way am I engaging with Mia.

I suppose she is Gorgeousgirl but I can't know that for certain.

'Phones away,' Mr Robbins says as he comes into the room. 'I shouldn't have to tell you.' I'm not going to look at him, but he sounds annoyed.

All the chatter stops immediately.

Kavya looks at me and raises her eyebrows. 'Tell him,' she mouths.

'You can't be serious,' I mouth back. How can she possibly think I could say anything with Mia in the room? Kavya is losing touch with reality. That makes my heart leap.

I rush to be first out of registration so Mia can't get to me and on the way to first lesson a younger boy I don't know comes up to me. 'Have sex with me, Poppy,' he says, his face all leery and grinning.

Horror runs down my spine and I don't know what to say, so I rush away from him, feeling myself go hot and red, hearing the laughing following me. I consider hiding in the loos but decide to be braver than that...be strong...not let Mia get to me.

But each lesson change is a nightmare – more stupid comments that make me flinch. I charge through the corridors, desperate not to meet Mia. By lunch time I'm exhausted, and I shut myself in a cubicle in the toilets.

'This is crazy, Poppy,' Kavya says, leaning on the door of the loos. 'What about telling Mr Robbins this afternoon? He'd find out who posted it and give them hell.'

'How can I possibly tell with everyone there?'

'Then go and find him in the staff room or in the art block.' I can hear the irritation in Kavya's voice, and I start crying.

'I just don't feel safe telling.'

Kavya sighs. 'I can understand that. Sorry if I'm being too pushy. Harry said to tell you he hopes you'll stay for rehearsals tonight.'

'He spoke to you?'

'He was trying to find you. I'll come with you to rehearsals if you want.'

'Yes. Please. That would be great.'

'Come out. Please. I want to comfort you.'

So I unlock the door and we hug.

We go to afternoon registration, and everyone seems a bit calmer and so I stop panicking quite as much. I stare at my feet as I go to afternoon lessons, but I don't get any stupid comments.

Maybe I've made it through the worst?

I'm glad I didn't skulk at home today. I probably would have cut myself.

I hear Kavya's words in my head. 'You're a strong woman.'

Chapter 22

The almost kiss

Somehow I get through the day and Kavya comes with me to after school rehearsal. I know she's hoping I'll tell Miss Singh about Promiscuous Poppy.

The hall is stuffy with everyone there, chatting in groups, waiting for Miss Singh. Kavya and I are sitting right at the back, on the top of the tiered seating. I feel safer with my back to a wall.

Messages on Snapchat ping into my phone, but I'm planning on ignoring them.

But the reality is I'm addicted to reading them. I tell myself not to take them seriously. But I glance down.

Do us all a favour and kill yourself.

The world stops for a moment as I stare at my phone. It's from Gorgeousgirl. And it's disappeared already so I decide not to tell Kavya. I look around the hall for Mia. She's surrounded by the Bitch Brigade and looking at me. Holding her phone.

She waves her phone at me and grins.

I'm pretty sure she's Gorgeousgirl.

Scarlet stands apart from the main group of the Bitch Brigade. It really is time she defected.

My brain is full of nagging worry that Harry might think the Promiscuous Poppy post is true.

Reggie's gang are shouting and laughing, fooling around as always on the stage. They've been better than expected today. Not too many stupid comments.

Last week Mia had to do my scenes at rehearsal as my understudy. She and Harry were clearly enjoying acting together.

They were good.

Mega-annoying.

Then I had to rehearse with Haq, Harry's understudy. That was okay because Haq is funny and relaxed and we get on well.

Mia and Harry got very close in the scene in the middle of the play where Harry has to carry logs for firewood and where Miranda and Ferdinand fall in love with each other. They got too close – Harry almost kissed Mia.

It's as if they were copying the actors in the BBC DVD of *The Tempest* we all watched with Miss Singh. I had to stop watching the DVD and stare at my shoes because Ferdinand got much too close to Miranda, and watching Harry and Mia getting close on stage, in a similar way, last week was agonising.

Now Mia's got her talons into Harry it's only a matter of time before they're an item. Perhaps that's why she did the Promiscuous Poppy thing? If Harry thinks I'm a slut that would give him a reason to choose Mia.

Not me.

Today I have to do that same log scene on stage with Harry. He's seen Promiscuous Poppy so he might be quite different with me. He's come into the hall and is standing near the stage and Reggie's gang. And as I watch him, Harry strips to the waist like Ferdinand on the DVD. Kavya's beside me grinning because I can't not stare at his taut body.

Is this Harry's response to Promiscuous Poppy?

Miss Singh comes into the hall and walks to the front and Kavya and I walk to the front too.

'Oh, Harry,' Miss Singh says, but she's laughing. Tell him to put his shirt on, Miss. But she doesn't.

Miss! Tell him to put his shirt on! I feel myself blush. How can I act with him like that?

'Good on yer, Harry!' Reggie shouts. He grins insanely at me. 'Are you ready for him, lover girl?' His minions smirk.

I know I'm strawberry red. But at least Reggie doesn't refer to Promiscuous Poppy in front of Miss Singh.

The Bitch Brigade glance at me, laughing, thumbs working at top speed on their phones. I suppose more Snapchat will come to me.

I dare not look at Mia.

How can I cope with Harry's nakedness?

I feel maggots eating my insides.

I don't want Harry to get too close to me on stage.

I do want Harry to get close to me.

On stage.

Or anywhere else.

But Harry's being dragged into the popular kids' gangs. He often sits with Reggie in the cafeteria at lunch time, the Bitch Brigade near them, with plenty of interaction between the two groups. They seem to enjoy their status – as if they've reached the pinnacle of what it is to be a human being – to be Popular.

Kavya leans into me, 'I can see you can't keep your eyes off him.'

'Log scene again,' I say, ignoring her. 'It's so hard.'

'Getting easier though, isn't it?' She puts her hand on my arm.

'Yeah.'

That's a lie. How can it be easier with Harry's torso shining at me? And it's the most embarrassing scene ever because we keep looking into each other's eyes and we fall in love.

It's all too overwhelming so I leave my body and drift off with Dad...The sky is bright blue and there's just the slightest breeze...He's smiling at me. He makes everything magical.

'Earth to Poppy!' Kavya whispers in my ear. 'You're on!' Xavier and Harry are staring at me from the stage. I swear I lose time.

'Come on, Poppy,' says Miss Singh. 'You look miles away.'

'Rehearsing my lines in my head,' I lie. I know my face is burning as I run to the stage, but I breathe deeply as I go up the steps and wait in the wings. I cling to the burgundy curtains, trying to stay in the present.

Harry's neck muscles tense as he carries the logs. His words are perfect. My brain flashes, 'TOTALLY GONE BLANK' at me.

Panic.

But I walk out from the wings anyway. I have to offer to help him carry the logs.

Got that bit right. He's too chivalrous to let me lug wood of course.

I'm tense near his nakedness. How am I going to carry this scene off in December with hundreds of people watching me?

Xavier as Prospero is lurking behind us, staff in hand, working his magic to make Harry and me fall deeply in love.

'*What is your name?*' says Harry.

'*Miranda,*' I breathe.

Harry tells me he's a prince – maybe even a king now his father has probably died in the storm. *'For your sake I am this patient log man.'*

I hate this bit. I have to look at his beautiful green eyes and say it. *'Do you love me?'*

Harry's amazing. He does his long reply where he says he'd be lying if he said no.

He's too close to me.

His chest and arms glistening. He's wearing a bit too much after shave – or deodorant – some kind of sweet musky smell – and I try not to gag.

I have to pretend to cry, but a real tear runs down my cheek. I wipe it away – embarrassment making me cringe.

Harry raises his eyebrows.

I have to keep going.

'I am your wife if you will marry me.' I manage to get out the whole speech, a lump forming in my throat threatening to stop me being able to say anything.

'Young love!' calls Reggie and I hear Miss Singh hiss back at him to be quiet.

'Here's my hand,' Harry says, reaching out.

'And mine with... my heart in it,' I say, glad my voice is working but knowing we must do that dramatic pause, looking into each other's eyes.

We pause.

His body's almost touching mine.

My heart thuds.

His lips are glossy as he leans towards me.

I feel Carl's wet lips pressed to mine and I freeze.

I hear someone screaming. And it's me. I'm not in my body but floating above the stage looking down on myself still screaming.

My legs give way and I'm lying on the stage floor. Kavya's beside me. And Miss Singh. And Harry. 'Sorry! So sorry, Poppy,' he's saying. 'They...on the DVD and I thought...'

'What happened? What's wrong?' Kavya's holding my head on her lap. 'You're ok, Poppy. Look at me. You're ok.'

'Here's her water bottle,' says Scarlet.

'Drink,' says Miss Singh. Kavya's holding my head up and puts my water bottle to my lips.

In my head words and images clash against each other.

Carl's wet lips and his voice: *Kiss me back you little slut.*

Harry was leaning towards me...

I hear Mia. 'Always said she was a psycho,' and the rest of the Bitch Brigade snigger.

Reggie and the minions are laughing.

'This isn't funny,' says Miss Singh. She's kneeling beside me, and I want to reassure her. But that's crazy. 'Stand back everyone,' she says.

'So sorry, Poppy.' Harry's still beside me.

Sorry? He didn't actually kiss me.

I start to cry. 'I'm ok,' I say, but my voice comes out high pitched, hysterical. I feel so stupid.

I hear Miss Singh tell Harry to leave. But he hovers. I wish I could explain – and I want him to hold me. I'm feeling myself drift away, running into Dad's arms.

Miss Singh is talking to me. Patting my arm.

'Scarlet,' she says, 'go and see if Rachel's in her room and ask her to come.'

Oh, please, God. No! Not School Shrink.

'The rest of you, please go home,' says Miss Singh. 'We'll leave it there for today.'

Mia and Harry leave the hall together.

The noise in my head is less and I prop myself up on my elbows.

'I'm ok,' I say.

'Course you are,' says Kavya. She helps me sit up. Gives me a tissue.

'Do you hurt anywhere?' Miss Singh looks worried. 'I'll have to write this up as an accident, but I don't know what happened. Was it Harry leaning in like that?'

'It was just a funny turn,' says Kavya. 'Up you get.' I grip onto her as I stand.

Carl's face smashes through my head.

If you tell anyone, I will kill you.

Miss Singh drags a chair in from the wings and I sit.

I'm crying again but my body rests against Kavya, sitting next to me, and I'm sobbing.

'Can I help?' It's Rachel – School Shrink and before I know what's happened I'm moving along the corridor into School Shrink's little room. I'm still holding Kavya's hands, and nothing makes any sense. I'm facing Rachel. Her face is kind. Plucked eyebrows but hardly any make up. She's wearing red today.

I don't know what to say to this woman.

She's smiling.

Talking.

I could just tell her everything.

Go on. Risk everything. Tell her what's going on.

But I can't. I feel far too ashamed. So I talk some drivel.

All lies.

Slut.

Chapter 23

We have to talk

Kavya comes all the way home with me because I'm still feeling wobbly after talking to School Shrink about the almost kiss. The wind is blowing leaves off the trees, and I try to tell myself how much I like autumn, the colours, the lushness of blackberries, and our apple and plum tree in the garden at home. But I just feel myself burning up at the memory of screaming and collapsing onto the stage.

How am I ever going to explain that to Harry?

I hate myself.

'We have to talk about what just happened with Harry,' Kavya says.

'I can't talk about it.' Even to Kavya. I can't explain because I don't know what happened.

The silence between us is painful.

'I know you're really upset about the Promiscuous Poppy thing. I know you know everyone's talking about it. And then Harry...doing...whatever he did. Tell me how you're feeling...please.'

'Kav, I can't talk about it.'

I can't even look at her, but she does her I-love-you-anyway hug and puts her arm around me and I melt into that.

Kavya gives my shoulder a squeeze. 'I know you don't want to talk about it, but...probably...the collapsing...whatever...was probably about what Carl is doing to you.'

I grunt.

'You really need to tell someone, Poppy.'

'No...I...' I'm out of words.

'I'll help you. I'll do anything I can. So just think about it, Poppy. Please.'

I grunt again.

'He's a criminal. Remember that. He belongs in jail.'

I'm silent.

Really? Carl could go to jail? I suppose I know that, but I keep pretending I don't, and I shut it out of my head.

I'm going off the idea of being Miranda. Perhaps I should just let Mia have the part? If I let her, that might stop the Bitch Brigade bullying.

I wish I hadn't said anything to School Shrink just now. What am I going to say to her next week? I wish I could remember what I've already said.

Lying has disadvantages if you don't have a super-human memory.

I keep seeing Harry's lips coming towards me. For an instant I know they are Carl's lips, but I shut that thought out. I try to rub my face to take the memory away. I don't understand why I screamed. I'll never live it down.

Did Harry try to kiss me because of the Promiscuous Poppy stuff? Did he mean that he believes that's what I'm like? He said he didn't. But was he telling the truth?

'Poppy isn't feeling well,' Kavya says to Mum when we get in. 'Maybe an early night? I'll do the paper round in the morning so she can have a lie in.'

'Oh,' Mum says, her lips thin and her voice sharp. 'I need to leave for work soon, so I was expecting Poppy to dish up. It's in the oven.' I cringe at the way Mum never makes any effort to hide her dislike of Kavya. And Kavya is just her usual straightforward self, confident and honest, despite the dagger-looks Mum throws at her.

'It's ok, Mum. I'll do it,' I say, giving Kavya a shut-up-right-now look.

'Bed straight after that, then,' says Kavya frowning at me.

'And JoJo needs to be fetched from next door in half an hour, have his tea and be put to bed,' Mum says. 'And Carl will be in about six thirty to eat. I'm sure you can stay up till then.'

'I'll be fine, Mum.'

'I'll be off then,' Kavya says. I can tell she's miffed at me but I have to keep Mum sweet. 'Bye everyone,' she says, and I reach out and hug her and she pulls away from me. I wish Mum would let her stay.

'Poppy!' Zara appears at the top of the stairs, still in her school uniform. 'I need to talk to you about something.' She waves her phone at me.

Mum frowns.

'Ok,' I walk upstairs.

'Half an hour then get JoJo,' Mum says.

We both go into my room.

'You've seen all this promiscuous stuff on Insta, I guess,' says Zara, shutting the door. 'I doubt Mum will see it, so you're probably safe.'

'Yes. Saw it. Not true.' I say. Words won't focus properly in my head.

Zara leans back against the door. 'I know it's not true! Have a bit of trust in me,' she says, staring at her phone. 'I've managed to take down some of the replies. I'm trying to see if I can take down the original photo with you...you know...but it's gone viral, and I can't see how to do it. It's everywhere.'

'You've taken stuff down from Insta?' I say. 'How?'

'You're not the only one who can do tech, Poppy,' Zara says.

I don't want this conversation with Zara. 'Look I've had a whole day of it, so...' I could just curl up and sleep right now.

'But this other stuff. Tonight,' says Zara. 'There's a rumour going around that you swooned over Harry.' She grins at me.

'Is the door closed properly?' I whisper. 'Look, I collapsed. I thought Harry was leaning in to kiss me like on the DVD we watched. I...I...don't quite know...' I'm saying too much.

'So you really did swoon!'

'No...I...'

'But new Harry's gorgeous!' Zara says, grinning.

I laugh and that breaks the tension. My little sister is getting interested in boys.

Zara steps towards me and grips me on both shoulders. 'So it's true you collapsed because you're totally and utterly falling over in love with him?'

'No!'

'And you were so freaked out you had to go and talk to School Shrink? True?'

'Who says?' I'm so tired.

'School rumour,' Zara says, waving her phone. 'Was it weird talking to School Shrink?'

'I don't want to talk about it.' I want to lie down and sleep. 'It was just a funny turn...I kind of fainted. Probably didn't eat enough lunch or something.'

'If you say so,' says Zara. 'But I'm going with the theory that at last my School Nerd sister is doing something normal for once and falling for New Harry. He's so cute!' She grins at me, waves her phone, and goes out.

I lie back on my bed, thinking about what Kayva said. That I need to tell someone about Carl.

Mum?

I don't know if I dare.

But at least I've got a mum. The memories of Kavya's mum getting thinner and thinner flood my mind. Kavya was so brave when she died.

I didn't know how to help.

Useless.

I fetch JoJo from next door and give him his tea, bath him and put him to bed. Then Carl comes in and we eat Mum's casserole. It has far too much chili in it, but Carl likes it.

How can I tell someone about him? And who do I tell?

'I don't feel well,' I say, leaving most of my meal on my plate. 'Is it ok if I go to bed?'

'I'll help clear up,' says Zara. She smiles at me and reaches out and holds my hand.

'Of course,' says Carl. 'You go to bed. Do you need painkillers or anything?'

'No thanks. I need to sleep.'

Hopefully I've given him a strong enough message to keep away from me.

My head aches and I wonder how I can face everyone at school tomorrow. Whatever could I say to Harry?

I try to sleep but there's too much to think about. I can't get the thought out of my head that Harry tried to kiss me because he saw the Promiscuous Poppy message.

And believes it.

I know Kavya is right. I have to tell someone about Carl. But jail? Mum would never forgive me. And how on earth would we manage without his money? We'd have to go back to another tiny flat like that awful one we lived in after Dad left.

And it's not just Mum who'd be angry. Zara would say it's all my fault.

Oh God, why did you make life so complicated?

Are you listening to me?

Chapter 24

Meeting Harry

The next day I'm nervous about going to school and facing people who saw me making an idiot of myself, falling over yesterday. But Kavya and I need to get together for our presentation on revenge in *The Tempest*. If we can get it right, Miss Singh would give us a 7, 8 or even a 9 grade.

But I've made a fool of myself so often and somehow life goes on. That's what Mum used to tell me anyway, back then when Mum and I used to talk. Before money and wine took over her life.

Life was so uncomplicated back then when I was twelve.

Eighty-two days until Zara is thirteen.

I feel myself heat up as I get closer to school. I put my head down, get through the main doors where a wave of voices hits me. I try to weave through the crowded corridors unnoticed. Our tutor room is empty except for Xavier sitting at the back staring at his phone.

I sit at my desk, get my phone out and look up revenge in *The Tempest*. We only have five minutes to do our presentation and we have two more weeks to get it finished. We're taking the line in our presentation that it's better to let things go than to take revenge. Reggie will shout us down, of course. He's already told us that in his presentation he's going to say 'an eye for an eye' and that you must always take revenge.

Sometimes I wonder about taking revenge on Carl, but that just makes me terrified, and my mind goes blank. Anything I do might just make everything worse.

I can tell Miss Singh quietly in religious studies that I can't go on being Miranda. I'm pretty sure that will make Mia back off from taking revenge on me. But it hurts that I have to do this.

I keep reading on my phone as a few people drift into the classroom. For a moment they are silent, but then the usual buzz of voices starts up.

I sense someone's come right up to me. I daren't look.

A note drops on my desk.

Meet me. Twelve o'clock. Just inside the double doors into the hall – by the blue lockers. H.

Goosebumps rise on my arms.

I turn. Harry walks out of the classroom.

The room is silent, and I look around at stunned faces. Jaws dropped open. Perhaps what just happened doesn't quite fit in with what's on their phones? But they can't know what was on the note.

Thumbs are busy on phones. Something will be all round school soon. I've never been so interesting.

But what will Harry say to me at twelve o'clock? I'm not sure I can face him. But I want to face him. Be with him.

But what if he tried to kiss me because of Promiscuous Poppy? What if he and Mia are planning my ultimate downfall?

Kavya's beside me, slipping into her chair. 'You're the colour of a strawberry,' she whispers. 'What's going on?'

I show her the note and we're both grinning when the Bitch Brigade walk in, all false eyelashes and lip gloss.

Mia has this way of looking down her nose at me. If only she had nasal hair sticking out, then I could comment on that. I try to ignore her, but I know I'm grinning because I'm meeting Harry at twelve and she doesn't know.

'What've you got to smile about?' Mia says. She waves her phone at me. 'Did you see what people think of you? Not really in touch, are you?'

I think she probably doesn't expect me to reply.

Then her nose is close to mine. Expensive perfume surrounds me. 'You can't be Miranda, you freak. Not with a face like yours and your ridiculously short hair. Not when you clearly can't cope. You're falling apart. So give it up. Right now. Let those of us that can actually act be the star of the play.'

That's the moment I decide I will be Miranda! I'm staring into Mia's face and from nowhere a snorty giggle erupts out of me.

For a nanosecond fear shows in Mia's eyes. But her lips curl and she spits 'Psycho' at me and goes to the back of the room with the courtiers. Scarlett gives me an uncertain look.

'Morning everyone.' It's Mr Robins. I jam my phone in my bag. He's ready for work in his paint spattered apron and tidy beard. Wearing sandals, with socks, as always, even in winter. He sits at his desk and does the register, but he keeps glancing at me.

I didn't like him much when we started high school in Year 7. He was quite strict but seemed not to see how Mia was bullying other girls – like me, and Kavya. So I thought he was yet another Mia-blind teacher like at primary school. But when they found out I was bunking off school when I was thirteen, he was unbelievably kind. Blew me away. One day I showed him a photo on my phone of Biscuit, and he showed me one of his dog, Barney, a Battersea Dogs Home rescue, all fluffy and brown like a teddy bear.

When the bell goes and everyone is leaving, Mr. Robins calls me back. 'OK, Poppy?' he says. I take hold of Kavya's hand so she'll hang back with me. 'Miss Singh told me about the incident on stage yesterday. I think the school counsellor will be sending you a time to see her. And you know you can always talk to me, don't you?'

'Yes, Sir.'

'Any time. Get me out of the staff room – come to the art block.'

'Thank you, Sir. But I'll be fine.'

'Poppy, if I had a pound for every time you told me you'd be fine, I'd be on a yacht on the Mediterranean, painting like Van Gogh.'

I grin at him and he turns to Kavya. 'Same goes for you, Kavya. You can find me any time.' He looks from Kavya to me. 'Look after each other. OK?'

I think Kavya's smile at me means you-could-tell-him-about Carl. But I shove that thought to the back of my brain.

The morning drags and my stomach churns the whole time. What's Harry going to say when we meet? I can't even concentrate in religious studies with Miss Singh. We're talking about the bad people in *The Tempest*. Was Antonio born bad? Or did he become bad because of what happened to him? And why does God let bad things happen to good people?

Why does God let Carl do it to me?

What is Harry going to say? How can I explain me falling down?

Kavya and I made a plan that she'll lurk by the new lockers in the corridor at twelve and I come and find her afterwards. 'Or don't find me – just be with Harry,' she says.

When the bell goes at twelve, Kavya hugs me and I head to the hall. I don't think I'm being followed. I push through the crowd around the blue lockers then go through the double doors into the hall into the silence. The musty warmth from the hall surrounds me, the sun spilling through the huge windows.

He's not here. Was it all a practical joke? Something to make me feel stupid? Did he plan this with Mia, and she's going to come and jeer at me? Maybe they're an item now and they planned the attempted kiss and it's a way to make me give up Miranda?

My mind is racing and I'm finding it hard to breathe. In for five. Out for nine.

It's five past. He's not coming. It was a set up after all.

Then he's there, his green eyes smiling at me. His backpack over one shoulder. His blazer flapping open.

His musky smell isn't worrying me today.

'Sorry! Got held up – Reggie wanted to talk,' he says. 'The vultures saw me give you the note this morning.' He looks straight at me. 'I wanted to check you're OK...I was worried about you...sorry I tried to kiss you.'

I can't look at him. He's a bit too close to me.

'I'm so sorry. Poppy?'

Then I'm staring into his eyes and I grin at him.

'It's OK,' I say. My voice is a bit gravelly. 'Don't know why I had that funny turn.'

'So you're OK?'

'I'm fine. Really.'

'I was so worried I'd done something really bad...sexual harassment or something.'

'No. No. Well, maybe it was...but...It's OK.'

'It was just a joke – after we saw the BBC DVD.' He runs his hand through his hair. 'I shouldn't have done it. Sorry.'

'It's really OK. You don't need to keep apologising. But –'

'What?'

'You said Jack showed you...those posts...that I sleep with anyone?'

'Yes, but I didn't believe them.'

'So that wasn't...why you kissed me?'

'No! No, not at all...Oh...so sorry. I was just being a stupid idiot. Will I see you tonight at rehearsal? Will you be OK? I promise no kissing when we have to do the log scene again.' He's laughing, but not at me, so I laugh too.

'I'll be there.'

'Let's go to lunch separately,' he says. 'I don't want people gossiping.'

Why doesn't he want to be seen with me?

'Reggie's being very odd.'

'He's always odd,' I say and a high-pitched giggle bursts out of me. Mega embarrassing.

'And Crabbe and Goyle still treat me like an alien. See you later.'

Then he's gone so I lean back against the wall. How weird was that? Is he just being nice to me because he's sorry for me? Or does he like me? He doesn't believe Promiscuous Poppy. Was he genuine? I think he was, and we're rehearsing tonight. So I get to stare into his eyes again.

But Mia will have a plan to take revenge because almost certainly she will have found out that Harry met up with me.

But I'm not going to let her get to me.

Possibly.

Chapter 25

Childline

Kavya and I meet up at her flat every day to get the words right for our religious studies revenge presentation. She makes hot chocolate, and we sit on the bed in her blue bedroom. We have to do a PowerPoint and mostly we agree on what we'll say. Neither of us think taking revenge is a good thing.

When we finish for the day, Kavya puts her arm around me. 'I so wish you'd tell your mum about Carl. She'd want to know.'

'She won't believe me.'

'Carl has brainwashed you to believe that.'

I love it that Kavya is so gentle and cares for me, but she's not seeing how hard it is to say something.

I feel so ashamed.

It's all your fault. People will know that.

'You don't ever talk about taking revenge on Carl,' she says.

'Huh! What could I do? It would only make it a million times worse. And anyway, I thought we were saying that taking revenge is a bad idea?'

'Yes,' she says, laughing. 'We're definitely saying that, but we're making it mega clear that people should get justice when bad things happen to them. And you'll only get justice if you tell on Carl.'

I know she's right. But how can I ever pluck up courage to tell Mum? And anyway, what are the chances she'll believe me?

Kavya goes to make us more hot chocolate. I sit on her bed, my head a whirling mass of chaos. Prospero in *The Tempest* doesn't take revenge because he chooses to be kind and forgive Antonio – which I think is a bit weird – and we say that in our presentation. But if people chose to be kind instead of making other people's life hell, school at least would be a better place.

'OK,' says Kavya. 'I hope we get a 9.' She hands me a mug then she gets her laptop. 'I want to show you what I've found online. Look. Someone had the same problem you have with Carl. Look what she says.'

I peer at the laptop.

'See,' Kavya says, 'this girl says her mum was brilliant when she told her about her stepdad and the police came. She's happy now.'

'But you hate the police,' I say.

'Only because of how awful they were to Mum and me when Dad died. But they can't all be idiots. Anyway, I know you know the Childline number to ring cos we did it in PHSE and I remember you were there. People are waiting at the end of a phone, Poppy, just there so people like you can ring them. I'll text it to you.'

Kavya: 0800 1111 Ring them.

I stare at my phone.

'Maybe ringing Childline will be easier than telling your mum?' Kavya says. 'Just don't give them your name. You could call yourself something else...'

'Amelie. That's who I am.'

'OK...Poppy, you surprise me every day...Amelie?'

'Yes, Claude Monet's daughter – the man who painted my poppy picture.'

'I think Monet just had two sons...Whatever. Ring Childline Poppy. You'll feel better. I know you will. I...I feel responsible...cos of just me knowing...if you ring...you know...if an adult knows as well as me...it would share the load.'

She hugs me and guilt seeps into my head. I've put too much on my best friend. But I could ring and not give my name.

'OK, I'll do it. Just to shut you up.'

'I'll be there with you when you ring – if you want.'

'Er...no...but thanks. I'll do it on my own.'

When I get home Zara's in her room playing her flute, Carl is out, JoJo is still with Mrs Bernstein next door and Mum is on her phone in the kitchen with the radio on. So I should be OK to ring Childline. I put my desk chair against my bedroom door anyway and sit at the furthest end of my bed, as far away from the door as possible, facing the wall.

No one must hear me.

Maybe I should have let Kavya be with me? Too late now.

I take a deep breath. Punch in 0800 1111. My hand is shaking so much I can hardly hold my phone to my ear.

There's a voice. 'Hello, you're through to the switchboard at Childline.'

I can't make any words come out of my mouth.

'It sounds like you're finding it quite hard to speak at the moment. I'm going to put you through to a counsellor who can support you.'

I still can't speak.

There's another voice. 'Hi there, you are through to someone you can talk to.'

I still can't get words out.

'Don't worry. Just take your time. I'm here to listen.'

My brain goes empty.

I try the breathing exercises School Shrink taught me.

'My stepfather,' I blurt out. 'He makes me have sex with him.'

I can't believe I said that.

'You know that is wrong of him to do that, and none of that is your fault,' she says in a voice so kind I want to cry.

But I just keep quiet because it is my fault.

What does she know?

'You're really brave for speaking out about what's happening to you. I'm wondering what it would be like to speak to an adult that you trust?'

'No one will believe me.'

'I want you to know that Childline believes you...'

'I've got to go.' I've said too much, and my head is spinning with shame. I never meant to say so much.

'Remember you are not to blame for what your stepdad is doing to you. We are always here to listen and support you – twenty-four hours a day, and seven days a week.'

I switch off my phone. My breathing is rapid, and I lie down. But I did it! I want to tell Kavya, yet I'm not up for talking to anyone.

I stare at my poppy picture. Go into it.

Be little Amelie for a bit.

The next day I call for Kavya in the morning and tell her I rang.

'You're a star, and I love you.' She hugs me.

'The woman said I was brave. And to tell someone. So I'm thinking I could tell Mum.'

'Brilliant!'

'I'm hoping I can be really brave...it's not long till Zara's thirteen.'

'Go for it girl. You do it...better than letting Carl...you know.' She rubs her hand across her scalp. She's had another two-millimetre haircut from Anjali.

'She won't believe me. Carl said Mum wouldn't.'

'You might be surprised.'

When I think about the reality of telling Mum my whole body shakes. Part of the problem is that Carl might see me talking to Mum on the CCTV monitors in his shed. If he ever plays back what has gone on in the house while he's out. Presumably he does.

Snooper.

He won't hear any sound though. He'll just see me talking to Mum. I wish I knew how Mum is going to react.

That evening I put my chair under my bedroom door handle again and go online with Childline and read some of the posts. Loads of people have all kinds of problems and others make suggestions for what they could do.

In the next few days I go to Kavya's flat and we read more Childline posts together.

One day, someone called Kylie – bet it's not her real name – says she told her mum, and it worked out.

'See? It all worked out for another person telling their mum.' Kavya takes my hand. 'Come on. You can tell your mum. I'll come and be with you if you want.'

'Best not to. You know what she's like with you.' I take Kavya's hand. 'You're so good to me and I'm so sorry about the way my mum treats you.'

'Don't worry about it.' She grins and hugs me.

'You know what? I'm going to do it.' I ignore the surge of fear that runs down my spine. 'I'll tell Mum tomorrow. Yes...tomorrow.'

'Promise?'

'Promise.'

That night at home I get out my secret diary from under my bed. Gran gave it to me one birthday and I love that I can lock it with the tiny key so no one can read my thoughts or poems. I write what I could say to Mum. My hand trembles. But I'm going to tell her.

I hear Carl's words replaying in my head like some demon music track that's driven by magic and impossible to stop. *No one will believe you. Your mum will be furious if you tell her. She'll know you're just being your usual hysterical self and making a fuss. She knows you've always had a thing for me, so she'll know it was your fault and she'll throw you out.*

I'll kill you if you tell anyone.

As I walk home the next day, I try to do deep breathing.

But if I tell Mum, will she protect me? Or reject me? I want her to put her arms around me and hug me just because I'm me.

But I don't want Mum to know what I did. How it was all my fault.

How I kissed Carl.

But I'm ready to tell Mum. Just the bits she needs to know. I just have to take a deep breath.

Then say it.

Maybe Mum will believe me and it'll all end. I'll be free. We can get back to how we used to be.

Before Carl.

I try not to think about how we'll manage without his money.

I put my bag down next to the hall table. I can hear Mum in the kitchen with the radio on. I can tell JoJo must still be next door, and I know Zara will be in her bedroom getting her homework done. She always likes to do that as soon as she gets home. I take a deep breath.

This is it.

I walk into the kitchen. It's almost dark, Mum's body silhouetted against the patio door. I switch the lights on, and they reflect on the shiny black granite surface.

Biscuit clatters in from the garden. She jumps up and puts her front paws on my legs and I hug her and feed her.

'Mum, I want to talk to you.'

She doesn't look up.

'I'm listening.' She keeps on rolling the pastry for the chicken pie. Her glass of wine beside her on the kitchen work top. She stops and sweeps her long hair back, leaving a smear of flour down the side of her face.

I wish she would stop cooking and listen. Maybe I should switch the radio off?

My limbs feel rigid. I glance up at the CCTV camera in the corner of the kitchen.

Your mother will throw you out. Hear that? Throw you out.

I hear Kavya's voice. 'You have to tell, Poppy.'

'Er...Mum...I'm not sure how to...er...' My sentences I'd practised have fallen out of my head. I can't look at her.

'What? Come on. Spit it out.' She takes a slug of wine.

'I...er...'

'You're pregnant!' She glares at me.

'No, Mum, course not.' My hand goes to my stomach. I'm a bit bloated. Pre-period. I suppose I could tell her that Steve gets stuff for Carl to inject me every few months but now isn't the moment to say that.

I feel as if maggots are eating my throat.

Breathe.

'You sure?'

I nod.

She bites the skin down the edge of her thumb making it bleed. She didn't used to do that. 'What then? Come on. I haven't got all day. I'm working tonight...it takes so much time to do Carl's favourite meal.' She lays the pastry over the chicken mixture in the dish, then trims the edges. 'He does love his chicken pie. Don't just stand there. Poppy! Tell me.'

'Well...you see...when you're out at work...Carl comes to my room...' I falter. The Monet picture of the poppies floods into my head. I sink into the picture and I'm in the field, running my hands along the tops of the grass, the sun shining, playing with friends, free.

'Poppy. You go off somewhere with the fairies. What do you want? Tell me!'

'Carl...he...'

Little slut. Asking for it.

'I don't know why you treat Carl the way you do. He's fond of you. Look at how he's taking you to Manchester at half term.' She turns and puts the pie in the oven. 'I'll set the timer to end at six thirty when Carl gets in. You serve it, with some salad.'

She starts to clean the kitchen surface. Bites the skin next to her thumb again. It bleeds and she licks it. Then she stops cleaning and turns to me.

'Look, Poppy, why don't you and I go clothes shopping some time, eh? Come with me one day when I'm off handbag shopping maybe?'

It's hard to breathe. I try to gulp in air.

'OK,' I say. 'I'd like that.'

'But you have to stop all this nonsense,' she says, frowning at me, 'Carl's so hurt that you won't help him with the new robot. He says you're so good at it...and he likes you to do the controls at Robot Wars. He really thinks he can get to the final next year.'

'Mum...Carl hurts me...'

'He makes you work hard. We want you to go to uni.'

Blood is hissing through my ears. I have to tell her.

'Mum...please listen. Carl...makes me do things I don't want to do. I say no but –'

'Listen my girl,' she says, turning towards me. 'You need to learn some gratitude towards Carl.' She takes another gulp of wine. 'He bought us this house. You've got your own room, for goodness sake. He looks after us. His business is doing great...and all you can do is make up lies because you misunderstand the situation.'

'Mum! I don't misunderstand! If Gran were here, she'd listen to me.'

Mum glares at me, like she always does when I mention Gran. 'What? I don't understand what changed between you and Carl, I really don't.'

'That's what I'm trying to tell you – '

'He's not the kind of person you get on the wrong side of, you know.'

'I know that Mum...I've seen the way he treats you...'

'That's none of your business.'

'But I'm scared of him too, Mum.'

'I'm not scared. It's just that he...well...' She drains her glass and pours herself some more.

'Mum, when you're out...he hurts me...he...he...sort of...he makes me...you know...he touches me.'

How can my mother not guess what I'm trying to say?

She twists her hands around so she can bite the skin down the edge of a finger.

'I don't know what you're talking about. You're just making things up...turning me against Carl. I know your tricks. It's me, me, me, all the time with you.'

'Mum!' Guilt shoots through me and I have to gasp for breath. My fault. My fault. I feel my knees go weak.

She drains her wine glass.

Tell her!

'Mum, please listen!'

'Oh, you –'

'Mum! Listen!' She stands still and looks straight at me.

'It's Carl...he...he makes me –'

'I don't want to hear any more of this.'

Chapter 26

Red wine

My chest goes so tight, I feel I can't breathe and the glare of the light shining off the granite worktop hurts my eyes. But I must keep going.

'Mum! Please listen! Carl makes me have sex with him!'

Mum's wine glass smashes on the floor. Red wine seeping towards me like blood. Splinters of glass spread across the floor. 'Look what you made me do!' she says, her voice hard and angry.

Oh no! JoJo! Biscuit! Bare feet!

And Carl will see that on the CCTV.

'Sorry, Mum.' I feel I can't move. Biscuit looks up from her basket. 'Stay,' I say to her. 'Stay!' I want to hug my little dog. Hold her close to make the bad feelings go away.

The blood moves towards me.

Mum stares at the blood too. 'Look at all that mess,' she says. Her body slumps forward and she leans on the work surface.

I hear Zara's footsteps on the stairs, and she bursts into the kitchen. 'Oh. I heard a crash. Are you two arguing again?'

'It's fine,' says Mum. 'An accident.'

'We're fine, Zara. Don't worry.' I just told my sister the most enormous lie. But she must be safe from all of this.

'Go back upstairs, Zara' I say. 'I just have to sort out something with Mum.'

Mum is glaring at me. 'Maybe Zara could make us all a cup of tea.'

'No! Mum, this is between you and me. Please go upstairs, Zara.'

My sister's face is full of worry, and I know she's desperate to know what's going on. She looks at me. Then at Mum. She hovers for a moment, twists her plaits in front of her face, turning them in her hands as if she's working out what to say. Then she goes out, thumps upstairs, and slams her bedroom door.

Mum reaches up and gets another glass. Fills it with wine.

'Carl just wouldn't do things like that,' she says. 'Somehow you've got it all wrong.'

'No, Mum, I haven't got it wrong.'

'Look, you're obviously not happy. You need help.'

'I'm asking you for help, Mum.'

'Well, stop lying then.'

'I'm not lying! Carl rapes me!'

'You are lying,' she says, and her hand swings around and hits my cheek. For a moment I'm unsteady on the wet floor. Tears flood into my eyes and I clutch the side of my face, taste the blood in my mouth.

But I feel nothing because I've done it. I've said it, but my head is spinning, and I hold onto the black granite of the breakfast bar to steady myself.

'You need to clean up this mess,' Mum says, her voice slurred and tense. 'I'm going to watch the television.'

The heels of her slippers clack on the floor as she leaves. My hands are trembling, but I get a floor cloth out of the cupboard, and a dustpan and brush.

Biscuit whines.

'Stay there, my darling,' I say, not caring now that I'm crying. Then I sweep up every tiny shard of glass and wrap it in newspaper, so that everyone is safe. As I squeeze the last of the wine out of the cloth one of the shards pierces my wrist.

I watch the blood drip.

I breathe in for five. Out for nine.

I've told Mum now.

Without her finding out about me kissing Carl.

Little whore.

I hear Mum has the TV on in the lounge. I put a dab of antiseptic cream on my wrist where the shard of glass stabbed me. I long to escape with Biscuit, but I'm so tired, I just want to go to bed. I know I might cut tonight.

I'll try not to.

Possibly.

But it's no different from Mum biting the skin on the side of her thumb.

Someone needs to get JoJo from next door.

Carl'll be home about six thirty. Then Mum'll leave for work. I'm going to ask Mum not to tell Carl what I said about him. Not yet anyway. I can't face the thought that she might have known before I told her.

If she tells Carl tonight, I could be dead by tomorrow.

I'll kill you if you say a single word.

If Carl kills me, I can't protect JoJo and Zara.

I go out into the garden with Biscuit to clear my mind. As I stand there watching her, it starts to rain, big heavy drops, thundering down onto the patio. God, I need your help right now.

Do you hear me?

I look up at the CCTV camera. Carl will know I stood here. He knows exactly what I do in the house every day. He'll have my row with Mum in the kitchen on tape too. And the row I might have in the next few minutes with Mum. Good thing there's no sound.

I'm soaked in just a few moments so call Biscuit and go in. I hug her and tell her to stay in her basket.

She does a complaining whine. Sometimes I think she knows exactly what's going on.

I get myself a glass of water and creep into the lounge. Mum is slumped on the sofa, legs up, gripping her wine glass. I know what I said must have been a shock.

'Mum. You OK?'

'No. Since you ask.'

'Please don't tell Carl what I said.'

Silence.

'It's important you don't tell him, Mum.

More silence.

'I'll get JoJo, shall I?'

'Yes,' she says. 'Get out of my sight. Get him, give him tea, bath him and put him to bed.' She turns back to the TV, ignoring me.

I go outside and stand in the gap in the hedge, almost in next door's garden. It's still raining, and I look up at the sky for a while, unable to stop my tears. I thought I would feel relieved when I told Mum, but it feels as if I've made everything worse.

But I must get JoJo from Mrs Bernstein and get him to bed. Although there are still things to say to Mum before Carl gets back. I must get her to promise not to say anything to Carl. So I'll need to get Zara to look after JoJo.

I ring the bell next door.

'Hello, Poppy. How lovely to see you, dear. Come in.'

I keep looking down, so she won't see I've been crying. 'Hello Mrs Bernstein.'

'Oh, my dear, call me Esther, please.'

Despite having JoJo with her all day, she looks so calm – although the boys are screaming in the lounge. 'We've had such a good day,' she says, reaching up and tightening her head scarf. 'Playgroup had a visit from a farmer, and we saw chickens and goats, didn't we?' she says as she sorts out the boys' argument. I stand by the lounge door, trying to get rid of Mum's angry face from my head.

'Mine,' shrieks JoJo and runs away from Ruben with a toy police car.

'I'll get JoJo's coat and bag,' Esther says, looking straight into my face. 'Oh, Poppy, you've been crying. Oh, my dear. Sit down.' She puts her arms around me. 'The boys will play for a bit longer. What is it?' She sits beside me.

'Nothing,' I say. 'Really, nothing.'

Liar.

She takes my hand. 'I remember being fifteen. It was difficult. All teenagers struggle.'

I mustn't let myself cry again.

'Yes. 'S'pose that's true. I'll be fine.' I smile at her.

The front door opens and Mr. Bernstein walks in. 'Hello everyone. Finished early today.'

'Daddy!' Ruben shouts and grabs his father's legs.

'Hiya Poppy,' Mr Bernstein calls, waving at me and hanging up his coat and hat.

'Pops. Peece car.' JoJo climbs into my lap still holding the police car. I hug him and try to put his coat on, wishing our house was more like the Bernstein's.

'Mine!' Ruben shouts and he grabs the police car.

JoJo screams.

'The police car is Ruben's isn't it, JoJo?' Esther rubs his back. 'Leave it here and play with it tomorrow.'

JoJo lets out a high-pitched wail, so I lift him and his things and head for the front door.

'Come back and see me any time, Poppy,' Esther says. 'I mean it, my dear. A problem shared is a problem halved.'

I stop for a moment in the gap in the hedge. Could I tell her?

Mum would be furious.

Even more furious than she is already.

Chapter 27

We need Carl

'I'll look after him,' Zara says when I ask her to mind JoJo. 'We'll play Lego in his room. But I want to know what's going on.'

For a nanosecond I wonder if I could just tell her everything. But I don't know what to say to a twelve-year-old.

'It really is something between Mum and me...sorry...one day maybe...'

'OK,' she says, 'but you owe me one.' She scoops JoJo into her arms and I'm so proud of my little sister, staying calm while Mum and I argue.

I creep into the lounge. Mum is still lying on the sofa with a bottle of wine on the coffee table beside her. 'I wondered...probably best if you don't tell Carl what I said.' I watch her. Waiting to see how she will react. 'With you going out to work tonight and all that...what if the two of us think about what's best to do next?'

This is my moment to get her to see Carl must go.

She gets up slowly from the sofa. Swinging her legs round, her eyes fixed on me.

I catch my breath. Now what?

'You misinterpret everything about Carl,' she says, advancing towards me, the wine sloshing around her glass, 'but you listen to me, my girl. He works his socks off for all of us. He gives you everything you want even though you don't help him with the robot. And he'd be devastated by what you've said. I know you're lying.'

'I'm not lying.'

'Like you swore blind you weren't lying when you played truant all those times a couple of years ago? That kind of "not lying" you mean?'

There's a long silence. I try to get my breathing calmer. Try to prepare myself for one of Mum's outbursts. Not that I blame her after what I've said. But I think she's not going to throw Carl out.

It's all my fault.

'I don't believe a word you've said,' she says in an earthquake voice that rumbles through my head. 'You're trying to split our family up.'

'No!' My voice struggles to get out of my throat. How could she think that?

I know I lied. Bunking off. Age thirteen. So confused all I could do was wander the streets. Forging notes for school. I wish I could have told someone about Carl. But I didn't know how to. Didn't have the words.

Asking for it.

'Mum, this is different. I'm not lying. When I was thirteen...that was when Carl started on me...on my birthday. You went out with Zara for her gymnastics class. He...pushed me down on my bed –'

'Shut up, will you? Just shut up about it.' Mum hits me across my face again.

I freeze.

She drains her glass. Puts it dangerously near the edge of the coffee table.

She sways. I almost reach out to catch her, but she staggers upright.

'If it started when you were thirteen, why the hell has it taken you this long to say anything? Eh? Why? Cat got your tongue? Or time to make up filthy lies? Twist the truth for your own ends?'

'No, Mum, I –'

'You're just angry at Carl for him being firm with you...I understand you, you see.' She wags a finger at me. 'I know what you're up to.'

If you tell your mum, she'll know you're lying. She'll throw you out.

'Gran would have understood.' I know I'm being too loud. 'Gran would have listened to me.'

'You have a rosy view of that psychotic woman. And you lie and lie! I don't know what I've done to deserve a daughter like you, I really don't.'

Molten magma builds up, ready to explode. I switch channels in my head. Think of Gran. Gran, holding me. Hugging me. Me holding the edge of her sari. The feeling of childhood. Soft. Safe.

But Gran always said that honesty was the best policy. No Gran. What's best is only to say what adults want to hear.

'I won't tell Carl what you've said. It would hurt him. And if you're not careful, my girl, on your sixteenth birthday you'll be out on your ear. August 31st next year you leave home. You'll never make it into Year 12 unless you stop all this nonsense.'

I can't stop a gasp bursting out of my mouth and my body feels too heavy for me to hold up.

She'll throw you out. She'll always believe me.

'You make Carl unhappy, so if all this nonsense goes on you should let Carl and me be happy with JoJo and Zara. We're a family we are. It's you who messes it all up.'

Yeah. Right. Happy families.

I'm crying hopeless tears, too many to wipe away. My head is throbbing. I want to keep swallowing, but the spit is stuck in my throat.

'So watch yourself, girl. Stop lying. Get your head down and work instead of all this gallivanting off to run – all this nonsense about acting, meeting your friends. You're not that bright, Poppy. If you want good exam grades, you're going to have to work hard.'

Thanks for the vote of confidence, Mum.

A million words spin around my brain. Getting a degree is my escape. And I do work hard. Plan A. Uni with Kavya. Being together.

I realise my breathing has gone crazy – I'm panting too fast. Get a grip.

But she won't tell Carl.

Not tonight anyway.

My fault. My fault. My fault.

Chapter 28

Finding Dad

The next few days I feel exhausted all the time and change between trying to be extra helpful to Mum and at other times keeping out of her way. I'm so stressed that I end up not giving enough time to revise for a chemistry test – so I know I won't get an 8 or 9 in it. I'm getting too many 6s.

Plan A. Get mostly 8s in the summer exams. Secretly I'm hoping for at least one grade 9, the old A star. But my head is in chaos, and I can't think straight and I'm worried this will go on for weeks if Mum stays mad at me.

Now I have another aim within Plan A. Try to be nice enough so I don't have to move out of home on my sixteenth birthday. How could I possibly get to uni if I have to do that? I wonder about ringing the kind Childline lady again, but I'd get someone different probably. But that would be OK.

I thought I was doing the right thing telling Mum. But I have a feeling that I've made everything much worse. But what if Mum tells Carl what I said? This is making me feel anxious all the time and I hate that – my heart pounding most of the day.

A few days later I'm sitting on Kavya's bed. It's our turn to do our presentation next week– about 'revenge' in *The Tempest* for religious studies. We've gone over it again and, as we're drinking hot chocolate, I tell Kavya what Mum said about me maybe having to move out on my next birthday.

'If your mum throws you out, you come and live here with Aunty and me. You know Anjali's always cool about everything.'

Immediately I'm crying. 'You're so kind to me,' I put my mug down and we hug.

'I'm angry with your mum,' Kavya says. 'You must be angry too.'

I'm snivelling into a tissue. 'I think I'm angry...but it's taken me a few days to realise that. And...you know...' I can't find any more words and start crying again.

'What?'

'I can't help wondering if my mum knows what Carl's doing – but she's too scared to admit it.'

'Oh, Poppy!'

'I've been wanting to tell you that for ages.' I lean on her shoulder and weep. It's all too much.

'You're right to be angry, Poppy – at your mum and Carl. Aunty always says that it's OK to feel angry – but don't do angry things.'

'I know that.'

We sit holding each other and as my tears dry up, I have one of my most mega brilliant thoughts I've ever had.

'If Mum won't listen to me about Carl, maybe I'll try and find my real dad? Now that's the start of a plan worthy of James Bond.'

'That sounds good. But...James Bond? What?'

'Oh, I've been wondering what he would do to bring Carl down. You know...if I was a super spy like Alex Rider – or something.'

Kavya snorts with laughter.

'Mum always calls Dad a loser. And he never even sends me a birthday card, so maybe he is a total no hoper. But he might believe me.'

He might come back and shove Carl out. There are only seventy-four days before Zara is thirteen. I know I'm crazy doing this count down...he might not...but he might.

I'll find my real dad.

Tomorrow.

The next morning I put my 'Finding Dad Plan' into action. I don't even know his full name so I'm going to have to do an internet search. Mum is taken in by my stomach clutching and groaning at breakfast. She gives me two paracetamol and I lie down on my bed, waiting for everyone to leave. Biscuit is snuggling up next to me and I'm trembling at the thought of meeting my real dad. Really meet him. Not just make him come into my head in my alternative universe.

Maybe it was all too painful for him that he never even sends me a birthday card? That's painful for me.

Zara knocks on my door and peeks in. 'OK?' She's done her hair in two bunches this morning, tied up with school-blue ribbon, making her look about ten years old. That's good when you live in Carl's house.

'I might come to school later,' I say in what I hope is a convincing I'm-in-pain voice.

'OK.' She smiles and I have a sense that she knows I'm faking it. My little sister is no fool.

Mum takes JoJo next door and I hear Ruben's high voice and JoJo's squeals as they greet each other. Then Mum gets in her car and backs out of the drive.

I count to three hundred, then creep into Mum and Carl's bedroom, Biscuit following me. I know where Mum's big brown concertina file is and go straight to it at the bottom of her wardrobe. There has to be information about Dad here. Biscuit snuffles into the bottom of the wardrobe too, but I push her away.

There are dozens of papers stuffed into the file, letters, birth certificates, divorce papers, school reports, Gran's will, then I find their marriage certificate. Dad's full name is Angus James Edward Stewart. That'll narrow down the search online.

Underneath the concertina file I find a photo album with a tartan cover and black pages. There are several photos of Dad. One of him standing next to Mum, wearing a green kilt. He has mousy coloured hair, and I remember his light brown curly hair and freckles.

I take care pulling a photo out of the album and find another one of him holding me. At least, I assume it's me, and another of Mum holding what must be baby Zara and Dad holding me in his arms. If I show him these photos, he'll know I'm his daughter.

I tidy all the papers back carefully into the file, so Mum won't realise I've been looking.

I go downstairs and have a blackcurrant drink and take it in the garden with Biscuit.

I throw the ball for her for a bit then go back to my bedroom and search online for Angus James Edward Stewart. Six of them but only two look in their forties. Then I've got him, his face grinning out at me. He has a jewellery and blacksmith business in Essex and there are pictures of metal gates, birthstone rings and necklaces, and an online map to show where his workshop is – not far from a station on the Central Line on the London underground.

I still have the silver bracelet he made and gave me on my fifth birthday so I'm sure it's the right person.

I go downstairs and have a bowl of cereal. I make a Marmite sandwich and walk to school in time for lunch.

All this flashing through my brain is making my heart beat fast and I have to see if Kavya will come with me to Essex to visit Dad. We could make that our way of disappearing for the Manchester weekend.

I sign in as late on the screen in reception and I wait outside the art block for Kavya, and we go into the cafeteria.

I explain my plan to go to Essex to find Dad instead of going to Manchester.

'It's a bit crazy,' she says, 'but I see why you're doing it...your mum being hopeless.'

'We were going to disappear on Manchester weekend any-way, but now it's perfect. We find my dad. He'll help me sort out Carl.'

'I'm worried you're getting your hopes up and your dad might let you down.'

I glare at her and finish my sandwich. I know Kavya could be right, but something tells me that Dad is going to care what Carl is doing to me.

I drape one arm over her shoulder, and I hear the hiss of 'lezzies' from the Bitch Brigade.

I deliberately kiss Kavya's neck. There's an 'ooooh' sound from the tables around us and Kavya and I collapse on each other, laughing. I can see Harry laughing too and he raises his eyebrows at me. So I raise mine back. Of course, he might think that Kavya and I are together and think I'm not interested in boys. But I suspect he doesn't think that.

At the end of school we walk together to Kavya's flat. 'I'll get Reggie to do our paper round that morning we go to Essex,' she says. 'But you know, your dad's likely to be in shock with you just turning up, though. He might not be there with open arms.'

I walk in silence for a bit, finding the noise of the traffic overwhelming today. Too much noise alongside the clutter in my brain. But we must get our escape plan right.

'So we vanish from the face of the earth, next week, that first Saturday of half term,' I say. 'Carl plans to leave the house at seven in the morning to get the nine something from Euston to Manchester so we'll have to be gone ridiculously early. He'll definitely get on the train because the tickets cost a fortune and he'll know he's powerless to find us.'

'OK.'

'Wow! That feels good,' I say.

'What?'

'Carl, powerless.'

Kavya laughs and hugs me. 'Good to hear you being a strong woman. I might have to tell Aunty, though. About the disappearing when she knows we're supposed to go with Carl. I don't like lying to her. She'll be cool with whatever we come up with.'

'She'd be OK if we deceive Carl and Mum?'

'You know I always like to tell the truth,' Kavya says, not looking at me, 'but I won't let it sound like a deception.'

I know she knows I lie but we don't talk about it.

'But no way can we both be in Manchester with Carl and Steve. I think it's OK for me to tell a little white lie to keep out of the grips of two creepy men,' I say, and she nods, hugs me, and we go into her flat.

Chapter 29

Destroyer

I'm a bit anxious around Mum because she still seems angry with me. I'm edgy that she didn't listen to me. Gran would have listened – would have heard what I was struggling to say.

And Gran would have done something.

Carl is being kind of normal so I think Mum can't have told him what I said about him.

But she might, I suppose. My tummy lurches.

Mum's in the kitchen chopping onions as I'm giving JoJo his tea. I offer to bath him.

'That would be helpful,' she says. She drains her glass of wine and pours another one.

I put lots of bubbles in the bath and Biscuit sits beside me as JoJo plays with his boats and ducks.

As I bath him and join in his laughter I begin to feel calmer.

I dry him, breathing in his baby shampoo smell. His forehead is damp as I kiss his curls and lie him in his cot.

'Sweet dreams, lovely boy,' I whisper. He puts his thumb in his mouth and with the other hand he pulls his teddy close to his face. I start his musical mobile and his eyes close straight away. I envy his ability just to sleep, but I'm glad his life seems to be without worries. Just the occasional longing for Ruben's toys.

I lean over the edge of the cot for a moment, listening, watching, holding onto the moment of peace and love, glad these still exist in our crazy world.

I just have to keep going. Keep doing what I'm doing.

I can hear Mum in the kitchen talking to Carl and the smell of her vegetarian chilli seeps upstairs. Mum calls out that food is ready, and I hear Zara go down.

Deep breath.

Down the hideous bald stairs, avoiding all the creaks. I place my feet carefully. It's the fifth one down that squeaks like a strangled rat. I think I could get down silently now.

Sixty-eight days to go before Zara's thirteen. I have sixty-seven days to get rid of Carl so he doesn't start on her. Or for Mum to make him stop.

Somehow.

My whole body shudders.

Biscuit leaps on me as I go into the kitchen and we have a cuddle, me kneeling on the hard cold tiles. She gives me her disgusted look. She does that when it's a vegetarian meal and she goes to her basket and curls up. No point lurking under my stool when it's chilli.

Carl's sitting at the breakfast bar, drinking wine, the shine of the black granite top catching the lights from the ceiling, reflecting the red of the wine onto his white phone.

He doesn't look up. He's talking on his phone, calm, smiling, sometimes running his hand through his hair that's greying at the sides. 'That sounds perfect. Thank you,' he says.

An ordinary guy.

Mum is getting the casserole out of the oven. She doesn't look at me.

I sit on a bar stool next to Zara. My usual place. I touch her arm and she turns towards me. I smile and mouth, 'You OK?'

She smiles back, but I can tell she's hesitant. I give her arm a squeeze.

Poor kid. I've made her life so complicated with Mum and me arguing and my Social Outcast status at school. We used to be mates.

Before.

Mum sits opposite Carl and they talk as they eat. Carl's had a big order for his robotic arms that will be programmed in factories to make cars.

'Serious money, Steph,' he says shovelling the chilli into his mouth and taking another slug of wine. I'll make another million profit this year again. Steve will too so we're planning another golf holiday for the two of us...usual place...in Spain. See, girls, if you work hard, you make money. Let that be a lesson in life for you both.'

I'm not sure how to respond. I glance at Zara. Neither of us say anything.

We probably weren't expected to comment.

'So you could give up work, Steph, if you want to,' he says jabbing his knife in the air and dropping blobs of chilli on the granite.

She takes another swig of wine. 'I like work, though,' she says. 'You know. Being with the others. We have a laugh. Something to get me out of these four walls.'

'I thought the night shifts were getting you down,' he says.

'Yowling cats do my head in, true. But I love chatting with my mates...and I love it that I can treat myself to a new handbag when I want.'

They both sink into silence, and their wine.

The chilli's too hot for me, and Zara's pushing hers around her plate and sipping water. Carl likes it this hot.

I find it unpleasant.

Actually, I hate it. So I just eat the rice. Almost certainly Mum won't notice. She's probably planning her next trip into central London for another clutch of designer handbags, each one of them costing enough to build a well in an African village where people have to drink polluted water.

'I need help with our robot, Poppy,' Carl's voice slicing through me. He sticks a white plastic toothpick in his mouth. I hate the way he digs around in his mouth and wipes the bits onto his clothes. 'Need you to help me with some of the circuits. Destroyer will smash the competition out of the ring next year. Total destruction of every robot that takes us on. Robot Wars champion!' He punches the air and laughs, but no one else does.

'I've got physics homework,' I say. This is true. 'Test next week.' This isn't true.

'Then a spell on the electronic circuits of our robot is just what you need.' Carl stands up, scrapes his stool back, squealing on the shiny floor. 'Come on. It's our robot, after all. We do it together.'

I know my skin is as hot as the chilli. 'I'd much rather do my homework.' I glare at him.

'Poppy!' Mum says. 'Give Carl a hand.'

I feel sweat run down my neck. 'You're always telling me to work harder! How can I get a good mark in physics if I don't revise and do well in tests? You know how hard I find it.'

'Oh, come on Poppy,' Carl says. 'It won't take long. And afterwards I can help you with your physics.'

I say nothing. I just stay sitting down staring at the breakfast bar.

Carl slides open the patio door and Biscuit darts into the garden, her tail down. She knows I'm anxious. She hates Carl. One day I hope she bites his hand off, although she tends to keep her distance from him. Shame. He'd be easier to manage with only one hand. I feel a laugh bubbling up at the thought of him as a one-armed bandit but know it will come out all hysterical so I hold my breath to stop it bursting out.

Carl waits by the open door.

'Poppy. Go with him,' Zara whispers to me, tears in her eyes and a look of horror on her face. She needs to learn to be a bit more defiant, but I stop for a moment, the cog wheels in my brain turn slowly. But I don't want to upset Zara.

'If you're not going to help,' Carl says, 'maybe I should get Zara to help me?'

'No!' I say. 'I'll come.' I get up.

'I wouldn't know what to do,' Zara says.

'I'll do it.' I smile at Zara.

Tears well up in my eyes at the thought of Zara 'helping' Carl. My heart is thundering, my brain working at a million miles an hour.

I don't believe he wants help with the robot.

Come and rescue me, Dad.

Perhaps I should just run?

My chest is tight, and I try to take deep breaths. The patio lights go on as we walk to his shed. I hate his enormous shed. Hate that we had to get rid of our trampoline to fit it in.

Hate him.

Biscuit is standing by her kennel. I have a few more seconds to decide whether I grab her and run. Run into the country park. Run and run and don't stop until my legs give in or I die of thirst. Or both.

He unlocks the security bars and the shed door and now no one is looking at us, he shoves me in. I know that look on his face. I know what he wants. And it's not about robot circuits.

Chapter 30

The white sofa

Carl drags me into the shed and locks the door. The keys are on a chain, and he puts it back in his pocket. I need copies of both keys.

My body surges with the beginning of a plan to prove to Mum what he does.

Could I find some kind of evidence on his computer?

If I get the keys.

There must be something I could find.

He shoves me down onto his new white sofa. If you're going to have a leather sofa with brass studs, it should be black. Not white.

He has no taste at all.

He sits at his desk in his black office chair.

I kneel up and crane my neck to look over his shoulder to watch him put his password into his keyboard. I think it starts with JoJo. Then some numbers.

Yes! I'll break his password. Somehow.

That makes me feel hopeful for a moment.

But the good feeling goes. What's he going to do?

Destroyer the robot is on the workbench, upside down, the hammer dismantled and lying amongst wires.

I get off the sofa and inspect it. I haven't got a clue how to mend it.

I creep back to the sofa.

How long will Carl make me wait?

I want my dad. I'll find him that Saturday of half term, and he'll rescue me from this torment. I lie back onto the Star Wars pillows Carl bought when we watched every Star Wars film one day.

Back then when Carl was my favourite adult.

I drift off with Dad...Across the bay, away from here...onto the island where I'm free to run amongst the wild flowers...

I pull my mind back to the present and think of seeing my real dad. What will he be like? Is he really a loser like Mum says?

I know I'm breathing too fast.

I focus onto Carl.

When he switched on his computer rows of screens above him lit up, fourteen screens taking up the whole wall of the shed. Of course – they're from the CCTV cameras around the house. Three screens aren't on.

On one of the live screens I see Zara come out of her bedroom and go into the bathroom. I don't think even Carl would get away with having a camera in the loo. JoJo's in his cot. Mum's in the lounge watching TV. Still drinking. I wonder if she knows Carl's watching her?

I'm panicking waiting for Carl to do what he wants.

I distract myself by staring at the robot's hydraulic hammer – Destroyer's main weapon. It smashes down onto the other robots, knocking out their electronic systems, killing them.

That's the thing about Robot Wars.

What the crowds are baying for.

Death. As violent as possible.

I try to take deep breaths to calm myself but the heavy smell of oil in the shed is nauseating.

Mustn't throw up.

I say some of Miranda's lines in my head. I like being Miranda. She's controlled and oppressed by the men around her, and far too obedient, but she's free – mostly. She has an island to wander around. And she's looked after by her dad.

Cherished.

But I suppose, in some ways, she's still trapped.

One of the three blank screens flickers on. It's me sitting on the big white sofa. I look around and locate the camera above me. Its red light is on.

He's going to film us.

I see why the sofa is white.

I shudder and feel the chilli rise up into my throat. No doubt he'll show the film to Creepy Steve. And who else?

I know what's coming and I'm shaking.

Breathe.

Try to hold down the raging volcano inside me.

The screen showing the back garden lights up as a fox runs across the patio. I get up and look out the shed window as Biscuit barks and runs towards the fox. It darts towards the hedge at the bottom of the garden and disappears. Biscuit stands for a moment, her tail wagging.

I long to bury my head in her fur and share her freedom. I can't stop the tears flowing down my face as I try to hold my feelings in. Biscuit sniffs where the fox walked, then goes back and sits outside her kennel.

Keeping watch.

Carl grabs me from behind, pushes me onto the sofa.

He flops down on top of me, breath exploding out of my lungs.

His hands creep around my body. It feels like maggots slithering over my skin.

His aftershave makes me feel sick.

Hard to breathe.

The memory of my thirteenth birthday invades my mind.

Happy birthday, Poppy. Thirteen today.

I retch. Choke and swallow it all back, the chilli burning my throat.

With no poppy picture to sink into I go numb, twist my head and stare at the robot on the work bench and space out.

Think of circuits.

Hydraulic hammers bringing an end to everything.

I'm floating above my body.

There's no escape. I know I have to deal with it. Keep him happy so he won't start on Zara.

I hate my body.

I hate me. Hate. Hate. Hate.

I'm bad. Bad. Bad. Bad.

I try to shut my body down. Breathe.

Can't control the tears.

Think of Biscuit. Feeling her love. Holding her. Hugging her.

Kavya. Hugging me. Daring to tell her.

It's all my fault. I sat on his knee when we made that merry-go-round out of his Meccano. As it spun around fixed up to the motor, I was in ecstasy.

I made popcorn in the microwave when he wanted to watch the cricket on the TV. Loving being with him. Sitting on his lap, putting my arms around his neck.

Laughing.

Shame floods through me at the memory of his head moving unexpectedly at the last minute as I tried to kiss his cheek. Our lips meeting instead. His lips thick and moist. My twelve-year-old embarrassment.

My fault. My fault.

I'll tell them what you did. Kissing me.

Asking for it.

My fault.

Slut.

I go to the island. Try to focus on the waves on the sea. Lose myself in the bigness of the ocean.

He sits up. 'You liked that didn't you Poppy?'

I can't see through my tears, his aftershave lingering in my brain, my body trying to shun off the feeling of him inside me.

'Say you enjoyed it.' His voice plunges into my body.

Snot is smearing down my face.

Hate. Hate. Hate. Hate everything about myself.

'Say you enjoyed it!'

I mutter 'I enjoyed,' and he walks back to his desk.

I don't want thoughts in my head.

Block them out.

But they start to creep in as I curl up at one end of the sofa – his smell clings to me. I try to breathe myself back together.

He gets money from his wallet and tosses it at me.

'Slut,' he says.

I want to rip the twenty-pound note into tiny pieces. But I don't. It'll go into the Plan A fund.

'And don't you say a single word or you're dead.'

I focus on the robot on the worktable. Our strong point was always our hammer that could smash other robots into pieces. Nothing but total destruction will do if you want to win through to the next round.

I bury my head in the Star Wars pillow.

My thirteenth birthday.

The day shame took hold of my body and my soul.

I built a wall around myself to keep my evil bits in and to keep everybody else out. I'm not worthy of Harry. Or Kavya's friendship.

I'm isolated. Alienated.

But I'm going to get a copy of those shed keys. I'll find that bit of film. Show it to Mum. Then she'll believe me, and he will have to stop.

And he'll never be able to touch Zara.

Chapter 31

Gangs

'Poppy, you're not listening.'

I sit up with a jolt. 'Sorry, Sir.'

Mr McKenzie is looking intently at me. 'I'm aware that amps and ohms may not have the appeal of *The Tempest*, but exams are in May. That's only seven months.'

'Yes, Sir.'

Physics feels as if it's been going on for hours and it's about yet more invisible stuff. What are amps and ohms anyway?

Harry turns and grins at me. 'I've made notes,' he mouths.

'Thanks,' I mouth back. It must be obvious that I'm not concentrating.

My heart has pounded all day, however much deep breathing I do. Every time Carl has a go at me it's as if I have to find the broken pieces of me that are scattered around. I have to sniff them out from the debris and get the fractured bits back inside me.

But I've also sniffed out my defiant self this time and I WILL find those shed keys.

My mind is racing with thoughts about me telling Mum a week ago what Carl is doing. I've thought about little else recently. And on top of all that, it's our turn to do our presentation on 'revenge' this afternoon in religious studies.

At last it's lunch time and I meet up with Kavya outside on one of the benches by the grassy area.

'Espionage is harder than you expect,' I whisper. 'I keep going into Mum and Carl's bedroom but his desk is never open.'

'So you haven't found Carl's keys?'

'Not yet.' I get my sandwich out of my lunch box.

'You won't do anything dangerous, will you?' Kavya puts her hand on my arm. 'Come on – let's just look at the start of our presentation. If we start confidently, it'll grab people's attention.'

'Do you think I'm the most awful hypocrite, saying that revenge isn't a good thing and then planning on downloading that bit of film to prove to Mum what Carl does?'

'That's not revenge, Poppy.' Kavya takes a bite of her sandwich. 'You're trying to get justice. And that's good.'

'It's not good to hate him, though. I wish I didn't. But I do. I want him to stop. I'm terrified he'll start on Zara.'

Kavya hugs me, 'I know. You're being a great big sister. Let's go over the start of our presentation. It'll take your mind off Carl.'

I'm struggling to control my breathing.

The religious studies room is stuffy as we all slouch in. It's good that we're doing *The Tempest* in RS as well as in English. There's a huge display on the back wall of the RS room about *The Tempest* with words like 'Slavery', 'Does God control the world?' 'Is it right to take revenge?' 'Are people born bad?' 'Why do bad things happen to good people?'

Miss Singh isn't there and I keep staring at the display. Everyone is on their phone when they shouldn't be, and heads together talking about Wolf and the Ashbury Road Gang. The police have raided some houses.

I'm not getting involved. It's more than enough for me that I have to go along Ashbury Road to deliver papers. I think I'm doing OK at my plan of Wolf never knowing I exist.

'Phones away,' Miss Singh says. 'You know the rules. Let's start with Poppy and Kavya, and their topic is "revenge",' she says, her smile at me encouraging and kind. I smile back. We move to the front of the class and Kavya puts her data stick into the computer.

I wish I felt better.

Our first slide shines onto the big white board at the front of the class. I stand to one side so everyone can see it.

Focus.

Mia is smirking.

Harry is smiling at me and I smile back.

Reggie is staring at me.

I take a deep breath.

'We're going to talk about some of the reasons why Prospero might have decided not to take revenge on Antonio in *The Tempest*,' I say. 'It was Antonio's fault that Prospero and Miranda were marooned on a desert island for years. Antonio never said sorry.'

Carl would never say sorry, I'm sure of it.

'Wanting to take revenge is a normal thing to feel when someone has hurt you.'

I think mostly people are listening. Kavya says her bit about the reason why Prospero just lets go of all his hurt, then I come back in with what we can do with our hurt when we choose to stay strong and not retaliate.

Mia does a loud sarky laugh.

'Mia,' Miss Singh says, 'do you have something to say?'

'Miss, no one thinks like that these days.'

'Yeah,' says Reggie. 'You have to be tough. Let people know that if they punch you, you'll punch them back harder.'

'But what if they have a knife and stab you?' Kavya's angry and glaring at Reggie.

'You have to train your gang to stab 'em back,' Reggie says.

'That is absolutely not how you deal with things, Reggie!' Miss Singh says sharply. 'I need to talk to you straight after class and I can see we need to invite the Community Police Officer in again. Now, Poppy and Kavya, carry on.'

'Thank you,' says Kavya. I can tell she's angry. 'We just wanted to end by saying how much better school would be if people were kinder to each other.'

'Huh!' Mia says loudly. 'Kinder!'

'Yes! Kinder!' Kavya says back.

'Thank you, Poppy and Kavya. You've done well.' Miss Singh writes on her tablet.

I'm hoping we were good enough for at least an 8 maybe even a 9. Kavya hugs me and I feel relieved to have got the presentation done. It was good to have some time when keys and Carl weren't dominating my thinking.

At last it's the end of school and time for the rehearsal.

'I'm helping Mr Robins with Caliban's monster mask,' Kavya says, her arms around me. 'It needs a few more gross boils. I'll come back to the hall and meet you after rehearsal...Poppy...are you OK?'

'Yes. Course I am.'

'See you later, then.'

But thoughts are rushing so fast through my brain I feel dizzy.

'Poppy. Physics notes from today.' Harry is holding out his notebook.

'Oh. Thanks. Thanks so much.'

'Are you OK?'

'Definitely.'

'Loved your presentation.'

Then he's gone.

I reach out for Dad's hand. Come and rescue me Dad. Too many words in my head so I clench my fists, digging my fingernails into my palms. I want to stay in my own world where I can be happy. But my sense of being disintegrated makes me tremble.

I have to get everything right tonight. We're doing a complete run through of Act IV so I don't have much to do, neither does Harry, just that mega embarrassing bit at the start where Harry has to say to Prospero that we won't sleep together till we're married.

I blush every time we get to that bit and Mia makes faces at me. I think she means that no one is ever going to want to be with me.

I must be perfect for Miss Singh.

She walks into the hall but the group around Reggie – Crabbe and Goyle – are still on their phones, agitated and loud. Everyone else looks at Miss Singh.

She listens and watches for a moment.

'Reggie,' she says, 'are you ready to do Act IV'

'Oh...er...Miss...'

Crabbe and Goyle are still staring at their phones.

'I know there's some local trouble with gangs,' she says.

'You could say that,' Reggie says.

She puts her head on one side. 'Then you'll be in the zone to be Stephano, Reggie, won't you? Time to get your drunken murderous gang on the stage. Come on. Phones away. You, Trinculo and Caliban, give it everything. You're drunk and searching out Prospero to murder him. Get inside Stephano's mind – be a perfect murderous gang leader, Reggie – and let's do a perfect run through.'

Reggie and his minions silently move up the steps beside the stage.

Then Harry's beside me, going up the steps right next to me. I didn't think my heart could pound any faster, but it does.

'You really OK?' he whispers, raising his beautiful brown eyebrows.

I nod. I must get in the zone to be Miranda.

'Right, everyone,' calls Miss Singh. 'Let's go.'

Chapter 32

The chase

The whole thing about the local gangs settles down and I'm so relieved. It could have got nasty. And at last it's Friday evening and half term has started. I pack a bag for the Manchester weekend and put it in the hall beside the little table with the landline phone on it.

Mum's in the kitchen, ironing Carl's shirts and her linen blouses. I have the chance to chat to her to try to get our relationship better. She's still a bit edgy with me so I know it'll be worth it to just chat.

'I looked at the weather app and Manchester is going to be dry but cold,' I say, 'so I've packed that lovely red jumper you bought me.'

'You'll have such a good time, I'm sure,' Mum says. 'Get some clothes with all that spending money – and make sure you get things that go together. Not just random things.'

I agree with Mum and chat to her as if as if I'm going to enjoy the Robot Wars final. I'm aware that we never actually did that clothes shopping trip she suggested. But Mum's more relaxed than I've seen her for a while. Perhaps because I'm playing the part of dutiful daughter.

Kavya and I agreed that we'd both pack bags, so we look convincing. But our actual plan is to get up very early – so I'll be out of our house before Carl is up. Kavya and I will meet at the tram stop on Sandyhills High Street and get the tram that leaves about five twenty. So we'll be well on our way to Central London before Carl is even awake.

'I hate lying to Aunty,' Kavya says, 'but I'll keep up the pretence of Manchester, then text her as soon as we're on the tram and tell her we've disappeared for the day – '

'Don't tell her we're going to find my dad.'

'Course not...I'll get Aunty to play dumb if your Mum or Carl ring her. They might all panic and ring the police, but if Aunty knows we're safe, she can stop your mum ringing them.'

I laugh. 'Police could be a disaster.'

Kavya shudders and grips my hand. 'Actually, I think it's best if I ring Aunty once I know she'll be up. If she knows we're safe, she'll keep her mouth shut. I'll tell her that I'm just helping you with something desperately important. She'll be cool. Don't worry.'

It's hard to act normally all evening and Mum doesn't query it when I say I want an early night.

It's hard to sleep.

I keep hoping Biscuit will be safe and that she won't mind me leaving her for a whole day.

I wake with a nightmare. Destroyer the robot is hitting me over the head with its hydraulic hammer. I can't get back to sleep so get up just before my phone beeps at four forty-five. I went to bed in my clothes so just pull on my trainers, put my phone in my running belt, pull on a grey hoodie and a warm jacket. I get my backpack out of my wardrobe.

The light is on in Carl and Mum's bedroom.

I freeze. Wasn't expecting that.

I smell his sickly deodorant.

Does that mean he's getting dressed already? Surely he doesn't need to be up this early?

But I have to go for it so I creep downstairs, knowing where I mustn't tread. The fifth one down, the ninth, and step right over the last one.

The landing light goes on. Carl is staring down at me. 'What the...?'

I'm out the front door, through the gate and running down the road towards the country park, my backpack bouncing on one shoulder.

I risk a backward glance.

Carl is coming after me.

Across the tram lines. Into the park. Mustn't let him see where I'm heading so I go left and take the path that goes away from High Street – away from where I want to be.

I can hear his feet slapping on the path.

Have to go faster.

He's still after me. Surely he'll be out of breath soon?

I'm gasping.

Go round the lake.

Look behind.

He's closer.

Can I loop back to the churchyard? Maybe head out onto the road, into the other gate of the country park?

He's so close I can hear him shouting. 'You're dead! Dead!'

I don't know if I can keep going.

He'd get charged with murder. Prison.

Lungs heaving.

Heart breaking out of my ribs.

Am I going to die?

Almost at the road. Go left. In the other gate.

Realise I can't hear him anymore.

Has he gone into the bushes to pounce on me?

Can't see him.

Sprint to the churchyard.

I don't know where he is.

Stop in the churchyard, lean down with my hands on my knees.

Gulping air. Noisy breathing.

I throw up. Nothing there but stomach juices. Throat hurting.

Pounding headache.

I squeeze between some bushes and collapse, still gulping air.

Lie flat on my back.

Want to crawl into my secret space under the yew tree. Haven't been there for months.

But Carl might still be around.

I jump up and jog back across the park, looking behind me all the time. I'm taking the route around the edge of the park which is more open, just in case he's lurking somewhere in the bushes. I jog past the running track, past school, up to Sandyhills High Street where I dodge from shop door to shop door.

My watch says it's four minutes to the first tram. Didn't realise so much time had passed so I sprint. Kavya's there and I fall into her arms.

I still don't feel safe but between breaths I tell Kavya what's happened as we get on the tram.

I'm still struggling to breathe. 'Carl might be on the tram.'

'I didn't see him, so I don't think he is. I'll text Aunty to tell her we're safe but disappearing today.' Kavya focuses on her phone, but I can't help feeling as if the people on the tram are all after us. Enemies.

I keep checking up and down the carriage.

My phone beeps. It's a message from Mum.

Get back here right now.

I ignore it.

Please God, make Carl get on the train to Manchester without us. Can you hear me, God?

'Carl can't know we're heading for a train to Essex can he?' I say. My lungs still hurt and my knees keep trembling. I'm not as fit as I thought I was.

'No, he can't possibly know that. He might think we're going all the way on the tram to Wimbledon to run on the Common, or something. He won't think Central London.'

'We can't know what he might do next.' I pull my hood up.

Every time we get to a tram stop, I find myself shuffling lower and lower down in my seat.

My phone rings. It's Mum so I dismiss the call. Immediately a message comes through.

Get yourself to Euston station for the train. Anjali furious.

I show Kavya.

She gets a message from Aunty Anjali.

Just keep in touch and let me know you're safe. Poppy's in real trouble.

When we get to East Croydon we run from the tram into the station, buy a ticket from the machine and get a train almost immediately.

Kavya rings her aunty and that makes us both feel better because Anjali is so sensible.

I still feel wobbly when we get off the train in Central London, but we find a McDonalds for breakfast.

'You're still trembling, Poppy. I'm sure we're safe now.'

I nod. Do deep breathing.

'OK, just eat and drink. Try to relax,' she says.

We stay in the McDonalds for ages, but I start to feel edgy. 'We'd probably be a bit safer on a train to Essex,' I say. 'What if Carl's got the police looking for us?'

'That's unlikely, Poppy, I was thinking that Carl's not all that likely to ring the police...he wouldn't know if you might just tell them everything...about...everything.'

'You could be right,' I say, getting up and putting the remains of our breakfast into the bin. 'Come on. I'll feel better once we're on the train to Essex.'

On the train I'm thinking about Dad and how he's in my head every day, how I drift off with him during French lessons. Why didn't he keep in touch? Is he a loser as Mum says?

Images of Dad as I remember him come into my head and I get the photos out of my pocket. I was only five when he left us, so I don't remember much. I look at the picture of him with all of us on the beach in the sun, eating ice cream, Zara tiny in Mum's arms, and me on Gran's knee. I don't think Dad and Gran much liked each other. I think she was glad when he left. I think I'll recognise him...his freckles...light brown hair...I'm drifting down the river...

'We're here,' says Kavya, so I shake myself out of my dream world.

My heart begins to race as the doors of the train open. 'Have I done a really stupid thing?'

'I thought you might think that,' says Kavya. 'Come on. It's not even nine o'clock yet so we'll need to walk around for a bit.' She links arms with me and drags me out of the station.

I have to stop and lean against a wall my heart is pounding so badly. I look at my phone and there are about a gazillion texts from Mum, some from Carl and dozens of missed calls.

I'm in deep trouble. And now I'm not sure if I can face Dad.

But I have to.

'But what if my Dad isn't there?'

'Come on, girl,' says Kavya. She's got her determined face on. She takes hold of my hand. 'Let's explore.'

I can do this. I'm not pathetic Miranda.

We're in a small town, lots of trees, the usual shops: a café, estate agents, nail bar, newsagents and a pub. We walk around for a bit, buy some orange juice at the newsagents and some chocolate.

'It's nine thirty-five am,' I say. 'Carl should be getting on the Manchester train with Steve. Hope he is anyway.'

'He'll know he can't find you.'

'Yeah. I think he'd rather see the Robot Wars finals than search for us. He'll want to size up the best of the competition for next year. He's spent a fortune on Destroyer. He thinks he'll win and be on TV.'

'And no one knows we're here, Poppy, so relax. We'll go and find your dad. Come on. His workshop should be open by now.'

I do School Shrink's deep breathing. What if I can never go back home because Carl is too angry with me? Would he kill me?

We follow the route on my phone, past a motor bike shop, and a builder's yard with bricks and timber.

There he is. 'Angus Stewart, Blacksmith and Silversmith' on the board outside. I look inside into the darkness. He's silhouetted against the light of the fire, hammering down onto an anvil. Is that him? I'm not sure.

I tell myself I must breathe. Feel blood gushing through my ears.

Kavya gives my hand a squeeze.

My mind is racing, memories, images of the boat, the island. Puffins. The waves crashing onto the rocks.

This man is real. He's not some fantasy or illusion.
I don't know if I can do this.

Chapter 33

Dad's workshop

I'm standing at the door of his workshop, cold seeping through my bones, looking into the darkness and the light of the fire. A man who I think is Dad walks towards the fire holding what looks like a long metal pole. I can't get a good look at his face. He puts the end of the pole into the flames, his back to me now.

Then he turns and puts the metal he's melted in the fire onto the anvil and he starts beating down with his hammer. It's going to be a bit warmer in there – so I almost take a step forward – but I hesitate. Is it Dad? It feels as if my heart is trying to leap out of my mouth.

Then he moves, and in the light of the fire I think it's him.

I take the photos from my pocket. I might need to convince him I'm his daughter. Ice cream on the beach, me sitting next to Gran. Him detached from us all.

My mind is racing.

Breathe.

'OK?' Kavya whispers.

'Not really.'

'Is it him?'

'I think so...but...I don't know if I can do this.'

'We can just go back to London if you want.' She takes hold of my hand.

I have a moment to decide.

I pull her forward and we walk into the warmth of the workshop.

'I'll be strong Miranda,' I say. 'I don't need to be feeble...I'll say exactly what I think.'

I'd better be sure it's him first so as we get closer I focus on his face. Yes. It's definitely him.

'Dad,' I say. It feels so weird for me to say that word.

'What?' he says, looking up. 'Hello. Can I help you?'

'I'm Poppy,' I manage to get out, although my throat is threatening to close up.

Silence. He looks at me, puts his hammer down and puts the metal he was hammering hissing into a bucket of water.

'I'm your daughter. Poppy.' I hold out the photos, my hands trembling.

The flickering of the fire seems to change what I'm seeing. One minute everything seems bright and OK. But then there is semi-darkness and the smell of fear.

My breathing has gone wrong. It's as if I'm panting. I feel I might throw up. He's staring at me, his mouth open.

He glances at the photos. 'You were cute...a lovely child...' He looks up at me. 'Why've you come, Poppy?'

'If...if I asked you for help...would you help me?'

'Do you want money?'

'No.'

'Are you...um...pregnant?'

'No!'

I step towards him. I'm still holding out the photos. We're all still for a moment.

'I'm Kavya, Poppy's best friend. She really needs your help.'

'Come and sit down, both of you.' He puts a light on – a single cord with a bulb – and wipes his forehead with the back of his hand. He's shorter than I remember him, but his brown hair and freckles are the same as the image of him in my head.

He tells us to sit on some wooden chairs beside a small table cluttered with mugs and opened packets of biscuits.

I stare at the mess. But we're sitting down. He's going to listen. I wish he'd given me an enormous hug.

'Coffee?' he says.

'No thanks,' I say. 'I don't much like coffee...'

'Kavya. Would you like coffee?'

'No thanks,' she says. 'Can't stand it. I hope you'll listen to Poppy. She really, really, needs help.'

'Does your mother know you're here?' He keeps rubbing the back of his neck.

'No.'

Then I realise I should have said yes to the coffee, even though I hate it. I don't know how to make this go any better. But at least I'm here and we're talking.

'We made a clean break your mum and I...eventually...I had contact at first, but...your mum...she...er...so we ended up agreeing no contact.'

'I need help.' My fists are clenched and I'm trying to calm my breathing. Be strong Miranda. Just go for it.

'Your mum is the best person to help you.'

'She won't.'

'Oh, God, Poppy.'

Another adult that calls on God but possibly isn't praying – not asking for guidance to know what is the best thing to do.

'I can't get involved. Sorry. It's the no contact thing...I'm sorry.'

'No contact. That's why you don't even send me a birthday card?'

'I did send cards at first...but...' He's looking at his hands in his lap. He has a bald patch on the top of his head. 'Then...your mum...we decided no contact was best.

'I thought I wasn't good enough...why you left...I thought it was my fault.'

'No, Poppy...no...it was me and your mum...our fault. Never yours.'

'So will you help me?'

'It's your mum who should be helping.'

'I told you. She won't.'

I feel uncomfortable with him so close to me. I stand up. 'Don't you even want to know why I need help?'

'Oh, Poppy.'

'You walked out on us.'

'That's what your mother told you, did she?'

We're looking straight at each other. 'Yes,' I mutter, realising I had only heard Mum's side of the story – even then, she's hardly told me anything.

I don't know what to say.

'Poppy really needs your help,' says Kavya. She stands up next to me. 'Shall I tell him why?'

I have a split second to decide.

'No...No...uh...' I don't want him to know because I can't trust him. But I've come all this way...

'Girls, tell me if you want...I wish I could help...I think about you a lot, Poppy...but I really, truly cannot get involved. I have another family. We're happy...Children. A new wife...She doesn't know...I didn't tell her...And I'm not going to tell her.'

I feel like he's just punched me in the tummy.

'Don't I matter at all to you?'

'Of course you matter, Poppy. I told you. Your mum wouldn't want me involved...I think about you...It's just...I don't do emotion.'

'What the hell does that mean?' I know I'm too loud. Mum's right. He's a loser. But I have more brothers and sisters? I feel myself split. I want to stay and maybe meet Dad's new family. But being here is a disaster.

My breathing goes scratchy and loud, the heat from the fire overwhelming me. I step towards the door.'

'Wait, Poppy,' Kavya takes hold of my arm. 'Look...Poppy really needs your help. If you knew – you'd want to help – please.'

We all stand looking at each other in a moment of silence. I know then that he won't help.

'This is hopeless,' I say. I grab Kavya's hand. 'We'll go. Thanks for nothing.'

'Poppy...I...' Dad gets up, his chair grating backwards on the stone floor.

'Poppy!' Kavya grabs my arm. 'Give your Dad a chance to speak!'

'No, he's a loser,' I mutter. I drag Kavya out of the workshop and into the cold street. My insides bubble like a volcano about to explode.

'Loser!' I yell at the world. Kavya hugs me and I'm crying on her shoulder.

'Come on,' she says. 'Let's find a café. Hot chocolate time.'

But I can't move forward. Can't see how to go on. My shoulders are heaving as weeping engulfs me. I can't stop the flaming magma boiling up, threatening to destroy everything. I came all this way and never really gave him a chance.

I mess everything up.

But he's not someone I can trust – and he's not going to rescue me.

We find a small café and the hot chocolate helps.

A bit.

I keep thinking that I didn't get that right at all with Dad. I could have done better. I think probably Kavya thinks that too.

'I didn't give him much of a chance, did I?'

'It was a tough situation. Do you mean you want to go back and talk some more?'

'I don't know...he really didn't want to get involved...loser.'

'Maybe he truly feels that your mum would be mad at him...and what about his new wife? He must feel he just can't be involved?'

'Maybe.' I stare into my empty mug wondering if a second cup was going to help.

'Why didn't he help me?' Then I'm crying and I want to get out of the café so I get my backpack and leave. Kavya runs after me.

'I'm so angry!' I yell. Kavya holds me and we stand on the pavement with people looking at us.

'Come on,' Kavya says. 'Let's walk.'

'I don't want to walk!'

'What then? Go back to your Dad?'

'No! I'm so angry at myself for messing it up!'

'You didn't mess it up. Your dad did. Doesn't do emotion! Huh!'

We stand with our arms around each other, my anger still churning inside me.

'You know what, Kav? If my mum and dad won't help me, I'll trap Carl myself. I'll get rid of him. Even if I die doing it.'

If you tell anyone I'll kill you.

'We...mustn't do anything dangerous...but...I'll help you,' Kavya says.

'I knew you would. But what shall we do?'

I've asked myself that question a billion times and my mind goes blank as always. But this time it's different.

I'll get Carl's shed keys. Break his computer password. Download his film of me and him to show Mum. Although the thought of her seeing Carl on top of me is hideous.

But I'm going to do it. He won't know what hit him.

Chapter 34

Back home

I spend the train journey home frustrated with myself for my failure with Dad. I handled it badly. I went all that way – then just gave up because I judged him a loser.

I could have told him it's only sixty-five days before Zara is thirteen.

I should have told him that.

My countdown calendar for Zara is beginning to freak me out.

'I could have let him make us coffee.' I reach out and hold Kavya's hand. 'I could have pretended to drink it. Maybe I could have met his new family.'

'Maybe you will one day. He was quite closed off though, wasn't he. Didn't want his new wife to know about you.'

'I messed it up. If I'd talked more to Dad then maybe he would have helped me.'

'I don't think you could have done it any differently, Poppy. He had his mind made up...didn't have any warmth about him at all.' Kavya has my hand in a firm grip and I can tell she's angry.

Then it occurs to me that Kavya could have said more to Dad. She must have known I was struggling, sitting there with a man I hardly know. But of course, it wasn't her fault. It was mine.

'I wonder what he meant that he doesn't do emotion?' I say.

'Maybe it's a man thing.'

'Maybe. Bit weird though.'

'This whole morning has been weird.' She squeezes my hand.

As we get off the train at East Croydon and head to the tram stop my brain fog is clearing. Oddly I keep thinking about Harry. Sometimes I see his face in my head, and I wish I was with him.

But we'll be home in half an hour and I'm worrying how Mum's going to react. I'm going to have to phone her, partly because I need to check that Carl actually went on the train. It would be a nightmare if he decided not to go to Manchester and he's at home. I can't face trawling through the dozens of text messages to find exactly what's happened. And there are some messages that are probably from Mia. I'm not going to read those.

'Mum'll be spitting mad at me,' I say as we get off the tram in Sandyhills High Street.

'Probably, and what will you do if she's drunk?'

'What I usually do. Keep out of her way. Or be a dutiful daughter and suck up to her.'

'You don't have to go straight home,' Kavya says reaching out and hugging me. 'You can stay at mine and put off seeing her till tomorrow. Come on. That might be best.'

'I think I'd better see her today, given the number of her calls I've missed. Anyway, I want to see Biscuit.'

'Come to mine if it's at all difficult. Don't just stay at home.'

'Sorry I'm being such a loser. I know she'll take my phone.'

'Let's ring your mum now and I'll walk to yours with you.'

'Yeah. Get it over with.'

I wait till everyone has left the tram-stop platform and ring her.

'What do you think you're playing at?' Mum's voice is loud but wobbly. 'Where are you now?'

'At the tram-stop on High Street.'

'You get back here right now, my girl. Hear me? Now!'

'OK.' Going into obedient-mode seems the best way through this. 'Did Carl go to Manchester?'

'Yes. And to say he's angry with you is putting it mildly.'

At last the call ends.

Kavya raises her eyebrows. 'Drunk?'

'Of course. Better go now,' I say.

'I'll come with you.'

'Maybe not come in. It might be worse if you're there.'

'I know I'm not her favourite person,' Kavya hugs me, then keeps up positive encouragements. But the thoughts in my head are churning chaotically again, clanging against each other.

'Whatever happens, Poppy, you've done well today. You asked an adult for help. But...you know...you could talk to Aunty. I know she'd listen.'

I don't quite know how to answer. I think of Harry. Then Dad is in my head.

Sandyhills High Street is heaving with shoppers and nose to tail traffic that's blasting out all kinds of noxious fumes that I'm breathing into my lungs. I'm finding it hard to listen to Kavya and I'm thinking the worst.

Mum has never, ever, been predictable.

She could throw me out. But I'm not sixteen yet.

If you tell your mother she'll send you away. You'll end up in a children's home. She'll see you're just a troublemaker with a vivid imagination.

'If it all goes pear-shaped can I come to yours tonight?' I'm struggling to squeeze my voice out loud enough for Kavya to hear above the traffic.

'Course you can. I said so, didn't I? Shall I wait outside your house?'

'Er...no...you go. She might take for ever with her yelling. She'll take my phone so I might just turn up at yours. Is that OK?'

'Course it is. Aunty's always cool about everything. Except drugs.'

When we reach my front door, I want to hold onto Kavya for the rest of my life. But I have to face Mum.

The sweet/sour smell of wine fills the kitchen. She's slumped on a stool at the breakfast bar, a glass of red wine beside her. Of course.

Carl isn't here.

Biscuit runs towards me, her toenails clacking on the floor and I kneel down and cuddle her. She licks my face and into my ears. I tell her to stay in her basket.

Mum's staring at me, her eyes red-rimmed. I'm not sure it's good or bad that she's been crying. 'Zara and JoJo are next door.' Her voice is loaded with threat.

My breathing goes chaotic, heavy. Loud. Fast in and out, and I feel a cold shudder down my spine. But maybe this will be the time that Mum finally believes me about Carl?

Mum's mouth and eyes are arrow slits, and I'm ready for her to take a shot at me. 'I can't believe a word you say.'

That was inevitable. 'I told you I didn't want to go to Manchester.' My voice is thin and hazy as I try to control my panicked breathing.

She'll know you're lying. No one will believe you.

She's shouting at me, but my breathing is loud and blood is pumping through my ears, noisy, telling me to be careful. Then I'm not in my body anymore, I'm floating up near the fancy lights Carl bought and I'm watching Mum's mouth move.

I try to focus. Mum says that Carl looked for me for ages and almost missed the Manchester train. He's rung her a few times, blaming Mum for me not going.

Guilt hits me. I don't want Mum to suffer because of what I do.

She says 'phone' and holds out her hand. I knew she'd take it. I put it on the black granite worktop.

'I still haven't told Carl what you said about him,' she says. 'I probably won't because he'd be too angry – because one thing you can be sure of is that he is absolutely furious with you right now. Why are you trying to destroy our family when Carl is so good to us?'

'Mum, he wanted me to go to Manchester to abuse me – '

'I don't want to hear any more of your stories.' She refills her glass, emptying the bottle. 'He'd never do such a thing. He's an ordinary man, with a good business, making lots of money. He wouldn't do that, Poppy. He loves you – despite how rude you are to him.'

'I'm rude to him because of how he treats me! He threatened to kill me if I told you.'

'That's enough. Go to your room and stay there.'

I'm fully focused now. My body calmer. And she's drunk.

'I went to see my dad. Essex. You're right. He's a loser.'

'You went to see him? How did you – ?'

'On the internet.'

'How could you be so stupid...deceitful – '

'You wouldn't help me. I hoped he might – '

'Go to your room this minute! You're grounded!'

In your dreams.

I have a moment to decide. Obey her and then maybe I can start the hunt for Carl's keys today or get the hell out of here.

'Biscuit!' I yell and she runs after me. I grab her lead, my jacket and my backpack and we're through the front door and down the road, Mum calling for me to come back.

No. No. No.

Once I'm down the road a bit I clip Biscuit onto her lead. I sort of wish I'd stayed and started the key hunt. But I can do that this coming week. The most likely place for the keys is the bureau in Mum and Carl's bedroom. Kavya and I could sneak out of her flat tonight. No, I can't. Mum would hear me in her bedroom. But I'll get the keys and download him raping me. It's going to be awful showing that to Mum.

But I must.

All that stuff about obeying your parents and teachers is all very well, but when they're drunk, or stupid, or evil, then obedience doesn't apply.

That's my decision. Me. Poppy Grace Stewart, and if the adults around me are too useless to do anything to help me, then Kavya and I will do something.

Get Rid Of Carl. GROC. Sounds a bit like a dangerous swamp animal. And I'm going to make GROC work.

But I'm dreading him coming home.

Chapter 35

Kavya speaks up

I go the quick way to Kavya's along the streets, but it's not quick because Biscuit wants to stop and sniff at every lamp post. My heart is galloping as I realise I might be in even more trouble now because I ran away from Mum.

I ring the bell to Kavya's flat, at last beginning to feel a bit more relaxed.

'How was your mum?' She gives me a hug.

'Mad as hell. So I ran away.'

'As in never going back?'

'No...as in...not wanting to listen to her drunken rant.'

'Hot chocolate time.'

While Kavya makes us drinks I cuddle Biscuit and think through my tiny beginning of the idea to download what Carl does to me so Mum can see – although that feels hideous – but I've got to go for it. I know he starts his password with 'JoJo' and he's probably just used JoJo's birthdate, or something equally feeble. How come I'm scared of someone who seems to use such hopeless passwords?

I'm a bit worried that Kavya could think it's all much too dangerous. But I'm going to do it anyway.

There must be spare keys to the shed and I'm pretty sure I can find them. It's hard to know what else to do, but I run through some spy films in my head. Pretend I'm James Bond. Except it's all so complicated.

As we're drinking our hot chocolate on Kavya's bed, Aunty Anjali comes upstairs to tell us Mum rang her. 'She says she sent you to your room, but you ran away.' Anjali's face is strained but kind.

'Correct,' I say. 'But you won't send me back, will you?'

'You put me in a difficult position, Poppy,' she says. 'But it's you who must decide. You're always welcome to stay here.' She squeezes my arm. 'But, to be honest, I think you need to ring your mother. Actually, I told her you'd ring her later.'

'OK. I will,' I say, taking a sip of my too hot drink.

'Is everything OK Poppy?' Anjali strokes my hair.

'Yes.'

'Poppy, what's going on?' Anjali stares intently at me.

'Nothing.'

'Poppy!' Kavya's voice is loud and harsh. 'Tell Aunty!'

'Tell me what?'

'Nothing. Really there's nothing.' I glare at Kavya.

'I think there is something.' Anjali stands beside me. I stare at my feet.

'OK,' Anjali says, 'But stay and eat with us, though your mum might ring you first of course. But both of you come downstairs when we close in fifteen minutes and help clear up.'

She goes back down to the salon, and I divert Kavya onto talking about Mum.

'You're gonna have to grovel,' she says.

'Mmmm. She might hit me.'

'Oh God help us.'

'I get the feeling God won't help, though,' I say.

'If she hits you, come back here.'

'Thanks.'

'Love you,' she says, hugging me.

'Love you too.' I know I'll only make a good plan for Getting Rid Of Carl with Kavya to tell me what's likely to work and what's just one of my fanciful ideas. I smile at the thought of the GROC, a stinking odious swamp monster getting caught.

Found out.

By me and my best mate.

We go down and sweep the shop floor at closing time, scrub the white hair-washing basins, put the used towels into the washing machine. Biscuit gets in the way but that makes us all laugh.

I couldn't manage life without Biscuit.

I'm still running through some James Bond films in my head. And Mission Impossible...recording Carl...that would trap him with his own voice. If I had a licence to kill I suppose I could do what the Ashbury Road Gang are rumoured to do and carry a knife and stick it into his heart when he throws himself down on me. But then I'd be put in prison for murder. Or would a judge think that it was self-defence given Carl was abusing me? But Miss Singh said the statistics show you're much more likely to be stabbed if you yourself are carrying a knife.

So I won't stab him.

While Aunty Anjali cooks a meal we squat on Kavya's bed, and I tell her about Getting Rid Of Carl and my latest plan for finding the keys to his shed.

'I even thought about stabbing him – '

'What! No! No! No!'

'But I won't.' I say, grinning. But I curl up and hug my knees because my insides keep wobbling. I cuddle Biscuit and think about Harry to distract myself.

Kavya pulls the sleeves of her hoody over her hands and gives me one of her intense looks. 'You'd end up in prison if you stab Carl.'

'I know. So I won't do that.' But inside I'm thinking it's what he deserves. 'Anyway, you know in spy films when the goodies lurk outside a house in a van with all their listening devices, well, the best I've come up with so far is to borrow Mum's little voice activated recorder she had for her Open University course. Put it under my bed and it'll record his odious grunts and groans.'

'Wow!' Kavya says.

'Do you reckon that might work?'

'Depends what Carl says – and does.'

'Last time he took me into his new shed so he might not do it anymore in my bedroom.'

Then I'm crying, big hot tears streaking down my face. I try to wipe them away with my sleeve, but there are too many. 'It's never going to stop, is it? Never ever! Oh God help me.'

Kavya holds me, lays my head on her shoulder and hands me a tissue.

'I'm so angry that you have to put up with it!' she says. 'So angry! Look, couldn't we tell Aunty? You know she's so cool about everything.'

'No! Not a good idea.'

'Ring Childline again! Come on, Poppy! Tell them who he is!'

'No! The best thing is to record him. Play it to Mum, then she'll know I'm not lying and she'll throw him out. Not me. At least...I hope she might believe me then.'

Then I'm crying again, snot pouring down to my lips. I can't get my head around the thought that even then Mum might not believe me. I can't think about that.'

'I don't think Mum will notice I've borrowed the recorder.' I blow my nose, breathing deeply, gritting my teeth, trying to switch off my feelings. 'It's in her chest of drawers with her notes from the course. She doesn't use it anymore. So it will just sit under my bed. Obviously if he takes me into the shed, I can't do anything about that, but I can check in their room every day to see if there's a shed key...one day his desk will be open.'

'And?'

'Go to the shed when he's out and download his CCTV recording of what he does to me.'

'Oh, Poppy, that sounds much too dangerous. What if he catches you in his shed?'

'But I'll have it all downloaded, and – '

'No Poppy. No! The voice recorder maybe. But trying to get into the shed?'

'I'll find a time when he's at work.'

'Look, Poppy, I don't often say this...I want to support you...but I think you're quite wrong about this. Don't do it. You're not an MI5 spy.'

'But I'm so desperate I'll do anything.'

'Then let's ring Childline. Right now.'

'Oh...'

'Tell them his name and what he does.'

'I can't.'

'Then tell Aunty. You're safe here. Carl can't get to you.'

'Mum will never forgive me for telling,' I whisper. 'She'll hate me even more. Please let me just do it my way.'

We sit for a while holding each other. I love to feel Kavya's warm breath on my cheek.

My plan with the voice recorder will work. I know it will. Getting the key is a bit of a risk. But I can get it.

I ignore the herd of elephants charging through my innards.

Chapter 36

Ring your mother

After I've eaten with Anjali and Kavya I know I can't put off ringing Mum any longer.

We both climb onto Kavya's bed, Biscuit between us.

'Cuddle up close,' I say, 'so you can hear what she says.' My hand is trembling.

'Where are you?' Mum says, her voice slurred.

'I'm still at Kavya's flat.'

'How dare you just run off when I ground you.'

'Sorry, Mum.'

'I'm furious with you about Manchester...and seeing your dad...then running from me.' She hiccups. 'Furious! You hear me?'

'Yes, Mum.'

'Your dad's a loser.' I hear her gulp down some drink. 'Don't get him...hic...back in your life.'

'He doesn't want me in his life.' It hurts to say that and my body freezes.

'Oh,' she says. 'Good.'

I don't know what to say to her because thoughts are crashing around my head.

'And we need to talk about Carl...he does so much for us...you come home after eight thirty and I'll...hic... get JoJo and Zara in bed by then.'

'OK.'

She ends the call.

'Oh God, I don't know why I'm crying...but she's going to listen to me...I think.'

Kavya hugs me. 'Come on. It could be worse.'

'Yes, true,' I say and wipe my eyes. 'She was talking in logical sentences at least. But by eight thirty tonight she might be beyond that.'

Anjali insists on walking me home with Kavya, but they don't come in. It's about quarter to nine. Zara must be in bed and Mum is sitting on her bar stool at the breakfast bar, a glass of red wine beside her and a bottle, almost empty. The kitchen is a mess, dishes stacked on the black granite surface, the sink full of glasses and mugs, JoJo's bright plastic bowls still with his gloopy food in them.

Biscuit takes herself out into the garden.

'You've deigned to come, then,' Mum says. She sways. This is going to be awful. A wave of trembling sweeps over me.

I put the kettle on and make strong coffee.

Mum drones on but she starts sipping the coffee. Her head is wobbling as if it's too heavy for her to control.

Then she abandons her coffee and pours herself more wine. Looks daggers at me so I don't say anything. She drains the whole glassful, then empties the rest of the bottle into her glass and drains that too.

We stare at each other.

My phone is on the kitchen counter and it pings as a message comes in.

'Good thing I know your phone password...I've been reading your messages.'

'Mum!' I make a mental note to change my password as soon as I can.

'You should tell school about these texts. One of them was telling you to kill yourself. That's bullying, that is. Show your teachers.'

'No, Mum. That would just make everything much worse.'

'Then I'll tell school.'

'No!' Nightmare scenario. Mum complaining to school I'm being bullied. Mr Robins seeing the messages.

'Who's sending those texts? she yells.

I stare at my trainers.

'Tell me,' she says, her voice full of venom.

'Mia,' I whisper.

'Mia! Mia? I can't believe such a lovely girl would do that. It's another one of your lies.'

'If you don't believe me, Mum, neither will the teachers. The messages will all disappear, so I'll have no proof. Rather like I have no proof of what Carl does.'

Mum looks away. 'I've been thinking, maybe you should go on the pill. I'll make a doctor's appointment. You and me.'

'OK.'

'I can't have you pregnant.' Her eyelids droop. I'm not going to tell her about Carl injecting me.

'Come on, Mum, let me help you up to bed.'

She lets me support her upstairs and I get her onto her bed.

I'm not undressing her. I move her legs onto the bed and cover her with the blanket from the foot of the bed. Her eyes are shut and she's breathing deeply. I decide to get her onto her side in case she's sick. She's so heavy, but I manage it.

Carl's desk is shut but I creep over to it and try to pull down the lid. It's locked. Of course, he wouldn't leave it open while he's away. Mum stirs and groans so it's not the moment to get the voice recorder.

I go back downstairs and grab my phone and go into the garden to change my passcode and be with Biscuit. She's nosing around the bushes and fruit trees at the bottom of the garden, but she rushes over to meet me bringing her ball.

I throw it for her, then stand on the patio and look at more messages. I don't want to look at them, but of course I do. It's like picking a scab. I know I shouldn't do it and it hurts like hell, but it's as if I have to do it.

Have to feel the pain.

Have to admit that Mia has power over me to hurt me.

I put my phone back on the kitchen counter and lock up the front and back doors.

Biscuit's clingy, so I take her up to my bedroom. It's against the rules to let her sleep with me, but I'm beyond caring.

Chapter 37

Grounded

The next morning I wake hearing the church bells. It's Sunday and JoJo is singing in his cot. 'Pop,' he calls. 'Jack and Jill. Aw faw down. Pop.'

Biscuit leaps on me and licks my face so I push her off and go to JoJo. I pull back his Toy Story curtains, loving his smile as he holds up his arms to me.

'Beautiful boy,' I whisper, kissing his warm neck. I take him downstairs wanting time on my own with him before battles with Mum start again.

Biscuit goes out through her dog-flap and JoJo is telling me about Peppa Pig and George's dinosaur, while I make porridge and have another look at my phone. I read through the new messages. They're from about seven different accounts but I think they're all from Mia and maybe Isobel and Flora too. Probably they need to keep in with Mia or maybe she'd turn on them too. I wonder if Scarlett has defected yet and if she's a target now as well as me?

They're keeping up the rumour that I have sex with anyone with these messages. This still hurts me and makes my stomach lurch, but I don't know what I can do about it. I'm hoping Harry still doesn't believe it.

Probably people like Reggie and Xavier don't care.

But Harry would care.

Maybe.

Somehow I feel so distant from Harry. What am I thinking? Of course Harry is distant. He won't be interested in me.

What would Zara make of these messages? If she reads them – they're probably all round school. She hasn't mentioned it recently. I can't face a conversation with her about it.

I put my phone back on the counter next to Mum's handbag and help JoJo with his breakfast. If Mum just keeps my phone in the kitchen that's not too bad.

'Biscuit!' JoJo squeals as she comes in from the garden. He deliberately drops a spoonful of porridge on the floor for her. She licks it up and I give her some of her proper dog food which she wolfs down then goes back under JoJo's highchair.

I love these moments with JoJo and Biscuit. They are the best bits of my life because they stay the same – mostly – and I feel safe with them.

I get some of my half-term homework from my school bag and do it in the kitchen. It's so hard to concentrate because I keep wondering how I'm going to get Carl's keys and Mum's little voice recorder.

It's after eleven before Mum appears. I make her coffee and toast.

'Mum. Can I take Biscuit for a walk?'

'Why are you asking?' she says, so softly I can hardly hear her.

'I...I wasn't sure how much I was grounded.'

'Grounded?' She looks up at me.

She's forgotten. A rush of happiness flows down my spine. 'So can I have my phone now?'

'No,' she says. 'Course you can take the dog out. Too much poo in the garden.'

I want to point out that I'm good at picking it up but I call Biscuit and I'm out the front door before she changes her mind.

Mum's still sitting at the breakfast bar when I get back, so I make beans on toast for everyone and more coffee for Mum.

After lunch Zara takes JoJo to the swings at the park and I sit down facing Mum.

'Mum. We have to talk. Am I still grounded?'

'Yes.'

'Are you going to tell Carl about me going to see Dad?'

She stares at me but says nothing. She's hunched over her coffee, her face grey and etched with more lines than usual. The Botox isn't working very well.

'I need to know, Mum. If you tell Carl I went to see my dad, he'll be angry.'

If you tell anyone I'll kill you.

Might Carl think that when I ran away from him I was going to tell someone? If he thinks that I'm in real trouble. But I suppose he might worry about that all the time.

'Carl is furious with you for you disappearing instead of going to Robot Wars,' she says. 'Running away from him like that. What on earth were you thinking?'

I'm not going to answer that. 'So will you tell him about my dad?'

In the silence I try to get my breathing under control.

'I won't tell him you went to see your dad.'

'Thanks, Mum.' That fear is back on her face. I must be right about her being as afraid of Carl as I am.

I don't want to think about Monday morning when Carl comes back. Probably the whole of half-term week will be ruined.

That sense of needing to cut myself creeps up my spine.

No. I'm going to stop thinking like this. I'm going to make my life better. Stand up for myself.

I'm not really sure how to do that, though. I divert my mind by thinking about Harry. His eyebrows. His cute lop-sided smile.

I go upstairs and go online on my laptop and look at the Childline website. I read about others who struggle like I do. My brain can hardly take it all in, but I make the decision to ring up again when I can.

Yes. I can make my life better.

While Mum's slumped in the kitchen I creep up to her bedroom and sneak the little voice activated recorder out of her drawer.

I sit on my bed working out how to use it. It's easy. When I put it under my bed it picks up even my quiet voice.

I'm ready for Carl when he comes for me.

'We're walking round to the café,' Mum shouts upstairs. 'Poppy? Do you want to come?' It's Sunday late afternoon and am slogging at homework, wishing I could text Kavya.

Zara bursts into my room. 'Mum says we can have milkshakes and burgers. Come on.'

Everyone will be out of the house. I can use the land line. Mum will never know I made the call. And I'll have time to do a search for Carl's keys.

'Er...no...I've got so much homework.'

Zara looks disgusted. 'You've got all half-term to do homework. Come on.'

'No...I...'

'You're such a weirdo.'

Then she's gone and I hear the front door shut.

I must do it before I change my mind. I'm downstairs to the landline and ringing Childline.

'You're through to Childline. How can I help you?'

'What would happen? I mean if I tell someone my stepfather is making me have sex with him?...I mean...he says he'll kill me if I tell...but someone would stop him wouldn't they?'

'You'd be safe. Do you want to tell me a bit more about it all?

The woman's voice is kind and soft.

'I think Mum would never forgive me...and I'm worried he'll start on my younger sister when she's thirteen like he did with me.'

'Do you think you might be able to tell a teacher that you trust?'

'But will it be safe? I mean...can he get to me and kill me?'

'Your stepdad would be taken away, Poppy. You will be safe.'

I put the phone down.

Is she telling the truth?

I'd be safe?

We'd all be safe?

Would we?

But Mum would be spitting mad at me.

So would Zara.

Our whole family would collapse.

I can't let that happen.

Chapter 38

Carl returns

It's Monday morning of half-term and I have a private conversation with Zara in her room. I feel she deserves to know about our dad.

'I don't remember him at all,' she says as she puts her flute away. 'I've seen him in some photos, but I have no memories. I suppose I would like to meet him.'

'One day, maybe,' I say. 'He has another family now and he hasn't told his new wife about our existence.'

Zara starts crying. 'Oh! Oh...how can we ever – ' She sits on her bed and reaches for a tissue.

'I don't know.' I sit next to her and put my arm around her. 'I didn't give him enough of a chance really...I should have stayed longer but I was so...well...I don't know. It was all a bit of a disaster.'

'I'm glad you told me. Thanks. I don't think of him, you know.' She dries her eyes.

'That's OK. I...er...Carl will be back from Manchester in a few hours.'

'Be ready to be grounded. Mum says he's furious with you.'

I smile and squeeze her arm and leave her room. I'm glad I talked to her. But my ears are buzzing, and I can feel adrenaline rushing around my body at the thought of what Carl might do and say. So I sit in my bedroom trying to finish some chemistry homework and revising for a geography test after half-term about tornadoes and hurricanes and how they're formed.

But it's hopeless so instead I check Mum's voice recorder is under my bed. Play a bit of it – just me talking to Biscuit. I put it back under my tennis racket and hockey stick. The truth will come out and Mum will get rid of Carl.

I think.

She might not because we couldn't live here without his money.

I sit and stare at my poppy picture. I go into it and I'm playing with the other children and I'm happy.

It's just after eleven thirty when I hear a taxi, then the slamming of car doors and the wheels of Carl's case on the drive. Mum greets him and then there's his inevitable shout. 'Poppy, get down here right this minute.'

My knees feel weak. I wish my dad was here.

When I open my door, Zara opens hers and runs to me and hugs me. She's crying so I hug her tightly.

I'd better obey Carl. But I've put on my running clothes and my trainers. And if anyone hits me, I'm heading to Kavya's. I don't care what the fallout is.

I creep into the kitchen. I wish my heart would calm down.

Biscuit goes through her dog flap into the garden. If I run, I'd want her to come with me.

They're both standing there, arms folded. Carl's case on the floor and his camera bag on the granite kitchen work surface. Had he planned to film Kavya and me?

I shudder.

'How dare you run away from me,' Carl says. His voice is menacing and I can't look straight at him. 'And if you think you're getting away with what you did, you've got another think coming. No going out for the rest of half-term at all except to walk the dog. No more pocket money, for at least a month. No meeting with your friends. None of this acting nonsense. No play rehearsals. No performances. No contact with that friend of yours – whatshername – Kavya.'

I say nothing.

I can't be Miranda?

I don't know if I can survive the rest of term if I have to be me.

I try to swallow, but can't. I feel my knees trembling.

'Come with me, right now, to my shed.'

For a moment I consider not obeying, but I'm too frightened of what he might do, so I follow him across the kitchen.

He yanks open the patio door and at the shed door, he puts his camera bag down and gets his chain with all the keys out of his trouser pocket.

He must have a spare set. And I will find them.

As he unlocks the security bars and the shed door, Biscuit nudges my foot and wags her tail at me.

'Later,' I whisper to her.

He goes to his desk, puts his camera bag down, sits at his computer. I move silently towards him – crane my neck up over his shoulder.

I'm right, I see him type JoJo to start his password. Could he really be so stupid as to use JoJo's birthdate?

I turn away so he won't suspect I'm watching him.

Breaking into his CCTV system could be quite easy. My insides smile, although I know what comes next.

After a few minutes he gets up and comes towards me. I just have to get through this, so I switch my body off.

When he's finished he gets up off the white sofa. 'No money this time,' he says. 'Maybe for ever. And if you even think of disobeying me again or telling anyone about us, I'll kill your dog.'

My stomach lurches. I spin around and stare at him.

'That got your attention didn't it?' he says, his lips curling into a smile.

I feel the strength go from my body.

'I'll go out right now and get rat poison. That dog'll eat anything, won't she? I'll put poison on some meat and she'll wolf it down. Dead in a matter of minutes. So keep your mouth shut.'

Carl goes out in his car. I'm too numb to do anything but I sit at my desk and pretend to be doing schoolwork. When his car comes back, I watch him from my window. He's holding a small package.

This poison could be the end of my happiness.

My life.

But my brain won't work so I lie on my bed. I know this is a moment to get my secret diary out and write a poem about the darkness that is surrounding me.

But I don't.

Zara brings me a drink of blackcurrant squash. 'Mum says you can take Biscuit out,' she says. She touches my arm. 'OK?'

'Course,' I say, doing my best fake smile.

I walk Biscuit around the country park. Mum says I have thirty minutes. No more.

It's raining and there's no one around.

I watch Biscuit, trying to pick up on her joyous busyness as she sniffs every blade of grass, her tail wagging as she picks up scents. But there is a great pit of sadness underneath my life. It sags into all the corners of my being, bigger than me, swallowing me up, consuming me. I feel I can almost touch it, yet it is also veiled and unpredictable. The sense of alienation sits in my stomach, never moving.

Silent.

I stand beside the lake, as sadness wraps itself around my throat.

What if Carl kills Biscuit? What if I just walk into the water? There's no one around to see me.

I try to make the cog wheels in my head think this through. What would it be like to die? Would the water flow into my mouth? Would it be quick?

But what about Kavya? Zara? Wouldn't they wish they'd done something to help?

Would it hurt them?

Maybe that's just how it is. They'd be hurt but I'd be gone.

They'd get over it.

Maybe.

I feel my body fill up with dread – of staying alive and facing my awful life.

I breathe deeply, as if I want to go on living.

But I don't.

Please God. I really don't want to go on. I'm not worth helping.

Biscuit makes her soft yipping sound. Nudges my foot.

Wags her tail.

At me.

I can't leave Biscuit. What would she do without me? I have to protect her from Carl.

What am I thinking? I can't leave Zara and JoJo! And Kavya. Course I can't. I have to protect Zara. And I think they love me...I'd make them sad...Kavya would feel guilty...

Maybe a better plan is to find that pack of poison and throw it away?

I must find the keys.

I must download the images of me from the CCTV on his computer.

I must.

If I'm going to stay alive, I will prove what Carl's doing.

Nothing else matters.

Sixty-three days before Zara is thirteen.

I find a park bench and sit and hug Biscuit.

I'd never manage life without her.

Chapter 39

No Miranda

I spend the rest of half-term wondering if I really need to obey Mum and Carl. But all I can think about is rat poison. Carl could be putting it right now onto something Biscuit would gobble up. I search everywhere for that little package, but he must have locked it in his shed or the bureau – which is locked every time I manage to get into his bedroom.

I must find those keys.

It's agony without my phone and I'm not allowed to go and see Kavya. She knows that Mum will go crazy if she rings me on the landline.

I beg Mum to make Carl change his mind and let me be Miranda, but her hands tremble as she holds her glass of wine. 'I can't do that,' she says, her voice gravelly and so quiet I can hardly hear her.

I know I'm right that Carl is intimidating her too.

But if I'm not Miranda, I won't be rehearsing with Harry. Mia will. And that feels terrible.

Before school on Monday morning, I avoid meeting up with Kavya because I think she'll say I should stand up to Carl and be Miranda anyway. But she doesn't know about the poison.

It's agony telling Miss Singh I can't be Miranda anymore.

'Why?' She looks hurt and I can't answer her. So I escape. Then Mr Robins asks me to meet him at lunch time in the art room.

'You're saying you don't know why you've given up being one of the stars of the play?' He's stroking his beard and I don't want to look him in the eyes. 'Is it pressure from home?'

'Sort of.' I'm desperate to tell him everything. But I know I just can't. The image of Carl arriving home with the little package of rat poison flashes into my mind.

'Would you like me to talk to your parents?' he says.

'Oh...no...that would make everything much worse.'

'I'm starting to worry now, Poppy. What's going on?'

'Nothing...nothing to worry about. Really.'

Mr Robins looks unconvinced, and I escape from him outside to one of the benches by the field, my head full of the Childline lady's voice. 'Tell a teacher you trust.' I wish I could tell him. But the poison...

'Found you.' Kavya sits down beside me. 'I got held up in the art room.' She puts her arm around me. 'What's all this that Reggie's heard about you giving up being Miranda?'

Silence.

She's holding both my hands in her hands.

I tell her everything. Boring half-term in my room. No phone. Going into Mum and Carl's room several times a day to see if Carl's desk is open to find the keys to the shed.

Carl's plan to kill Biscuit. Trying to find the packet of poison.

I love the feel of Kavya's arms around me, and she dries my tears.

'It was hard without my phone. But I went on the Childline website on my laptop and rang them from the landline when everyone else was out.'

Kavya's words explode out. 'Brilliant Poppy! Please just tell someone!'

'But you know why I can't.'

'Oh, you and your reasons!' She jumps up and grabs my arm. 'Poppy, let's get Zara...right now...run and get Biscuit, and tell Aunty. Everything. Come on. Let's do it now.'

But we don't because my whole body trembles at the horror.

I will kill your dog.

At afternoon registration Harry leans over to my desk.

'You're giving up Miranda? What happened?' he whispers, his green eyes searching my face.

'Can't talk about it.' I feel myself blush.

'Was it something I did?' His eyebrows almost meet in the middle as he frowns.

'No. No. Course not. I just can't...you know.'

'Please come back. I'll really miss you...like being with you...acting with you.'

My body tingles.

I'm not breathing.

Harry likes being with me.

I try to swallow, but can't.

Mia gives me triumphant grins several times a day, but I tell myself I don't care. Over the next few days the bullying is less, so I'm glad of that, but I'm missing seeing Harry and I listen to his voice in my head. 'I like being with you'. But now he's rehearsing with Mia.

He'll like being with her more.

School has become a nightmare. I stagger from class to class, aware of Harry sometimes looking at me. I consider asking him for help with our physics project on energy transfers, but I don't have the courage.

Every day I go into Mum and Carl's bedroom to search for a spare set of his keys – if a spare set exists. I've taken to sneaking in while everyone else is at breakfast, but every day the desk is locked. But sometimes it has been open in the past – when I've brought clean laundry in and put it on the bed it's definitely been open. And I've seen keys. But maybe they are somewhere else now? I check the bedside cabinet and drawers in the new posh bedroom furniture Carl had fitted recently.

I must find those keys.

Every day I note the number of days till Zara is thirteen.

Chapter 40

Carl makes a move

November is damp and cold and it's awful not being part of the play and being someone else. But I often pretend I'm strong Miranda, speaking my mind.

And one day I'll prove the truth about Carl.

Somehow.

He's being louder than usual, laughing in that forced way he has. He watches me whenever I'm in the same room as him. That's seriously spooky and all the time I have a kind of premonition that he's up to something.

I'm hoping it's not him planning when to use the poison.

Harry asks me at registration if I'm OK. 'How you doing?' he says. 'Wish you'd come back and be Miranda. We all miss you.'

That sounds like a lie.

'Long story,' I say.

'Oh,' he says, his eyes searching my face, so I have to look away. I wish I could sit and talk to Harry. Really talk.

At last the weekend comes and I wonder if Harry might do parkrun on Saturday. Mum and Carl say I'm not grounded anymore and so I can do it if I want to – but I can't have my phone back yet. Kavya and I decided yesterday at school that we had too much homework so we wouldn't do parkrun. It would be just my luck that today Harry will be running – and I'll miss him.

Carl says he's working in his shed on his robot for next year's Robot Wars. I slog at my desk on maths for ages before giving up and decide to take Biscuit out. Mum's taken Zara to gymnastics, and she and JoJo will go on to the Arts Centre as usual. I smile at how excited he gets going to the crèche while Mum does her yoga. Then she meets with her friends over coffee, and they play badminton sometimes, although I've noticed Mum is doing that less these days. And she's putting on a bit of weight.

Probably all that wine.

It's pouring with rain, but I don't mind. I love the fresh new smell as I walk Biscuit our usual five-dog-poo-bins walk, straight across the country park to the lake, twice round it, across to the swings, then back home.

I'll need to dry her when we get in, so she doesn't leave muddy paw-prints on the floor. That would annoy Mum and Carl.

Whatever I do I seem to annoy them. Perhaps they really will throw me out once I'm sixteen.

It's been another awful week. Rain most days and it's harder to talk to School Shrink. I've run out of things to say to her.

Biscuit is sniffing at something, and I leap through the long grass just in time to stop her rolling over in fox poo. Her favourite delicacy to smear across her back. Or eat. The vet laughed when I told her about this. 'That's dogs for you,' she said, and she was such a happy person I spent a week wondering if I'd rather be a vet than an engineer. Dealing with cute dogs all day seems fun.

I've just finished going round the lake when I hear my name and turn. Zara is running towards me, her arms flailing in her usual crazy run.

I grin. She'll never be a runner with that style!

'Poppy!' She's screaming. 'Couldn't find you!'

Something's wrong. The tone of her voice isn't usual.

My stomach tightens.

Biscuit stiffens, her ears twitch.

'Come on!' We run towards Zara.

I open my arms and her face is full of terror as she runs into my hug. She clings onto me. 'He...He...tried.' Tears run down her face and she's gasping for breath. The sweatshirt she wears over her leotard is half off – gathered around her neck, one arm naked. Her hair tousled and turning frizzy in the rain. She puts her arms around me and her head collapses on my chest. Her body's heaving.

She barks out some snatched words, but I can't make any sense of them.

'What are you trying to say?'

She throws up, choking. Spits. Wipes her face with her arm.

'Tried...pushed me...punched...'

'Who punched you?'

'I punched Carl! Came into my bedroom!'

My body starts to shake. My insides implode and I'm screaming in my head.

'No! No!' I grip onto my little sister as guilt surges up from my stomach.

'Punched him...Ran,' she gasps.

My mind is reeling. I didn't protect her.

We both weep on each other, hugging, gripping, until Zara's chest stops heaving. I can't find the words to comfort her.

The anger inside me is boiling up. I could kill Carl.

A scream bursts out of me. 'This was never meant to happen!' I cling to Zara. I failed her and there's a tornado inside me, unstoppable and destructive. 'But...thought you were at gymnastics?'

'I had such a bad sudden tummy ache...Mum brought me home.'

We cling to each other, crying.

A woman with a purple bobble hat approaches with a chocolate Labrador on a lead. The dogs bum-sniff. Biscuit's tail wagging.

'Can I help, girls?' she says.

'No. No, we're OK,' I say.

'We're not OK!' Zara yells.

The woman looks worried but I try to smile at her, dragging Biscuit and Zara away.

'We're just on our way home. Er...thanks. We'll be fine. Bit of a fight! Nothing to worry about.' I pull them down one of the smaller paths that run through the woodland.

The woman lurks for a while, but we go further into the woods and lose sight of her.

'What happened?' I say.

'I hit him. Scratched him. His face.' She shows me her hand and there's blood under her nails.

'What did he – ?'

'He...tried to pull my leotard off...pushed me onto my bed...'

'Did he – ?'

'No! I kneed him in the balls.'

'So he didn't – '

'Rape me?' she says. 'He kept...trying to get my sweatshirt and leotard off...but I'm not sure...He touched me between my legs...his face when I kneed him! He couldn't walk! Just crunched over in agony!'

Zara collapses on my chest and we're both crying again.

'I'm so, so sorry. I tried to protect you.' I grip her harder. How could I have let this happen?

'Why are you sorry? It's not your fault.'

It is my fault.

'He...well...he...' My brain is whirring in the chaos. 'I...I didn't want him to start on you.'

'You knew...he'd try...?'

I nod. I try to squeeze words out around the lump in my throat. 'He does it to me.'

'Then why the hell didn't you say something?' she yells, pushing me away, her eyes full of rage. 'You could have said!'

'Shhh,' I say, reaching out to pull her into a hug, but she shoves me back with both hands.

'Why didn't you say?'

'I couldn't...I tried...Mum wouldn't believe me.' I look away, embarrassed. Gran would have expected me to have done better. I reach down to comfort Biscuit to hide my angry tears. Her tail's down and I can see she's upset.

'You could have tried harder!' Zara yells at me. 'You mean you let him do it?' She shoves me again. 'I escaped this time,' she says, 'but what about next time?'

My inside is whirling. I'm disorientated and feel sick.

'Is that what you meant that day when you went on about Pantosaurus? You knew he might...?'

I nod.

We hold each other.

She's shivering with cold.

Red hot words are bubbling up inside me. 'Come on. We go back right now and confront him!' Something tells me this is crazy but I'm going to do it anyway. Great sobs fill my throat. 'We stand up to him right now!'

I take deep breaths. Try to calm myself. But the rage inside me gets hotter.

'I'm not sure,' she says, 'I mean he just tried to pull my clothes off...he didn't...actually do anything.'

'He touched you where he shouldn't!'

'Mum'll be back later. Let's – '

'No. We go now! I have to get you dry and warm anyway.' I grab her hand and stride down the path.

Zara stops. 'Poppy, look, wouldn't it be better to wait till Mum's home? I mean...'

'Look, I'll go...better that way. You stay out of it...safe.'

'No. No. Best with both of us. I'm so mad at him.' She's looking more defiant.

My heart is pumping so loudly I can hardly hear. I want to get to Carl. Tear him apart.

We cross the tram tracks and turn into our road.

I stop. 'Let's think this through. Maybe...I really think it should just be me who faces him. It's too dangerous for you, so I'll do it. You run upstairs...get clothes on...get warm.'

'No. I'm not leaving you on your own. We do it now, together,' she says, her nails sinking into my arm. 'Come on!'

I hesitate. 'We need more of a plan. What if I talk first? You should go and put dry clothes on.'

No. I'm staying with you.'

School Shrink said to be more assertive. Like strong Miranda.

'OK,' I say, 'we go together. With both of us we should be safe. We tell him...he must leave the house because we're going to tell Mum...she'll believe us now. And just so you know, I really tried to protect you. Because I love you.'

'Love you too,' she says, hugging me.

My spine prickles and my knees feel weak.

We stride up our road. Silent.

I know we could be doing the wrong thing facing Carl like this. What kind of mood will he be in after Zara ran away from him? What if he's angry? Are we doing the right thing?

I notice the Bernstein's car isn't there in the drive next door. Unusual for the Sabbath. Maybe they're seeing Ruben's Gran.

Leroy's fruit and veg box is in our porch.

I stare at this bit of normal life, swallow, let us both in through the front door, unclip Biscuit from her lead and she runs into the garden. I rush to the kitchen and grab my phone from behind the coffee machine where Mum hides it. Then run back to Zara and push my phone into my running belt.

Carl is in the lounge with the TV on. 'Hi girls,' he calls. His voice slurs so I know he's been drinking. 'There's a football match on later. Want to watch it with me? I'll get snacks and Coke.'

We look at each other.

My brain feels stunned for a moment.

Then we hold hands and walk into the lounge.

Chapter 41

The wine bottle

Carl is sitting on his black leather chair reading the paper, a glass of red wine in his hand. There's an opened bottle on a small table next to him. An empty bottle is discarded on the floor. Scratches on his neck are seeping blood onto his white designer polo shirt. The TV is on as usual, blaring some Saturday morning cookery programme. The cooks are laughing, chopping up a huge octopus and for a moment I can't take my eyes off the grey tentacles. The wobbling slitheriness making me swallow.

Gelatinous suckers.

Too many hands to get away.

Zara and I stand together, clutching each other. I hear her rapid breathing, feel her trembling. I want to hold onto her and squeeze the uncertainty from her of what Carl did.

I wish we had more of a plan.

Chaotic words tumbling through my head so fast I can't capture them, and the acid sweet smell of the wine hits my brain. I wish Mum was here.

I lean into Zara, my arm touching hers.

I can't make any words come out.

Focus.

Carl looks up from his paper. His forehead is sweating.

I squeeze Zara's hand.

'You...why did you do it?' she says, her voice quivering.

'Go away...do whatever little girls do on a Saturday morning.' Carl takes another swig of wine.

I stiffen.

'You...you touched me,' Zara says.

'What?'

'My private parts.' She's holding my hand so tightly it's painful.

'Oh my goodness, you have a vivid imagination,' Carl says, crumpling the newspaper down onto his lap. He turns towards us and does his arrogant smile, as if to say he's invincible.

'And you did it to Poppy!' Zara lets go of my hand and her fists clench.

'You have no proof.' He glances at the TV then looks at me.

I lock eyes with him. His brow furrows and his lips go thin. He puts his wine glass down on the small table and gets up tectonic-plate-slow and moves toward me.

Zara and I take a step back.

He knocks into the foot stool. Sways.

Redness is creeping up his neck onto his face.

He staggers and swears.

'Jealous, are you?' He's staring at me. 'Don't want to share me with your sister?'

'You're disgusting,' I say.

Cold is spreading through me. I know we should both get away from here, but I freeze.

He moves closer to me.

He's coming for me.

I smell the wine on his breath, and he sways again.

His eyes blaze and his neck muscles bulge.

I'm struggling to breathe. Facing him was a bad idea. 'Make a run for it' flashes through my mind.

But we can do this. I want to see him squirm.

'People will believe me now because of what you did to Zara.' My voice is calmer than the rumbling volcano inside me.

'You stupid little girls!' He blunders towards us, his hand raised, but we both dodge him.

He turns towards me.

For a moment my mind and body go dead, then I'm screaming at him, words unstoppable. 'You hurt my little sister! You shouldn't have done that! I hate you. Why the hell do you think you can just use our bodies...Mum will believe us now – '

'Shut up, you stupid cow.' He lurches towards me his hand raised. He tries to slap me, but I duck and he staggers across the room and falls.

Zara grabs my arm. 'Let's go!'

I shake her off because I can't hold the words in. 'I hate you...you selfish, loathsome idiot. You just take what you want. You're evil. I hated you from the moment you did it to me...on my birthday! I hope you go to prison!'

He's on his feet and lunges for me. I dodge him but he grabs me around my shoulders and my feet are swept off the floor.

I lose a sense of where I am, suspended somehow in some frantic world where I can hear Zara yelling but I can't get out of Carl's vice-like grip. Everything spins around me.

He slams me down on the sofa. He's leaning over me, the stink of alcohol on his breath.

Spit escapes from his mouth as he roars at me. His angry words rattle in my head and I'm trying to push him off.

He has both his hands around my neck.

He's squeezing.

Yelling.

His eyes piercing through me.

I can't breathe.

I know I'm going to die.

I'll kill you if you say anything.

Everything has gone fuzzy and out of reach, but I can hear Zara shouting.

I don't care if I die but how can I protect her?

Zara's almost on top of us and she's holding JoJo's little wooden chair above her head. Then she brings it down on Carl's head and his hands loosen on my neck. He falls sideways, cracks his head on the coffee table and rolls onto the carpet. Face down.

He doesn't move.

I can't bear it that he's so close to me.

I'm able to take a breath, then another. I finger my sore throat, tears falling down my face.

Zara's standing beside me holding the broken chair. 'Is he dead? Did I kill him?'

It feels like a whole day I'm there on the sofa, sobbing, trying to get air in my lungs, my neck and throat throbbing.

I try to get up, but my legs won't work and I'm too close to Carl, sprawled next to me on the carpet. But I must get to Zara. She's still standing holding the broken chair, horror on her face.

I heave myself up.

I put my arms around her.

'It's OK.' My voice comes out in a strained whisper.

'He moved!' she shouts, jumping backwards away from me.

I freeze.

Carl pushes himself up on his arms, then he crawls with remarkable speed towards the door.

We can't get out.

He grabs Zara with one hand and swings at her face with the other.

She's screaming, backing away from him towards the TV.

He's leaning over her, hitting her.

I grab the nearest thing. A wine bottle, next to the armchair, and smash it down onto the back of his head, the red wine running down my arm.

He falls on his side, closes his eyes. Motionless. Red wine spattered on the back of his shirt and on the carpet.

Zara takes hold of me, weeping, pee running down her legs.

'Is he dead this time?' she whispers.

I want to escape but want to know if he's dead.

'We must get out of here,' Zara whispers.

'We must find out if he's dead.'

I creep towards the body, not really wanting to touch him. My body shudders with revulsion. I nudge him with my foot to see if he moves.

He doesn't.

Chapter 42

Police?

I stare at Carl's body, slumped on his side, his knees curled up, eyes closed.

Driving rain clatters on the window.

I finger my sore neck. We have to get out of here.

My body has frozen. Zara grabs hold of me, her head resting on my shoulder, her body shaking with tears. 'Is he dead?'

'I'll check.' Please God, don't tell me I've killed him. Will I go to prison? Come on. I know how to find a pulse. I move towards him, touch his wrist, but shudder, pulling my hand back. Do it. Now.

His skin is clammy. At last I find a pulse. 'He's still alive! It's OK!' I pull away from him. Relief floods through me.

I can't see any blood on his head and don't want to touch him again.

'No blood...I think he's breathing. Yes. His ribs...moving slightly...look. I'll call an ambulance.' I fumble, trembling, getting my phone out of my running belt. 'Come on. Let's get out of this room.'

Zara puts her hands over her face, still sobbing. 'Will we...be...in trouble?'

'It's him who's in trouble.' I hug her again. 'You saved my life, hitting him like that with the chair. It's all going to be OK.'

That's a lie. This is a nightmare. Carl could come round any minute. Possibly. Or will he die? Focus. My hands are trembling so much I can't punch in 999 so I stop and pull Zara to the lounge door so we can get out quickly.

'Let's ring Mum first,' says Zara, tears in her eyes.

I look at the clock. Just after ten thirty. 'Mum's only just started her yoga class so she won't answer. Anyway, she switches her phone off. Class rules. We'll have to ring her later.'

'I want my Mum.' Zara's cries.

I want Mum too. But who would she believe? Do I ring her first or for an ambulance?

I hug Zara. 'Come on, we're safe now...knocked him out twice. Let's wait by the front door for the ambulance...won't be long...pelting with rain outside.' My voice still isn't right and my neck is painful.

'Should we ring for the police?' Zara's moving from foot to foot.

'Not the police,' I say. 'Too complicated.' Kavya would tell me not to go near them and somehow her fear of police has rubbed off on me. 'They might blame us.'

I long to ring Kavya. Have her arms around me.

'You mean he'll say we attacked him?'

'Maybe.'

My hands are still trembling, but I manage to punch in 999 and put my phone to my ear. The woman's voice is calm. 'Ambulance' I say. 'I don't want to give my name,' But I give her our address. 'He...er...fell and hit his head. He just fell.' I look at Zara. 'Yes, he's breathing...I have to go now.'

'Ambulance is on its way,' I say to Zara. 'Look and see if the Bernstein's car is back yet.' My throat hurts and I still feel Carl's hands pressing down on me. I try to swallow.

Zara opens the front door. 'No. They're not back. Do we need to wait for the ambulance? Or shall we just go?'

'You think we should just leave?'

I know from first aid classes that I should put Carl in recovery position, but I don't want to go back in the lounge and touch him again. And I know we've made a terrible mistake. I shouldn't have come back to the house. I shouldn't have confronted Carl and put both of us in danger.

'Mum'll be out of yoga by eleven thirty,' I say. 'It'll all be OK – she'll believe us now because it's both of us.'

She might not.

I glance at the time on my phone. It's only ten forty. Maybe we should ring Mum. I put my arms around Zara, trying to think it all through. I could ring the arts centre and ask to get a message to her. But Mum won't want us to interrupt her yoga. But that sounds crazy. Surely she'll want to know about this? Listen to us? Believe us? Maybe I should ring the reception desk?

I hear a groan from the lounge.

'You're both dead,' Carl yells.

We dive out of the front door and I pull it shut behind us – not locked so the ambulance people can get in. My heart is thundering in my chest. We sprint out of the gate and down the road towards the park, rain soaking us before we reach the corner.

'We haven't got Biscuit!' I say slamming my foot down on the pavement so I stop. Panic.

'We can't go back,' says Zara. 'He'll kill us.'

Chapter 43

Biscuit is lost

I can't make myself move further down the road. 'But...Carl might kill Biscuit.'

'No! Poppy...he won't do that.'

'I have to go back!'

'No! We have to get away from him.' Zara takes hold of my arm and pulls me behind her.

I want to go back, but I know Zara's right. I must get her to safety. Dread sits in my stomach. Please look after Biscuit. Please don't let him hurt her. Please, God. Please. I'll do anything. I'll stop lying. Anything! Please!

It's still raining and we cross the tram tracks and go into the park. Huge sobs are bubbling up inside me. But I have to stay strong for Zara.

Biscuit probably went out of the dog flap into the garden. I try to convince myself she'll be safe. The ambulance will take Carl away. Biscuit will be safe in the garden.

Maybe.

'Head for the den,' I say, as we run on along the path towards the swings. I'm soaked right through. I glance at Zara. Her eyes are still full of terror.

I can't stop my tears and Zara is making great heaving sobs.

'Carl doesn't know about the den, does he?' she says.

I stop, take hold of Zara while she gasps in air. 'I don't think so. How could he?' Her sweatshirt is still half off so I help her pull it on properly. She's soaking wet and I don't want someone to ask us why she's out in the rain just with her gym stuff on.

'He could be following us,' she says, her eyes wide. 'I'm so cold.'

We both look behind us, then tighten our grip onto each other. 'He's not following us,' I say. 'He was knocked out...twice so I'm sure he's wobbling around hardly able to walk – and he's drunk. The ambulance will take him.'

I hope I sound confident. Please keep Biscuit safe.

'What about Mum?' Zara's still trembling. 'Should we ring her?'

'I think yoga finishes at eleven thirty. She'll switch her phone on then.'

Zara follows me as we skirt around the spinney towards the den. It's so odd without Biscuit and just telling myself she'll be fine isn't working.

I take deep breaths. Don't let there be anyone in the den I pray as we wade through the wet grass, and round the blackberry bushes. I can see the fallen tree of the den.

I gulp back my tears.

The den is empty. I sit Zara down inside the trunk.

'Go further into the corner out of the rain,' I say.

She's sobbing so loudly I think if Carl came to the park he'd hear us. I sit beside her, hugging the tears out of her. Trying to rid my mind of Biscuit.

'You were so brave,' I say. 'You saved me. Shhh. It's all going to be OK.'

'How is it going to be OK?' she says, frowning at me, her voice angry. 'Did I get it wrong with Carl? He didn't do much really, just pushed me onto my bed and put his hand between my legs!'

'And he was wrong to do that...we'll be OK. Mum'll sort it.' As soon as I say that I know it's unlikely to be true. I take my jacket off and wrap it around her. 'I'll ring Kavya. She'll help us.'

'I think you should ring Mum first! Honestly. You and Kavya! You think more of her than you do our family.'

Zara's probably right but I'm hoping that her anger won't spill over onto me. I'm not sure I can handle it.

I phone Kavya, but my voice is pinched and squeaky as I try to tell her what's happened. 'We're at the den. We're soaked...freezing.'

'I can hear a siren,' says Zara. She grabs hold of me and starts crying again. 'They'll know we did it. We're in so much trouble.'

'Stay there,' says Kavya. 'I'll run. Five minutes.'

I cling to Zara. 'We'll be OK.'

'Stop saying that!' she snaps. 'What if we aren't OK?'

My brain is full of words, cogwheels whirring around my head so fast I can't work out what the words are. Except 'Biscuit. Biscuit.'

'You're worried about her,' says Zara.

I must have said 'Biscuit' out loud. 'Yes. He threatened to kill her.'

'You never told me that.'

I want to be strong for Zara but my body collapses and I'm sobbing on her shoulder. 'I couldn't bear it if he hurts her,' I say.

I try to stop crying. Must pull myself together.

We settle into silence, our arms around each other. We're both shivering.

Dad. My dad. Our dad. Why wasn't I more patient? I could have waited. Talked more. Got him involved. He might have helped with Carl.

There's the swish of footsteps through the long grass. Zara opens her mouth, but I put my hand over it. I'm ready to run.

But it's Kavya, her big brown eyes peering out from her purple hooded rain jacket. She climbs into the den and we do a recap of what's happened.

'This is crazy, all this talking, Poppy,' Zara says. 'We need to ring Mum!'

'I know! Don't yell at me. I'm just...well...It's that...she might not believe us. Well, me anyway.'

'You're both soaked,' says Kavya. 'Come to my house and get dry clothes and ring your mum then.'

'I want my mum,' says Zara, a look of such anguish on her face that my heart breaks for her. Shame runs through me. Perhaps we should have rung Mum earlier for Zara's sake?

Kavya hugs Zara. 'Of course you want your mum. Come home with me and we'll make a plan.'

'Mum'll believe me, at least, won't she?' says Zara.

I bite my lip. I get a bad feeling about this. 'Course she will,' I say, but my voice is tight and dry. And all I can think about right now is Biscuit.

Chapter 44

At Kavya's

It's still tipping with rain as the three of us leave the den. The wind is blowing so much that the raindrops are coming horizontally right into our faces. My clothes are soaked right through and Zara is shivering, still just in her wet gymnastics things and my jacket on top.

There are deep puddles everywhere and a stream of water is gushing down the side of the path towards the running track and school – those bits of my life where I used to feel safe. Will I ever get back to that?

We make our way along Sandyhills High Street where people are leaning into the wind, trying to do their shopping. A broken umbrella blows across the road in front of a bus, towards us, spikes exposed. I pull Zara out of the way, and it crashes into Leroy's fruit and vegetable display, knocking over some apples, then it skids up the road behind us.

For a moment I wonder if I should go after it so it doesn't hurt someone, but when I look at Zara's face, I know I must keep hold of her hand.

Please let Biscuit be safely at home. Please. Can you hear me, God?

I have to drag Zara up the steep stairs to Kavya's flat because she seems unable to make her body move.

'I won't tell Aunty you're here just yet, Saturday's such a busy day in the shop,' Kavya says, taking some towels from a cupboard. 'First thing, I'll lend you some dry clothes and get some towels.'

We go into her blue bedroom and she pulls some tops and jeans out of her wardrobe and chest of drawers. I start drying myself.

'No,' says Zara when I try to get her to change. However much I persuade her she refuses to undress – even in the bathroom – and she stays zombie-like. So Kavya gets a blanket and we wrap her and take her into the kitchen for a hot drink.

'Ring Mum now,' Zara says so quietly I can hardly hear her. 'I want my mum.'

'Five minutes,' I say. 'Then it'll be 11.30 and she'll be out of yoga.'

Zara starts to cry again. 'OK,' I say. 'I'll do it now.' But I know she won't answer so I leave a voice mail message. 'Mum, ring us back soon. It's urgent.'

Zara is still a zombie but eventually Mum rings back. 'Where are you?'

'At Kavya's. Mum, we really need you to come home. It's Carl – '

'Why the hell are you at Kavya's? What about Carl?'

'Mum, please come home and we'll meet you there.'

Zara grabs the phone. 'Mum... Mum...Carl...he...he...'

Is Zara going to tell Mum?

She stops talking and listens, then gives the phone back to me. 'She just keeps asking questions I can't answer. She's angry.'

'Mum, please come home,' I say.

'What the hell is going on? You're not supposed to have your phone.'

'I know that, Mum. But something happened. It's urgent Mum,' I say. 'Please. I can't talk about it on the phone.'

'I'll get JoJo from the creche now. We'll be at the house in half an hour.'

'We'll meet her at our house.' I hold Zara who is now curled up on the floor hugging her knees and weeping.

Kavya lends us jackets and we're just going down the stairs to the street when my phone rings. It's Mum.

'Poppy, I've had a call from the police. Carl's had a car crash. So I'm going to the hospital in Kent. I'll take JoJo to the Bernstein's first. You stay at Kavya's. Carl's badly injured. Must go.'

'Mum – .'

But she's gone and I sit down on the stairs, my head confused.

'What?' Kavya sits down beside me.

'Carl...he's had an accident...but how is he even driving when he's so drunk? We knocked him out. I thought the ambulance...this is so weird.'

'What's happening?' Zara slumps down on the stairs, so I go through what Mum said.

'But I want my mum.' Zara is crying again so we get her back up the stairs and onto Kavya's bed with a blanket and another hot drink.

'Let's talk in the kitchen,' I mutter to Kavya. 'None of this makes any sense. But I'm desperate to get back to my house to see if Biscuit is OK. I don't want to leave Zara, but – '

'You go. I'll be with Zara.'

'And the Bernstein's weren't at home when we left. I kind of want to...I want JoJo to be OK. I suppose Mum would take him with her if they aren't at home...but I want to check...I'm so muddled. We knocked Carl out. How did he get up and drive? And he'd had so much wine...and...oh...Biscuit...' I don't let myself cry. Must stay strong.

'Go. Zara will be fine with me. Then we'll have some lunch. Go.'

The rain has turned to a fine drizzle and I take the shortest route to home, down the High Street. I'm running as fast as I can to get to Biscuit. But I have this sense of dread sitting in my tummy.

I'll kill your dog.

Mum's car isn't there so presumably she's left for Kent. But the Bernstein's car is there – so hopefully they have JoJo. I creep into our house. There's no sign of Biscuit in the house. Or the garden. I check under the bushes in case she's dead – poisoned. I look behind Carl's shed and peer through the windows to see if he's shut her in there. But there's no sign of her.

Carl has taken her. Or he made her run off. Most likely he took her, and I feel my insides collapse. But I have to stay strong. I call next door and JoJo rushes to meet me, grabbing me around my knees.

'He'll be fine with us, so don't worry,' says Mrs Bernstein. 'I do hope Carl will be OK. Will you be OK at your friend's house? If not, you can come here, Poppy.'

'We'll be good with Kavya. But...it's Biscuit...I can't find her. She might have run off. But...well...I can't find her.'

Then I'm crying and Mrs Bernstein leads me to the sofa. 'I can't manage without Biscuit...I just can't.' It feels too much to explain about the rat poison and Carl attacking Zara this morning so I let myself cry, knowing later I'll have to be strong for Zara. But I don't have to be strong this minute.

'If Biscuit ran off,' Mrs Bernstein says, 'then she'll come home. So I'll keep checking for her.'

'Thank you,' I say.

She makes me a cup of tea which I drink with some difficulty – tea really isn't my favourite drink. But at least she's made it sugary and I'm so grateful for her care.

But I know Biscuit has gone and I don't know how to handle that.

Chapter 45

Telling Anjali

It has gone back to raining hard again as I leave the Bernstein's and head to Kavya's through the country park. Somehow I need to be OK enough for Zara. The wind is bending the trees making me feel some of them could fall onto me. It feels too much that the storm hasn't died down. Any good God would take pity on me and let the sun shine.

You hear me God?

Please look after Biscuit.

When I get to Kavya's flat, Aunty Anjali has her arms around Zara, who is still weeping. They are sitting around the little kitchen table with Kavya, and there's bread and cheese on plates but no one is eating.

'Now then, girls,' Anjali says, 'I'm hoping you want to tell me what's going on. Then we can eat, and you can all watch TV this afternoon and get an early night. A good sleep is always healing.'

'What about Biscuit?' Kavya looks at me.

'She's not at home. I think Carl might have taken her in his car. But I don't know.' I finger my neck where Carl tried to strangle me. 'My neck hurts.'

Anjali stands up and pulls back my hoodie.

'Let's ice that.' She looks almost scared and stands motionless just for a moment, as if wondering what to do next. Kavya gets ice from the freezer and wraps it in a cloth and Anjali puts it very gently on my neck.

Her voice is kind and something inside me changes. Then I know it. I know that this little kitchen is the place to tell our secret. My secret I've held onto for more than two years.

Our little secret. Never, ever tell or I'll kill you.

When we're all sitting close to each other, Kavya's arms around me, I tell Anjali everything, starting with Zara today, then my thirteenth birthday when Carl first attacked me, Childline, Carl in my bedroom, the poppy picture, the white sofa, Manchester, School Shrink, the keys.

I want to tell her everything.

Except that I kissed Carl.

You started it, you slut.

Then I'm crying huge gulping sobs as the words pour out in a messy torrent, all out of sequence. Zara hugs me, crying again. 'Why didn't you tell me?' she says.

How can I answer that?

'You've been carrying so much,' says Anjali. 'You just cry it all out.'

So I do and more of my words go on flowing out of me. Me cutting, Mum not believing me because of all my lying when I bunked off school so much after the abuse first happened. It all falls out of me, a waterfall of words, spilling out into that little kitchen.

'And he said he'd kill Biscuit...poison her...if I told anyone. He's taken her and she's dead somewhere. I can't find her.'

My words dry up.

Zara is still silent, but sniffling.

Anjali looks on her phone. 'Poppy, look, there's an NSPCC help line. Is it OK with you if I ring them? They will have some advice for us.'

I nod.

She rings up and I just can't listen. I know I'm spacing out, but I'm so relieved that now the truth is out there.

Anjali explains what's happened and that the advice is to ring the police.

Both Zara and I start crying again, and Kavya stands up, agitated. 'Do the police have to come here?'

Anjali pulls her into a hug. 'I know it's hard for you, my treasure, but you do see that we have to tell the police what happened? But we'll leave that till the morning. We might have to go to the police station I suppose...depends what they say. You all need a relaxing afternoon and a good sleep first.'

Kavya and I get Zara to choose a film to watch in the afternoon – *Monsters, Inc.* – and we end up laughing. Even Zara. Anjali cooks us a vegetarian curry, just like Gran used to make. Zara seems to have settled down at last but she's quiet and I know she's missing Mum.

That evening Kavya and I get Zara into Kavya's bed and then blow up two air mattresses for ourselves.

'It'll all work out, you'll see,' whispers Kavya as we both struggle to sleep that night.

'I know,' I whisper back. 'But I'm so upset about Biscuit. And I failed Zara. I should have protected her better.'

Kavya reaches across and hugs me and I'm so glad she's there.

'I hope when Carl grabbed Biscuit she bit him.' I can't help my tears. 'She's always disliked him.'

'She's a perceptive little dog,' Kavya says. 'She might be alive somewhere.'

'Maybe she even bit him so hard she drew blood.'

'We're together, though, Poppy. Our Plan A will work. We'll be together.'

'Yes, I hope we can still do Plan A. Together.'

'We should try to sleep now.'

But I can't. My brain is churning and I hate myself that I didn't make a good enough plan to protect Zara from it all. I want Biscuit back. I shouldn't have gone back to face Carl like we did. I should have known that.

Harry. I don't know what he's thinking. Or feeling. How could I ever tell him about all this?

The landline rings in the corridor, and I see the light come on under the door. I hear Anjali get up and answer the call. She listens and then says, 'Oh dear.' Listens some more, then, 'No, I don't think they should talk at the moment. Let them sleep now. They can stay here as long as they need to.' I hear her put the phone down. Then it's quiet.

Was that Mum? Has Biscuit been found? I wonder about getting up and asking. But I don't.

I want to cut myself, but I can't. Not here. I try to focus on Zara and her needs. I can perhaps ring Mum tomorrow and Zara can talk to her.

I wonder about Dad. I should have talked more.

Something within me is lighter. What Carl did is out in the open. But which of his threats will he carry out?

No one is going to believe you.

Will he come back and kill me? But now I've told Anjali, she would know it was him.

Please, God, don't let Biscuit be dead.

It felt so good to smash that bottle down on Carl's head. Glad I didn't kill him though.

In the morning Anjali makes us scrambled eggs and toast – and a big jug of hot chocolate with marsh mallows in it.

'Your mother rang in the night,' she says, looking a little uncertain. 'Carl is quite badly injured so she wants to stay with him at the hospital.'

'Did they find Biscuit?'

'Your mother didn't mention that.'

I try to stay strong but I'm not and I curl up in Kavya's bed while Anjali rings the police. I block my ears so I don't hear what she says.

The Magical Haircut is shut on Sundays so Anjali says we can just hang out and watch TV or whatever we want while we wait for the police. She says that a police officer will be here soon. So I wrap Zara in a blanket because she still seems spaced out and pale, and I sit her on the grey sofa in Kavya's lounge, clutching a red cushion on her lap and watching cartoons on children's television. I can tell Kavya's upset about the police coming to the flat but she's being brave and helping Anjali in the kitchen, so I sit next to Zara. I want to curl up with Kavya really, but I think Anjali wanted to talk to her privately.

Poor Kav. I've dragged her into my chaotic life and she's upset. It's too much of a reminder of them treating her dad so badly. And she misses her Mum.

I'm not taking in what the cartoon is about. I don't suppose Zara is either.

Now I've said all the stuff about Carl once, I know I can do that again.

At least I think I can.

With Carl in hospital maybe I'm a bit safe for now. And I think Anjali believed us so maybe the police will too?

But what will Mum say? Will Mum believe us now? Maybe she'll just drink more? Maybe if Carl says he didn't do it she'll believe him not Zara and me?

I shudder.

Chapter 46

The police arrive

'I know you're nervous about the police coming,' I whisper to Kavya 'but so am I. You know. Telling them.'

'You'll be OK,' she whispers back. 'You told Aunty. So you can just say the same words.'

'You're right.' But then I'm crying because of Biscuit so I lie down on my bed again for a bit.

Everything feels too much and all I want is Biscuit back, and never to have to see Carl ever again. Would my dad, our dad, want to know about all of this?

At ten o'clock the front doorbell goes. It's a woman police officer and as she comes upstairs to the flat, Kavya hugs me and slinks into her bedroom. I tell myself that all will be well. It's best now just to trust everything will be OK if we tell the police. Carl has probably already killed Biscuit and he can't get to us here in Kavya's flat.

'I'm Suzanna,' the police officer says, and she smiles at us and that helps me to relax as we all sit down in the lounge. 'I'm going to take notes,' she says.

'OK,' I say. I just have to go along with what she says.

Zara clings onto me so I get us both doing deep breathing.

The front doorbell goes again. 'That'll probably be the social worker,' says Suzanna and Anjali goes downstairs to the door.

'Good morning.' A woman in a purple poncho and wild curly hair comes into the lounge. 'I'm Ellie.'

I like her immediately with her cheerful smile and crazy hair. She has no make-up on, a handbag the size of Mount Vesuvius – and gorgeous knee length black leather boots. She pulls out a large note pad and perches on one of the chairs Anjali brought in from the kitchen, clicks her pen, crosses her legs and I feel safe enough to talk.

But inside my head I'm telling myself that if all this goes wrong, Zara and I could end up in care.

'I'm going to record what you say,' says Suzanna. 'I hope that's OK because it's important. We want you to tell us just in outline what has happened. You're safe here.'

I nod.

It's a little voice recorder. Like Mum's, that is uselessly sitting under my bed.

'Shall I stay?' says Anjali.

'Of course,' says Suzanna and Anjali smiles at me.

I'm ready to tell.

'Our stepfather has sexually assaulted both of us,' I say.

Suzanna nods at me and looks me in the eyes.

I tell her about my thirteenth birthday and then Zara speaks up and tells what Carl did to her yesterday. I'm so proud of her for talking. I'd expected her to stay silent.

'OK,' says Suzanna. 'You've said enough for me to know that you will both need to have a formal interview that we video. Nothing to worry about. We will want to know the detail and you will only have to say all the detail once – on the video.'

'Well done, both of you,' Ellie says.

Then I tell them about Carl filming me and that his computer password is likely to be JoJo's birthday. 'You could break into his shed,' I say and Suzanna writes in her notebook.

'I realise now that I should have told someone earlier,' I say. 'But he told me no one would believe me – and...he...he...said he'd kill me.'

'It's OK, Poppy,' says Ellie. 'It's out in the open now and you're safe. You've done well.'

I hug Zara tightly. We've done it. We've told.

Anjali makes everyone a hot drink and Suzanna smiles at me and says, 'Well done Poppy and Zara. I hope all goes well for you both.' We hear her go downstairs and out through the door.

Ellie stays behind and asks more questions.

'I want my Mum.' Zara isn't so pale but she's starting to cry again.

'Your mum's staying in Maidstone for a bit to be near Carl,' Ellie says. 'She's left JoJo with the next door neighbours.'

Zara starts to cry harder at this. 'Why won't she come home?' Anjali comes over to the sofa and puts her arm around Zara.

'I went to check on JoJo.' I say.

'I've checked on him too,' Ellie says. 'The neighbours let me into your house when we went in to get things for JoJo. There were lots of wine bottles. The recycling was overflowing.'

'It would be,' mutters Zara.

I glance at her, not sure what to say, but her face is now determined and strong. She sits up straight and looks at Ellie and blurts out, 'Mum and Carl drink too much. Mum especially.'

I feel guilty confirming Zara's right that they drink too much, but there doesn't seem much point in holding back now. I feel we can trust Ellie.

I know I need to ask. 'Will we all have to go into care?'

'Well – '

'The girls can stay here for as long as they need,' Anjali says and I want to throw my arms around her. But I don't.

'What will happen to Carl?' I'm staring at my hands. They're shaking. But I have to know. 'Will he come home?'

'That's for the courts to decide,' Ellie says.

'But if he comes home, I don't know if I can stand it,' I say. 'He almost strangled me yesterday. My neck still hurts.'

'It's OK, Poppy,' Ellie says as she looks at my neck. 'The most likely thing is that he'll have to leave the family home. We'll keep him away from you.'

Then I'm crying a loud mewling howl. 'He took my dog.' Everything I've said seems so insignificant except Biscuit is dead. I love her. How will I live without her?

Ellie reaches over and lays her hand on mine. 'I've got a dog,' she says. 'I understand how you feel.'

'Carl bought her for me the day after he...' Snot is pouring out of my nose. 'The day after I was thirteen and I thought he was saying *sorry I won't do that again*.'

Anjali goes and gets another box of tissues and when she's back Ellie asks me about Mum.

'Tell me about you and your mum?'

'I think I'm an awful daughter.'

'No you aren't,' says Zara. 'Mum just gets mad at us. She even puts JoJo to bed by half past five some days so she can go on her phone and drink wine.'

'She puts JoJo to bed early?' says Ellie.

'It sometimes seems she doesn't care about us.' Zara sits up straight and looks defiant. 'Why isn't she here with us, right now?'

Ellie writes on her note pad. I want to tell Zara to be quiet but I don't dare, and she's not looking at me so I can't do one of my shut up glares at her. I keep thinking that if we say too much about Mum, we really will go into care.

We might even be split up.

Chapter 47

Kindness

After all that has happened, Anjali says we don't have to go to school on Monday. She lets Kavya stay home with us and do some of her art GCSE coursework. There's no way I could have faced school because I'm still tearful about Biscuit. I can't see that changing the rest of my life.

Ellie comes to take Zara and me home to get spare clothes. Today she's wearing a huge rainbow jumper which makes me feel safe and she's still wearing the knee length black boots.

'I'll just check you're strapped in properly,' she says, leaning into her car. That's a bit like her treating us as five-year-olds, but with her wide cheerful smile, I decide not to complain. And because she has a dog too, she understands why I can't stop thinking about Biscuit. I'm not saying it out loud, but I so much want my dog to be on the doorstep when we get to the house.

But she isn't and I can't help my tears. Zara holds my hand as we walk into the hall – I'm glad my little sister understands. How odd it feels to be here and I lean into Zara and hug her. We're going to have to stick together.

'Upstairs and pack a few things,' Ellie says. 'For school and a few days of home clothes. I'll come up and help you.'

I shove clothes and as many schoolbooks as I can into my case, although the thought of having to concentrate on work feels awful. Maybe I can borrow Harry's physics notes to catch up? I keep wanting Harry to be with me, but I couldn't tell him about all this chaos. He wouldn't want anything to do with me.

After I've dragged my case downstairs I go out into the garden to search under bushes again to see if Biscuit's body is there. If Carl poisoned her she could have died here, all alone.

But her body isn't there. I knew it wouldn't be, and I sit on the ground for a moment to try to stop crying. I must stay strong for Zara.

Ellie comes out of the patio door. 'Have the police got Carl's computer from the shed yet?' I ask.

'I heard they found one in the wreckage of the car,' she says.

'Good. That should prove what he did.' I look through the shed window. 'They should break in and take that computer too.' I'm hoping there is evidence for the police to find to prove that Zara and I are telling the truth.

The front doorbell rings so I rush in. Someone might have found Biscuit.

It's Mrs Bernstein – Esther – with Ruben and JoJo. The boys are both wearing red Superman cloaks and rush up and down the hall yelling. JoJo smiles at us but is far too busy being a superhero to hug. So he's fine.

'I can hang onto him as long as needed,' Mrs Bernstein says. 'As I told you, I'm a fully registered childminder and I have him every weekday anyway,' she tells Ellie.

We're just leaving when Zara notices that the red light is flashing on the landline in the hall.

'A message,' Zara says and presses the play button.

'This is a message from The Ark Veterinary Practice in Swanley. Your dog, a Westie, has been handed in – '

'Oh Biscuit! She's not dead!' I'm crying again, but so happy I'm jumping up and down and Zara joins me. I put my arms around her – and her face has lost the haunted look she's had for the last few days. In that moment I know that everything will get better now.

'We must go and get her,' Zara says.

'Let's listen to the message again.' My inside is bubbling.

'Your Westie was found wandering the fields and a farmer brought her in. Her identichip gave this phone number. Please ring us back to let us know when you can come and fetch her.'

I keep bouncing around I'm so excited. 'She must have escaped from Carl's car when he crashed. I could ring Mum now on my phone and get her to go and pick up Biscuit.'

'Oh,' says Ellie. 'I'm not sure you should ring your mum.' For a moment I freeze. 'But Mum knows how much I love Biscuit. She'd want to pick her up for me.'

'I think she wants to stay by Carl's bedside,' says Ellie. 'He's so badly injured.'

'You mean he might die?' says Zara. That makes my insides lurch but I'm so happy about Biscuit that I swallow the weird feeling.

'I don't know if he's going to die.' Ellie looks a bit distant.

'I know what,' says Mrs Bernstein. 'Let's ring the vet back and tell them that Mr David Bernstein will fetch her...so you need to tell them that, Poppy. The vet needs to know it's not just some random person saying Biscuit is their dog.'

I'm so happy I can't think straight.

'Brilliant. Thanks Mrs Bernstein,' Zara says. 'Come on Poppy. Ring the vet and get it sorted.'

So that's what we do, and the vet says he's done X-rays and no bones are broken, but Biscuit does have a bit of a limp, but he doesn't think it's serious.

It feels like a miracle and Mrs Bernstein says that they will pay the vet bill. I argue a bit, but she insists. 'Let me do that for you, Poppy. You are such a special part of our family the way you look after Ruben, so we're very happy to do that for you.

'Thanks so much,' It doesn't feel enough just to say that, and her kindness is seeping into me and my body is relaxing.

'I'll ring you when David is back with her,' Mrs Bernstein says. 'I've got your mobile number.' I hug her, unable to stop crying, but I'm thinking about Harry and that makes me cry more. I wish he were here, right now.

On the way back in the car to Kavya's Ellie says that no one has told Mum yet what we've said about Carl. 'I think the police might wait until Carl is well enough for them to talk to him.'

'Do you think she'll believe us?' I say. Now Biscuit will be back with me in a few hours I don't really want to think about all the awful stuff.

'Who knows?' Ellie says. 'We'll have to wait and see. You can talk to her when she rings at twelve o'clock. But...maybe keep off the difficult things about Carl? I think your mum is really upset about him being so badly injured. And he'd taken his passport with him...she's a bit shocked about that.'

I don't say anything to Zara about my worry about how Mum is going to react when she knows what we've told the police about Carl.

I don't want to think about it. I'm going to think about hugging Biscuit.

At twelve o'clock Mum rings on Anjali's landline.

'How's Carl?' I say. 'Is he badly hurt?' I feel guilty that I haven't asked her this before.

'Very badly,' says Mum. 'But he's out of intensive care now. Thank goodness no one else was involved in the accident...and the car's a right off. Hope we get the insurance money. A new Porsche must mean we could get thousands.'

I can't deal with her talking about money, as if she's calculating how many new handbags she can buy.

I hand the phone to Zara who's tearful but chats for a while. Then her tone changes and she's asking Mum to come back, crying and beginning to sound hysterical.

Anjali comes and reassures Mum we're OK.

Zara storms into Kavya's bedroom, slams the door and cries.

I wonder if Mum can hear Zara? Will she come back? If I were Zara's mum, I'd come back and hug her.

But I'm beginning to see that our mother isn't like that.

But she used to be. Before Carl. I wish she and Dad hadn't split up.

That evening Mrs Bernstein rings to say Biscuit is back at her house.

I'm crying again. 'Thank you...thank you.' I put my phone back in my running belt feeling a bit weird because I don't deserve all this kindness from people around me. And Anjali said that it was fine for us to have my dog in the flat.

'Can I go and get Biscuit now?' I ask Anjali.

'Course you can.'

'Want to come, Zara?' I say.

'No. Watching TV.'

Kavya and I run through the country park and we're laughing and joking like we usually do. That feels so good.

When we get to the Bernstein's Biscuit runs round in circles and wees on the floor she's so excited. Mrs Bernstein laughs. 'The carpet's had worse than that on it.'

'Shall I get a cloth from the kitchen?' I'm horrified and feel so embarrassed.

Ruben starts chasing Biscuit, shouting, 'Wee wee doggy wee wee.' JoJo joins in and the two of them make enough noise for ten toddlers.

'Don't worry,' Mrs Bernstein says. 'I've got some special spray and I'll deal with it later.'

'The vet said they bathed her,' Mr Bernstein says, his face full of joy. 'She was caked in mud, and the vet reckoned she was thrown clear in the accident and she's lucky to be alive – the limp should gradually go but if we're worried, take her to your usual vet.'

'The limp doesn't seem to be affecting her,' I say as Biscuit jumps up at me for the hundredth time. I want to hug her, but it seems best just to let her run in circles until she calms down.

We thank the Bernsteins again and set off with Biscuit wagging her tail.

'Let's get back and get Zara to choose a film,' Kavya says as we go down the drive. 'We can all snuggle up together on the sofa under a blanket. I'll make popcorn and see if we can cheer her up.'

Mum doesn't see how kind Kavya is.

More and more I'm seeing that Mum could be in trouble with the social worker. It's her who should be cuddling up on the sofa with Zara.

That night I sleep with Biscuit in my arms and Kavya curled up behind me. Biscuit smells of antiseptic and I'm so happy I can't stop grinning. I think I told God that if he brought Biscuit back I'd stop lying.

I need to think about that.

Ellie comes to Kavya's flat on Tuesday. Kavya has gone back to school today, but Ellie and Anjali said that we could both stay home again. It turns out that Ellie knows Rachel.

'You know School Shrink?' I say.

Ellie laughs. 'We've been on training courses together. How to look after stressed children and teenagers. Now I'm just checking in quickly today. Do you both feel up to going to school tomorrow?'

'I think so,' I say. 'What about you, Zara?'

'Yes, fine. I'm missing my friends anyway.' Zara has perked up a lot and has had several messages from her friends asking where she is. 'I told them I had the flu.'

'Sounds a good strategy, Zara,' says Ellie. 'I've told school that there has been a family problem, but you might want to say something different to your friends, Poppy.'

'Which friends?' I say. 'Apart from Kavya, no one else will be remotely bothered. Didn't you know I'm School Social Outcast?'

'Oh,' says Ellie. 'Does Rachel know you think that? If not, you need to tell her. She's going to give you both appointments to see you soon.'

'I'm not talking to School Shrink!' Zara looks up from her phone, a shocked look on her face. 'No way.'

Ellie grins. 'You don't have to if you don't want to. But I think you'll find it helps. School tomorrow then. I'll pop in and see you again soon.' Then she's gone and I run down the stairs and catch her by the front door. 'Are we going into care?'

She looks confused. 'I don't know, Poppy. We'll do our best. I think if you can both get back to school tomorrow, you'll feel better.'

'If we have to...go into care, you'd keep us together, wouldn't you?'

'If I could,' she says. 'But it might not come to that. Your mum might be back soon.'

'When she comes back, she'll know what we said about Carl to the police, won't she?'

'Yes. Someone will tell her soon. They may already have told her.'

It sends shivers down my back when I wonder how Mum will react.

'But Carl won't come back, will he?'

'No. I'm pretty sure he'll have to live somewhere else.'

'Prison?' I say.

'That's for the courts to decide, but...I'm not supposed to say anything...but ...well...the police have found things on his computer...you'll be safe.'

I'm grinning and run back upstairs.

I've lost count of the days before Zara's thirteenth birthday. It must be forty something.

But I've done it. I think so anyway. GROC the slimy swamp animal has been trapped.

Hopefully.

Chapter 48

I've had the flu

It's good to be back at school on Wednesday. Ellie told me that Mr Robins and Rachel know the truth about what happened. Zara and I are going to stick to our story about flu.

As I approach the classroom I can hear lots of loud voices and I expect to be stared at as I go through the door. But no one even looks at me, except Harry. He smiles and I smile back. 'You want to borrow physics notes from Monday?'

'Yes, please,' and he smiles again, so I smile again.

'You OK?' His green eyes seem so intense, but friendly.

'I'm good,' I say. If I don't actually say it was flu then I'm not lying. I slide into my seat next to him. He gets a phone out of his bag. 'My mum let me have my phone back at last. But I had to grovel...promise that I won't do social media and stuff like that...er...can I have your number? It would be great to feel in contact.'

My insides go all jumpy and I feel myself get hot.

We swap numbers and get our phones away before Mr Robins comes in. I have Harry's number! But I think I should wait and let him contact me first. A tingle goes down my back. Harry might text me.

The rest of the week at school goes OK, much better than I expected. Mia seems to have backed off and mostly ignores me. That feels such a relief. And I'm waiting for Harry to text me.

'Your mother knows what you said about Carl,' says Ellie on Friday evening when she comes to Kavya's flat. 'Carl is much better, and he's been arrested and taken to a prison hospital on remand. So your mum is obviously in shock.'

'Does she believe what we said?' I say.

'I had a message from the person who told her and she thinks that your mum does believe you both. But obviously she's really upset. It looks as if Carl was trying to get to Dover to escape to Europe. He had his passport with him.'

'When is she coming home?' Zara asks.

'She's already home.'

'What? Why...?' I can't get my words out. It feels weird that Mum didn't ring us, and Zara and I cling to each other.

'I've talked to Anjali and we thought that I'd come Sunday morning and take you home. Let's give your mum a couple of days just with JoJo. She needs time to think.'

I feel Zara's arm slowly rub up my back and then go around my shoulder. 'Is she angry with us?' she says.

'No,' says Ellie. 'Not angry. She's had a shock. She is talking to me about how she's feeling and she's really looking forward to you both going home.'

Zara and I look at each other. I know she's hurting.

'Everything is going to be fine,' I say.

I only half believe that.

Ellie comes to get us from Kavya's flat on Sunday. Both Anjali and Kavya are hugging and kissing us.

'You are welcome here any time,' says Anjali as she bends down to stroke Biscuit.

'You're both wonderful,' Ellie says to Anjali and Kavya as she helps us down the stairs to the street with our cases.

'Missing you already,' Kavya calls after us and I collapse in giggles. But I'm worried about how Mum is going to be with us both. Now she knows. Now it won't be so easy for her just to say that I'm lying.

Ellie parks in our drive and Mum opens the front door, JoJo is her arms and she's smiling. Zara runs towards her and they hug in the doorway. It's a long hug and I hesitate.

Mum puts JoJo down and he's gripping my knees for a moment, then he's trying to hug Biscuit. 'Doggy wee wee,' he says and starts laughing.

'Come in everyone,' Mum says. 'Come on Poppy. I've really missed you.' She reaches out and her arms are around me and we're both crying.

'Why don't we all go in the kitchen,' says Ellie. 'Any chance of a cup of tea?'

'Blackcurrant for you, Poppy?' Zara says.

'Yes, please.'

Mum has her back to me as she fills the kettle.

My insides are churning.

'Poppy,' Mum turns towards me. 'I'm so sorry. I should have believed you.' She puts her hands over her face and weeps.

I run to her, put my arms around her. 'I'm so sorry I lied so much. It was when Carl first did it to me...I couldn't cope...so no wonder you didn't know if I was telling the truth.'

Being able to say that to Mum makes me feel relieved. She's believing us.

'I've done with Carl.' She looks straight at me, tears still in her eyes. 'What he did to you both was unforgivable.' I hug her again and let myself imagine life without Carl here.

We talk more with Mum, telling her about last Saturday, Ellie listening. 'Keep talking to each other,' she says. 'That will get you through this. Must go now but I'll call in next week one day after school.'

That evening is one of the best times I've had with Mum and Zara for ages. After we put JoJo to bed, Mum makes pizza and we all sit on the sofa and watch a film. Mum drinks a bit of wine, but now the lounge now feels safe and not that place of violence that it was last weekend. Mum is listening. She's being kind. She says that we may not be able to stay in our house without Carl's money, but wherever we go, we'll be together. And she keeps hugging me.

I'm so relieved that she believes us – and it feels as if that is all that matters at the moment. I've got my dog back. And my mum.

And I might even get a text from Harry.

But then there's a disaster. On the front page of our local paper is the story of Carl's car crash in Kent. His computers have been taken from his car, the shed and the office at his works.

He's been arrested for child abuse and he's in a prison hospital on remand.

Of course, the victims haven't been named but somehow everyone at school knows it's me and Zara.

'That's your stepdad?' a Year 9 boy says to me, pointing at the picture of Carl in the newspaper that's alongside the photo of his Porsche crashed into the motorway barrier. I look down and rush away. Not many people can have known who Carl was. I wonder if Mia is behind this? She'd recognise him in the paper.

But I can't know how Carl was recognised and I feel I can hardly breathe. I just want to crawl into a hole and hide for the rest of my life.

School social media sites go crazy, and I decide not to look at any of it.

So embarrassing.

School Shrink rings me on my mobile – which makes me wobble. It was good to chat with her, but my head is in chaos.

'I'll be fine,' I say. 'I'm not looking at social media.'

'See me in my room tomorrow. Come before school. Eight fifteen. Is that OK?'

'OK.' It's easier to talk to Rachel now I know she's friends with Ellie.

Somehow Zara copes with it all, although she keeps looking at all the posts on her phone.

I'm ready for my Social Outcast status to plummet to six gazillion below.

'There's lots of buzzing on Snapchat and Insta,' I say to Rachel the next morning, 'but I'm OK. It's just millions of selfies and gossip. I've told Zara not to look on her phone, but she does anyway. She says that some of the posts are quite kind and supportive, but I'm not going to look.'

'That's wise, Poppy. I want you to keep in touch and if anything is bothering you, come and see me. Is there anything else I should know?'

'Um...I'm a bit annoyed with myself...with Carl...saying I couldn't be Miranda...Do you think Miss Singh might let me go back to being in the play?'

'Ask her. I think she'll be pleased. And I'm pleased. What made you change your mind?'

'We got Carl.'

Mr Robins chats to me at registration. 'Miss Singh tells me you're back being Miranda. And you want to do that speech where Miranda is strong and tells Caliban what she thinks of him after he tries...you know...to rape her. Well done. I'm proud of you.'

'Xavier minds a bit – me having the speech back – but he said I deserve to be able to say it.'

'You find me if you need anything,' he says. 'Anything at all. OK?' I feel so lucky to have such a great form tutor. I'm a bit embarrassed that I didn't tell him about Carl. I could have done that.

Social media buzzes on my phone for a couple of days and I keep my head down, expecting Mia to explode.

But it all just dies down. I get friendly smiles – sometimes embarrassed smiles. I notice it first in rehearsals. Xavier nods at me. Jack says, 'Glad you're back, Poppy. You're a great Miranda.'

Reggie and his gang head towards me and I dread what he's going to say. He touches his quiff. 'You've had an exciting time.'

'Shut up. Right now,' Kavya snaps at him. 'You don't know what she's been through.'

'You think?' says Reggie. 'It's not just girls who get sexually abused you know.'

My heart tries to leap out of my throat. Has Reggie been abused? I really don't want to have to talk about it. But does Reggie need help? He always seems totally together.

Crabbe and Goyle look confused.

'Poppy, if you need anything,' Reggie says, 'you ring me. Kav, make sure Poppy's got my number.'

Reggie always seems fine...so confident...even if he does have a gang. 'Thanks, Reggie,' I say, trying to disguise my shock at his friendliness. But I'm relieved for Kavya's sake if Reggie and I can be friends.

'I mean it,' he says. 'Protection. Money. Dope. I can get my hands on anything.'

I giggle and feel myself calm down. Maybe I'm going to manage people talking about it.

'It's so good to have you back, Poppy,' Miss Singh says. 'Now then everyone, we've got three more weeks before the performances and tickets are selling fast – some performances already sold out – '

'Oh,' I say, 'my Mum hasn't got a ticket yet.' Then I feel heat rush up my body onto my face. I interrupted Miss Singh. I'll die of embarrassment.

'Don't worry, Poppy. See me afterwards with Mia and we'll make a plan of how you share the performances – to make sure your families see you.

I don't dare look at Mia. She flicks her hair over her shoulder. At the end of rehearsals, Mia stands beside me as Miss Singh sorts who will do which performance and writes it on her clipboard.

Mia doesn't look at me. 'My mum and dad want to come on Friday evening,' she says, 'and they've already got tickets.'

'OK,' says Miss Singh, 'so that means Poppy, you'll do the final performance on Saturday evening. I'll make sure you have tickets. Don't worry your mother about it. I'll make sure a few are available for your family.'

I realise tears are forming in my eyes and I wipe them away. Kavya comes closer to me. I feel her hand on my back.

Mia drifts off, joining her courtiers at the back of the hall. There's no backward glances. No whispering behind hands.

I'm feeling lightheaded so sit down on one of the plastic chairs for a bit.

'You OK?' Kavya says.

'Everyone...I can't quite deal with...people are being so kind.'

Then Reggie is there. 'You OK? Poppy, I meant it when I said – anything. Do you need me to put Mia in her place? We do protection, don't we guys?'

Crabbe and Goyle nod, fold their arms across their chest, and do their usual vacant stare.

I put my hand over my mouth to stop a giggle escaping, grab a tissue from my pocket and pretend I'm blowing my nose. But the giggle is still there.

'Reggie, you know what?' I manage to say. 'You're a star,' and a huge snorty giggle escapes.

As I walk home, Harry's there smiling beside me. 'I'm definitely allowed to join running club now. My mother has at last worked out that I need breaks from studying. So let me know when you're going and I'll come too.'

'Oh...yes...I'll check with Kavya...I'll let you know.' I realise I no longer have to plan my evenings around making sure Zara is protected. And letting Harry know when I'm going to running club feels like an invitation for me to be the first to text.

'See ya,' Harry says, and he's gone.

This is my best ever day at school.

Chapter 49

Life at home

We all settle into life at home without Carl. Mum is tense at times and she's still drinking sometimes.

'Ellie says you'll feel better, Mum, if you don't drink at all,' I say. 'And it won't cost as much.'

'I'm trying,' she says. 'You think I'd be able to – but it's not as easy as it sounds. I'm so confused. And upset. I should have been there for you.'

'It's OK Mum. It all worked out, didn't it?' I wish I could help Mum more. I feel guilty that I don't know how to help her stop drinking.

Ellie is helping Mum a lot. 'Try to get to Alcoholics Anonymous once a week, Steph,' Ellie says. 'It really will help.'

I asked Ellie yesterday if we might go into care if Mum can't stop drinking.

'I don't think it will come to that,' Ellie said. 'Your Mum is doing really well.'

I want to believe that is true.

Mum's selling her handbags on eBay because we don't have much money. Ellie says Carl will have to help us more, but at the moment money is tight. But I've got the paper round and I'm still babysitting Ruben and Leroy's little girl with Kavya. Mum is still working a few hours at the vets and when she goes to work, Mrs Bernstein has JoJo for a sleepover and she checks in on Zara and me about ten o'clock, which makes me feel safe.

I text Harry on the Tuesday nights that I can go to running club. But I know not to expect too much.

'My mother is still demanding I work every evening except Tuesday,' he says at club. 'She will most definitely explode if my exam results in August aren't totally mind-blowingly brilliant.'

'But they will be brilliant,' I say. I'm glad Harry doesn't ask me about the whole Carl thing. That's why it's easy to be with him at rehearsals and on club nights. We text sometimes about meeting at running club, but we're not texting every day or anything like that.

I wish we were.

I give Zara some cash because she needs new shoes and it's time she had bras, so I take her on the tram into Croydon to shop.

'Thanks, Poppy,' she says. 'I'd have found bra shopping really embarrassing with Mum the way she is at the moment.'

'I know what you mean. She'll get better, though. I think she was frightened of Carl in some ways. We need to give her time.'

Kavya and I get our heads shaved for free at The Magical Haircut. Mum frowns but doesn't say anything. That's unexpected and I'm relieved.

At school the following Monday Mia grins at me. 'You know that wigs itch like hell, don't you?' she says, when Miss Singh decides I must wear one for the performances.

I grin back, hardly able to believe that Mia's backed off me.

I remember Gran always said the truth sets us free and now I understand what she meant. It's been such a relief to have said it all.

I'm writing poems – which is helping – but I wish I could get Carl out of my head. I wish I could sleep better – not have the nightmares.

But we will get through it.

Chapter 50

The performance

Home is a less scary place now Carl isn't there, and it's easier to go out to running club because I don't have to work out if Zara is going to be safe at home. She is safe because Mum is there. I've been wondering about asking Mum if we can ring my dad and get back in contact.

I love being back rehearsing with Harry. He doesn't text me much, though – just an occasional one around club night and occasionally about schoolwork.

'Don't worry about it,' Kavya says when I complain and am wondering if I should text him much more. We're sitting on one of the benches by the games field eating our packed lunches.

'But I'm worried he'll hook up with Mia,' I say. 'They're so good together when they rehearse with her as Miranda.'

'Oh, but I think Mia is back with Jack. Didn't you hear?'

My heart leaps. 'Oh! That is wonderful! That's the best news ever! Do you reckon Harry will ask me out?'

'I don't think so. It's his demon mother. But after the exams – that's when he'll be free.'

'But that's months away! I can't wait till June!'

When we reach the week of the performances, someone puts up a Christmas tree with lights in the hall beside the stage. Mia and

I share the afternoon and evening performances, and she's definitely backed off me. Everything goes without a hitch. Everyone remembers their lines, the Spirit dancers are brilliant, and Enzo's singing and dancing is always amazing.

Then it's Saturday evening – the final performance, and I'm Miranda. The hall is stuffy with so many bodies in it, the murmur of hundreds of voices in the audience unnerving.

I've had my make-up done and I'm standing in the darkness at the side of the stage doing deep breathing, holding onto the burgundy-coloured curtains. It's reassuring to have the soft fabric in my hand. I'm enjoying a moment in the dark away from the busyness of the classroom where the girls are changing.

I scratch my scalp where the wig of long dark hair itches. I mustn't scratch during the play. Must stay focused. Don't drift off.

Whatever happens, God, don't let me forget my lines. Not with Mum and Zara in the audience tonight. I get goosebumps down my spine at the thought of Mum watching me.

When Mr Robins put up the scenery last week, I'm so glad he said how well Kavya had done this term.

'I couldn't have managed to build the boat or do the rest of the scenery without you, Kavya,' he said.

She glowed and I loved Mr Robins for being so kind to her. It's all been tough for Kav. I should have realised that earlier when I put so much on her. I feel bad dumping so much on her – then not letting either of us tell an adult.

A group of Year 13 girls doing a Btec course in sound engineering have downloaded storm noises for the beginning of the play. It's so loud. I must try not to panic like I did on Thursday night – though I managed to cover it up. I get unpredictable times of anxiety and Rachel says that this is normal and it should settle down.

Emma, one of those doing Btec, comes to find me and fits my microphone. She's wearing felt reindeer antlers and a red nose that lights up. 'You're brilliant, you know that, Poppy Stewart? The Btec crew are all behind you.' She flashes a white-teeth smile and she's gone.

I wish I could peek out of the curtains and see Mum and Zara, but Miss Singh told us not to.

The orchestra are tuning up in one of the classrooms...awful discordant sounds. But they are so good once they get going.

I hope Mum enjoys the play. She never talks about Carl now, although that awful Saturday when he attacked Zara was only a month ago. But I've heard Mum talking on her phone to her friends about getting divorced.

I like it that I can talk to Ellie and Rachel. Zara talks to them too now, and she's back to her old self. I think she's right that I should have told someone what Carl was doing – despite his threats. I feel guilty because if I'd told a teacher, Carl would have been stopped earlier and he couldn't have attacked Zara.

The police found all kinds of things on Carl's various computers. Lots of indecent pictures and films of children. And a few of him and me so that means there's evidence that what I've said is true. I'm relieved about that but it's hideous that people are looking at me with Carl. And Steve, Carl's weird sidekick, is being investigated as well, although he's not in prison. Steve is back at work keeping Carl's engineering works going so that Carl can give Mum some money.

I still haven't told anyone what I did that time with Carl. I know it was all my fault.

Can't think about that.

'You will come to the after-play party tonight, won't you?' says a voice beside me. My insides lurch. In the darkness I know it's Harry. 'Will you come?' he says.

'Not sure,' I say, trying to squeeze my voice out of my tight throat. 'Might go home with Mum and my sister.'

'Oh, please come,' he says. He looks strange with make up on, his green eyes huge with matching eye shadow and black eye liner.

My face will be glistening with sweat, despite the make-up.

'Yes, do come.' It's Mia. 'My house, soon as you can after the performance.' She looks so striking in her deep red dress, her hair up with flowers in it.

How can I face a party? 'Oh...Don't want to drink...I...um...'

'I'll call at the late-night shop and get juice and coke.' Harry reaches out and touches my arm and my spine shivers.

The orchestra comes in and sits down.

'Quiet, everyone,' says Miss Singh. 'Final chance to show the world what amazing young people you are. Go for it, guys.' The sailors and the King and his entourage take their positions on the ship.

The lights in the hall go down, the audience shush. Kavya and the stage managers start playing the noises for the storm. They've got a thunder sheet to shake as well and it's extraordinary how rumbles of thunder come from a piece of metal. I suppose that's more physics.

As Scene 1 ends, Xavier is beside me in his magician cloak, staff in his hand, ready for our scene. 'Good luck, Poppy. You'll smash it tonight.'

I can't conceal my surprise. 'Thanks...You too... Let's make it sensational.'

'Yeah. Let's be our best ever,' says Enzo, his wispy spirit costume catching the lights from the stage.

'You're not actually some wilting female, Poppy,' says Xavier as he throws his cloak back over his shoulder. 'It was good that you wanted the speech back.' The noise of the storm stops, and he marches onto the stage.

I keep trying to look where I think Mum and Zara are, but the footlights are too powerful, shining into my eyes.

When we get to the bit where Harry almost kissed me, I'm looking at him and he smiles back. We've rehearsed this a gazillion times. I'll be fine.

I'm safe.

I love being Miranda.

Looked after.

Cherished.

But I only just manage not to burst out laughing as Harry as Ferdinand gets close to me to tell me of his love.

I swallow. Please God, don't let me giggle.

Get a grip.

We get through that scene, everything going perfectly.

Reggie as the gang leader is so funny that people keep laughing and clapping, and he manages to stop speaking, waits for the clapping to stop before he goes on. Miss Singh will love that. And Reggie knows it.

Jack and William do their baddie roles so well they're almost chilling.

By the final curtain I'm exhausted, feeling my arm pits damp. The audience are standing and cheering as we take our third curtain call. Everyone who's helped is clapped in turn. Miss Singh is beaming, clutching a bouquet, and the orchestra takes a bow.

Kavya comes onto the stage and hands me a bouquet of white lilies. I'm so happy I'm crying and when we all get backstage everyone is patting everyone else on the back.

Can I go to a party at Mia's? Feels a bit of a risk, though now she's stopped the bullying...maybe.

I'm changing in one of the classrooms, so are the girls who were Spirits and dancers. Mia comes towards me, flowers still in her hair. Everyone is chatting so when Mia whispers to me, I know others can't hear.

'Well done,' she says. 'You're a good Miranda.'

'So are you,' I say. Where is this heading?

'I...just want to say,' she says in my ear, 'I have an older brother who tries...er...you know...to get in my knickers when he's home from the army.'

'Oh. Mia.' I'm not sure how to react.

'Just wanted you to know you're not alone.'

'Thanks...um...I...always thought I should say sorry about the Year 3 Nightmare Nativity thing – putting my shoes in the toilet then blaming you. You have good reason to hate me. I lied to the teacher.'

'You did.'

'Sorry. I did it,' I said.

'I knew it was you all along.'

'I know it was awful for you...'

'Yeah. It was. Mum was furious. But I'll forgive you. Just this once.' She raises her eyebrows at me, and she's laughing. 'But you're still a nerd.'

My inside relaxes and I'm laughing too.

'I'd like it if you came to my house this evening – I promise my big brother isn't there.' Her smile seems genuine. 'Let your hair down. Not that you've got much.'

I run my hand over my shaved head, grinning at her.

'I'm really trying to be less of a bitch,' she says. 'We girls must stick together. Come to the party. Please.'

'I'll see. I'll ask.' But I know I should go home with Mum and Zara.

I pick up my lilies and walk down the corridor towards the main entrance hall where the lights from a Christmas tree glow red and green. Kavya comes to meet me, and I hug her and tell her about the party.

'Mia came and asked me too,' Kavya says. 'Bit of a turn up. P'raps we should go?'

'Not sure. The flowers are wonderful, Kav. You're so kind to me.'

I see Zara and Mum. My heart is hammering so fast I can hardly breathe. 'Did you like it, Mum?'

'You were phenomenal,' says Zara, arms around my neck.

'Well done, darling.'

I hug Mum. She liked it. 'Mum, you smell of drink. You said you wouldn't. You promised Ellie.'

'Poppy, shut up,' Zara grabs my wrist.

'Did you drive, Mum?'

'I only had one glass and I'm fine to drive.' She sways. Kavya reaches out and supports her. Blood is hissing through my ears and my body is trembling.

'Mum! No! That's why Carl crashed, Mum. Didn't you learn anything from that?'

'Poppy, don't.' Zara is glaring at me. 'Come on. Let's go to the car.'

'No. Mum, you need a taxi. I'll ring for one.'

'I'm perfectly capable of driving five minutes to get home.' She staggers towards the door, getting her keys out of her bag.

'No.' I run after her, volcanic words forming in my head. 'There's an after-the-play party at Mia's and I'm taking Zara. She's not coming in the car with you. We'll bring her home later.'

I try to stop Mum, but she pushes past me and goes out the door.

'I can't believe your mother would just leave...' Kavya's frowning at me.

'Not now,' I say. I put my arms around Zara, but she doesn't seem bothered by Mum's drinking. I try to breathe. I need to calm down.

'I can go to the party?' she says. 'Really? Wow.'

'Do you think it's OK?' says Kavya. 'Taking Zara?'

'Yes,' I say. 'I'm sure Mia will be cool about it.' Of course I'm not sure, but with Mum walking off like that I don't care. 'Come on. We can go and look at Mia's bedroom. See what makes her tick. My money's on it not being pink.'

'You're on fire, girl,' says Kavya. 'Let's go to mine and pick up juice first.'

Yes. I am on fire.

In my head I see Mum's car crashed.

Don't think about it.

Glad I said sorry to Mia.

Chapter 51

The party

We head across High Street to Kavya's flat, waving and calling to other members of the cast going into the late shop.

Somehow Xavier is still wearing his magician's cloak.

'It's my mother's...she collects stage clothes,' he says when I query it. 'I thought I'd stay as God, controlling the world a little longer.'

'What a weirdo.' Zara whispers.

'We're all a bit weird,' I say. 'The world is weird.'

'You were so good – incredibly funny,' Kavya says to Reggie as he goes in the front door next to hers.

'I know,' he says. 'And more surprises to come.'

'What?' I say.

'You'll see,' says Kavya. 'Aunty. We're back.' We race upstairs. 'Poppy was utterly amazing!'

Anjali hugs us all and gives us cartons of orange juice for the party.

I ring Mum. 'Just checking you're OK,' I say, my body relaxing.

Silence.

'I do try not to drink,' she says so quietly I can hardly hear her.

'I know, Mum. You go to bed, and we'll see you later. I'll look after Zara so don't worry.'

Kavya and I look through her wardrobe but decide not to get changed into something more party-ish.

'We go just as we are,' Kavya says.

'Right,' I say. Although I was hoping to wear her long sleeved black sparkly top.

'You're definitely both weird, you know that don't you?' says Zara.

Zara's face is at peace. I'm so proud of her. 'You've helped me...little sister...the way you just got on with your life...'

'What would really help me,' she says, 'is if you could drop the nerdy-geek thing so my big sister is...more normal.'

'You won't say that when we get brilliant marks at GCSE in the summer.' My heart misses a beat at the thought of exams just five months away. Plan A. Got to get good results.

Kavya grins at herself in the mirror in her bedroom, runs her hand over her shaved head. 'I'm quite shocked Mia asked us to her party.'

'Maybe we're not the Social Outcasts we once were...maybe cos of Carl...now that's mega weird.'

Anjali offers us food and we eat quickly and I'm more relaxed than I've felt for years.

'Back by twelve?' says Anjali.

'Probably Mum would like us back by eleven,' I say.

'I'll be at Mia's house at ten forty-five, then I'll walk you home.'

'Thanks,' I say. 'I'll text Mum to tell her.' I think of flinging both my arms around Anjali because she's amazing. But I don't.

Anjali stands at the top of the stairs as we leave. 'Remember, no drugs girls.'

'Course not, Aunty,' says Kavya.

'Not my scene,' I say.

The streets are still busy and the three of us go up Sandyhills High Street to the posh houses where Mia lives. Her house has tall metal gates with Christmas lights glowing in the windows, and a large porch with pillars and pots of olive trees either side of the door – which is open.

We walk in. Dump our coats onto a pile on the chairs in the hall.

The lounge on the left looks crammed and has booming loud music. 'Let's find the kitchen,' I say.

Harry's there, leaning against the counter eating pizza.

'You came,' he says. 'Look at my stash of drinks just for you.' He waves his arm at cans and cartons.

He's wearing a black suit with tails, a white shirt, a black bow tie and a top hat!

'We didn't dress up,' I say. Wishing we had. I feel stupid standing there in jeans and a sweatshirt.

'I thought we could do with a bit of class,' he says, his lopsided grin making me feel a bit unsteady.

'I'm Harry.' He holds out his hand to Zara.

She takes it. 'I'm Zara. Please can I have a coke?'

'Of course,' he says and serves us all drinks.

Mia floats in wearing a sleek white dress, flowers still in her hair. 'You came! Help yourself to anything. My mother's nibbles are to die for.'

Mia floats back out again and I peer out of the kitchen door seeing her go into the crammed lounge area. The bass of the music is so loud it makes my innards churn and I'm not sure I can keep being here for another hour. Images of Carl flash into my mind and I feel uncomfortable.

'Let's not stay long,' I whisper to Zara and Kavya. 'We could ring Anjali to come early.' Even the thought of being near Harry isn't enough for me to want to stay.

'No! I want to dance,' says Zara and heads towards the music in the lounge. My twelve-year-old sister is much more socially adjusted than I am. I think of my countdown to her birthday. Just twenty-three days to go – and Carl is still on remand in prison. He can't touch either of us.

'Come on,' says Kavya grabbing my arm. 'Let's go and talk to Reggie.'

Even with the music I can hear Reggie's voice in the lounge, and he walks towards us.

I'm staring at him. He's dressed in a tight green glittery dress, red high heeled shoes, a long blond wig and full make-up.

'Reggie,' I say, 'you look...sensational. Wow!'

'I knew you'd look fantastic,' says Kavya.

Reggie puts an arm around her. 'Thanks for the shopping trip, Kav. I know I have to share you with Poppy, but we're friends for life. That OK with you, Poppy?'

'Yes. 'Course.' Though I'm not at all sure what the implications are for Reggie as he is this moment. How did he make his breasts so big?

'I did the make-up,' says Mia, gliding by.

'You're a darling.' Reggie blows her a kiss.

I can see Crabbe and Goyle lurking in the corner, glancing at us, holding bottles of beer.

'Ignore them,' says Reggie. 'I seem to have upset them. Kav, Poppy, dance with me.' So we fling ourselves around on the dance floor, feeling free, and Xavier, Jack, William and Enzo join us.

'Will you dance with me?' Harry's there beside me and I clam up.

'Course she will,' says Kavya.

'Go for it, Harry, boy,' says Reggie.

'Come on,' says Harry. 'Let's dance in the conservatory. More space.' We push through the crowd and I know I should have washed at Kavya's. Harry and I kind of jig around a bit but I keep my distance, worried I smell sweaty.

'Will you come out with me to see a film?' Harry's face is serious and he's looking straight at me. 'Don't know what's on. We could look on my phone and you could choose.'

I can't swallow.

'Have to ask Mum,' I say, my voice husky. 'But I'd like that.'

Then we both stop dancing and lean forward, hands on our legs, laughing. I don't know why it's so funny, but I enjoy feeling so free – and so relaxed.

'Let's go to the kitchen and get something to eat,' he says when the giggles finally stop. 'I've been waiting to ask you out all term, but my parents – you know – the extra tutoring. It's driven me crazy and if I don't get 9s for every exam in May...well...I know it's months away still, but will you go to results morning with me?'

'In August, you mean?'

'Yes. I'd like you to be there.'

'It could be scary,' I say picturing me with low grades and tears in my eyes. Plan A failing.

'Let's go in the garden,' he says when we're both clutching a bit of droopy pizza.'

It's so cold outside that I shiver, and Harry puts his jacket around my shoulders. Just like men do in films when the drippy female lead is cold. I almost tell him to put his jacket back on, but I'm rather enjoying being a drippy female.

Though I know I'm not one.

'All that stuff about your stepfather...is it OK to talk about it?'

'It's OK,' I say, although I'm not sure it is.

'Was that...when I almost kissed you in rehearsals and you collapsed...that's what it was about?'

'S'pose so.' My lips are trembling. I turn my head so Harry doesn't see. 'But I didn't realise at the time...how it affected me. School Shrink is helping me.' I try to take deep breaths.

'That sounds good.'

'And we have a great social worker. She's trying to help Mum stop drinking but that's not working very well.'

'Maybe it'll take time.'

'Yeah, but Mum's much better than she was.'

Harry grins at me. 'Sounds good. And...you'll come to a film – if your Mum is OK with it?'

'She will be...I think.'

'And I promise not to kiss you till you're ready.'

Then we're both laughing again, and he puts his arm round my shoulder.

But maybe I'm ready to be kissed now.

Chapter 52

A new life

Harry and I go out and watch one film before his mother puts pressure on him again.

'I have to stick to her rules,' he says as we walk home from school together with Kavya. 'But in the summer...after the exams...we could do stuff maybe?'

'Hanging out after the exams would be brilliant. But you'll keep coming to running club?'

'When I can. Gotta go. A new tutor for English is coming at four pm so I need to get home. Mum's idea...so that's another subject I'd better get a 9 in.'

Then he's gone, walking fast away from us.

'He's going to get 9s in everything!' Kavya says.

My best Christmas present ever was Carl admitting he did it.

'So you won't need to go to court,' Ellie says. What a relief! She must be the best social worker ever. And now Carl gives Mum money every month from his business, so we can stay in our house and Mum only goes to work occasionally when they are really short staffed and that works well for us all.

Mum asked us what to do about Carl's shed. I wanted to rip it apart. I feel trembly just thinking about it.

'But it could make a really cool den for us,' Zara said, and in the end I agreed with her. So Mum put the boxes of Lego and Meccano in the loft over the Christmas holidays, and she let us decorate the shed how we wanted. Mum gave the white sofa away on our local Freecycle and instead we've got bean bags and a TV. A kind man came and took away all the CCTV and that felt good.

Mum has gone back to being the mum I remember. She goes to Alcoholics Anonymous. At least she goes sometimes. Ellie and Mum get on really well and that helps a lot because it feels as if we've gone back to being a real family.

Mum makes pancakes for breakfast on Saturdays and does normal things like takes Zara to gymnastics, then takes JoJo and Ruben to the swings in the park and I do parkrun with Kavya, Harry and Biscuit.

JoJo started nursery school with Ruben and Mrs. Bernstein still has both of them often to help Mum out. And I'm chief babysitter to Ruben so my Plan A money is building up. Mrs Bernstein tells us again to call her Esther.

'Thank you. You're so kind,' I say, hardly able to say how much it makes me feel safe to have her next door.

We have mock GCSEs in February and Kav and I get a few 6s, some 7s, and two 8s. But Kav gets three 9s! She's amazing. Harry gets only 8s and 9s so he's happy. So is his mum. I feel so good about my marks that work seems to be easier – and even the invisible things in physics make a bit more sense.

Only a bit though.

We work hard all term and Kav and I work all through the Easter holidays, revising most days and running together every now and then. April and May is solid revision – with running and meeting up for watching a film when we know we've worked hard.

Just before the exams in May, Rachel made me a poster on her computer. It says, 'It wasn't my fault.'

'I love it,' I say. 'Especially that it has butterflies and birds on it. Kavya and I are going to make a big effort to save the planet, what with all the climate change and everything. We think the adults should be listening to us young people...'

'Good for you, Poppy. You've done so very well, you know.'

Then I'm crying, gripping the poster. Staring at it.

'Tell me what's going on, Poppy,' says Rachel. She hands me a tissue.

'It was my fault.'

'You've said that before so many times. Can you say why you think that?'

'I kissed him. Carl. On the lips.' I try to breathe deeply so I can keep talking. 'When I was twelve and we were sitting watching the cricket. He pulled me onto his knee, and I went to kiss his cheek but he turned his head...I kissed him right on the lips...all wet...it was my fault...a few weeks later was my birthday. And it happened...I feel...ashamed.'

'It wasn't your fault. He was the adult. You were a child. He had power over you and he misused that power. It was never, ever your fault.'

Get a grip.

Breathe.

'I'm not sure...why...so difficult to tell you that.' I feel a bit stupid.

'It's hard to trust,' she says.

'I'm going to decorate my bedroom over the summer. Take down my old posters and put this one up.'

'Good idea. Keep remembering. It wasn't your fault.'

The exams in May go reasonably well, but I was so sad with Harry's plans.

'My last exam is 6th June,' he says, 'and I'm going to Australia for the rest of the summer. My mum's brother has a sheep farm and I'm going out to help. It's miles from anywhere...sort of looking forward to it. Mum's idea. So I won't be sending postcards or anything. The nearest town is an hour away. I'll be back for results day, though.'

I didn't know what to say. This didn't fit with my fantasy of a few weeks after the exams when I could see Harry whenever I wanted. 'Oh...OK...Hope it's fun,' was all I could manage, and I couldn't look at him. Was he going all the way to Australia just to avoid hanging out with me?

'Nah, it's his demon mother again,' Kavya says when we're drinking hot chocolate in the new shed/den that evening. 'But he's back for results day. I'm dreading it.'

But then a wonderful thing happens. The owners of the café decide to go to Tunisia to see family for a few weeks leaving Reggie's cousin in charge, and Kavya and I get perfect summer jobs, waiting at tables, washing up and generally being helpful. The money is brilliant, and our Plan A money grows. Even better than that, Mum let's Kavya come to the house whenever we want so after our shifts we sometimes watch films in the den with Zara.

So although I didn't get my fantasy few weeks with Harry it was a good summer, and I began to realise that I feel more together. Carl is in my head much less, so I feel less shattered. I'm so glad that the money he gives Mum each month means we can stay in our house. And I feel more at peace with Mum.

It's GCSE results day tomorrow and I haven't heard from Harry all summer. I'm beginning to accept that he doesn't want to be with me. That makes me feel terrible – rejected and not good enough. But at breakfast I get a text.

Harry: Meet me at bike racks tomorrow 8.20 am?

It takes my breath away. I do some deep breathing to calm my pounding heart.

Poppy: OK.
Harry: Ask Kavya too?
Poppy: OK.

He doesn't reply to that, although I want to ask him about Australia. Well, actually I just want to be with him today, but I'm worried I'll seem too needy. So I don't text him again.

The next day Kavya and I wait by the bike racks so we can go into the school hall together to get our results. I've stuffed a whole load of tissues up my sleeve. Just in case my nerd status hasn't led to brilliant results and I'm bawling my eyes out.

For Plan A to work I need to look at my results and cheer.

Zara's away this week at a gymnastic training camp. She's thirteen and a half now. And safe. I find myself looking at her at times, so proud of her, so impressed at the way she lives her life. She's not a nerd like I am. And she still hasn't had a single spot on her face.

I've already told her I'm jealous of her skin and she told me she's jealous of me having a special friend like Kavya. Zara says she's in a group of good friends, but she'd love to have one special person.

'This is nerve-racking,' says Harry as he comes towards us. His face is tanned and he's got a white T-shirt on, denim jeans and fabulous white trainers. Why can't I look cool like that?

People are milling around the corridor, then the hall door opens, and the teachers are sitting beside tables with boxes of results.

Mr Robins has a suit and tie on today and he smiles as he hands me my future. I can hardly bear to look. My hands tremble as I open the envelope.

I've got mostly 7s. And one 6 for maths.

'I've got a 7 for physics,' I say to Mr Robins. 'I can tell my mum that's an A in the old grades. There is a God after all! It's a miracle!'

'Mr McKenzie told me to tell you that he hopes you'll do physics A level, and it has even more invisible stuff. Does that make sense?'

'Yes and no.'

Thoughts rush around inside my head at a million miles an hour. Carl's face leering at me. I try to switch channels in my head.

'You can be an engineer, Poppy.' Mr Robins is serious. It's a bit unnerving.

'I keep changing my mind about what to be.' I'm trying to stay calm. 'Keep wondering if I might be a social worker.'

'I'm so proud of you, Poppy.'

'I'm pretty proud of myself, Sir.' I grin at him and he grins back.

People are all around me, shrieking and laughing, so I join them, leaping up and down with Kavya. She's got mostly 8s and three 9s, just one 7 for English. 'After all that work we did on *The Tempest.* Rats!'

'It's just one 7, Kav. It's still an A in old grades.'

We're hugging and then I see Harry walking towards us, his face sad.

'OK?' I say.

He looks blank.

'Oh, Harry,' I say.

Then he's jumping up and down, flapping the bit of paper. 'All 8s and 9s,' he says. 'Got you there.'

Kavya and I leap around with him, hugging each other. 'My parents will let me do anything from now on,' he says. 'I'm free. Let's go to the café and celebrate. Hot chocolate and muffins on me.'

'I'll just go and see Rachel,' I say.

I have a few minutes with Rachel, standing near the stage at the far end of the hall. She tells me she's proud of me for overcoming so much.

'I'm going to paint my bedroom brilliant white,' I tell her. 'Because I'm aiming at making my life totally brilliant.' I really want to say virgin white, but that raises too many questions. Carl's face crashes through my brain.

There's a queue of people waiting to talk to Rachel, some of them crying, so I go to the café with Kavya and Harry.

'I did well enough to get into Year 12,' Reggie says. He serves us without making any stupid comments and I realise that I've become quite fond of him. I'm even wondering if I can ask him if I can touch his quiff.

But I know that's weird and I'm trying to stop doing weird nerdy things.

My sixteenth birthday is on the 31st August and Mum says I can have a party. But I don't fancy that. People might expect booze and I'm not up for that yet. I can't cope with the smell of it on people's breath. Anyway, I want to paint my room first.

'I'll help you,' Kavya says at running club.

'I really want to do it on my own,' I say. 'But let's meet to run most days.'

I must cleanse my room from all the befores. I still struggle to sleep, and sometimes I get nightmares, Carl chasing me, and I wake, sweaty and trembling. So I need my room to be mine.

My safe space.

I shut everyone out, including Biscuit, and rip off all my old tatty posters. I tear them into tiny pieces and put them in the recycling.

'That looked a good thing to do,' says Mum. She's peeling carrots for her special carrot and bean soup because she's decided we should go vegetarian.

Zara and I think that's great. Biscuit doesn't so we still feed her meat out of a tin.

'Don't put in too much chilli, though, Mum,' I say.

'I won't use any chilli.' she says. 'I know you and Zara don't like it.'

I hug her. 'I love you, Mum. And I love my little sister,' I say as Zara comes into the kitchen.

'Maybe you'll make your room so sensational that you won't want to leave home,' Zara says. 'I'm sure London has a great uni you could go to.'

'I might do exactly that,' I say and Zara claps. Although I might need to leave home to move on.

'I've got something upstairs for you,' Zara says and clatters up to her room.

'I made you a picture for your wall,' she says, coming back into the kitchen clutching some paper. 'But...if you don't like it you don't need to put it up...I just wondered...I got a 9 for my 'Peace After the Tempest' picture.' She turns the painting around. It's a rainbow against a dark sky.

'Wow! Zara. I love it. Thanks!' We hug and I feel so happy in her arms that I even find the words 'thank you God' going through my head.

I take the pots of white paint, brushes and the roller up to my room. I stand in the middle of my bedroom and realise that I have a pretty good life now. And I can make it even better – family and friends. I can make a new start. And I'll cope with the Carl-memories that suddenly come into my head.

I put the Monet poppy picture in my wardrobe. I think I won't hang it up again. That way I can't disappear into it. Can't keep remembering.

I'll keep my photos of Gran and Grandpa where I can see them from my bed. But I'm putting them on a cork board instead of covering the mirror. It's OK to let myself look at my reflection sometimes. I think Rachel has helped me to like myself a bit more.

It's so freeing to tell the truth. I feel lighter – but a bit of an idiot that I didn't tell someone sooner.

I sort under the bed. I give Mum back her voice recorder and she cries when I tell her why I took it.

'It's OK, Mum.' I hug her. 'It's all over now. We can have a new start.'

I'll keep my secret diary with all my half-baked poems. The world isn't ready for them. I'm less sure about keeping the craft knife. I haven't cut my arms for weeks now and hope I won't ever again. But I'll keep the knife. I might need it when I'm an engineer, so I put it in a box at the bottom of my drawer of running things. If I stop cutting maybe I could wear pretty strappy tops and short sleeved running T-shirts like Kavya does and that would make me feel good.

I get a text from Harry.

Harry: Can't wait to see you. Come to swings and hang out?

I don't reply immediately because I sort of want to be with him. But I so much want to do my room...I remember that first day he walked into the classroom and sat beside me. His cute lopsided smile and those green eyes. My body longs to be beside him. I most desperately want to write a poem. But not right now.

Poppy: Painting my room.
Harry: Can I help?

You have helped me, Harry! I'm full of hope that I can get myself back together, piece by piece – that one day I'll feel whole again.

Poppy: No.

Wish I'd said yes.

Harry: Hot choc @ caf @5?
Poppy: Oh, OK then.

Author note

Looking after yourself

You might have found some parts of this book hard to read. Can you do some kind of self-care? Maybe chat with a friend or watch a film. Remember, if you are worried about anything, you can ring

Childline 24/7 on 0800 11 11.

A note from the author

I started writing *Poppy in pieces* after listening to author and Children's Laureate Malorie Blackman in a workshop. She said, 'Write about what you feel passionately about.' I feel passionate about the amount of abuse that goes on in the world. One statistic from the UK is that 1 in 20 children are sexually abused – but some researchers say it's much, MUCH higher than that.

If you include other kinds of abuse – neglect, physical, emotional, spiritual abuse or seeing domestic violence – or experiencing bullying at school – the number of children affected by abuse is horrifying. Some say it affects one in four of us. Some say it's much more than that.

Poppy in pieces isn't an autobiography. I was much younger when I was sexually abused, but Poppy's emotions are like mine – and those of friends who are survivors of abuse. I love my survivor friends who I've met through Survivors Voices. The effects of childhood abuse can last into adulthood, and we support each other as we heal.

Childhood is hell for some children, and we could make it better for them if we all talked more about abuse – telling the truth about this horror in our world. I hope this book will give some hope to those children and young people who are struggling with guilt, shame, and the other devastating effects of any kind of abuse.

Some things to talk about with your friends

1. Some people might think that Harry's 'almost kiss' (chapter 22) was him just making a joke, but others might believe it was sexual harassment. What do you think? How would you decide?
2. Some might think that Miss Singh's reaction to the 'almost kiss' wasn't good enough. What do you think?
3. Do you think Poppy could have told someone about Carl earlier? What might have helped her to do that?
4. Some might think that by telling Kavya, Poppy put too much pressure on her best friend. Or was it a good thing to tell her friend?
5. If you were Poppy, what might you have done that was different?

Getting help

If you have faced any kind of bullying or abuse, **Childline** is open 24 hours a day, 7 days a week. They say 'We're here for all young people.

0800 1111, calls are free in the UK.

You can talk to Childline confidentially about any worry or problem you have, or go online https://www.childline.org.uk/

and search our message boards to get feedback from other young people.'

Survivors Voices is a community of adult survivors of any kind of abuse. We run peer support and creative writing groups, and we get involved in research and activism – anything that makes survivors' lives better. The website has information about abuse and other resources.

https://survivorsvoices.org

The author royalties from this book will be split evenly between NSPCC/Childline and Survivors Voices. In buying this book you support these two groups. Thank you.

Further reading

There are quite a few young adult books about abuse. These three are some of the best.

The girl in the broken mirror by Savita Kalhan. A gripping story of an Asian girl who is raped, and how she starts to recover.

A beautifully written book.

No virgin by Anne Cassidy, and

No shame by Anne Cassidy. Award winning author, Anne, captures the emotions of survivors very well in these two brilliant books.

Acknowledgements

Many people have helped me as I've written this book. Thank you so much all those in Penny Joelson's writing for children workshop at City Lit – and the spin-off groups that arose from that workshop. Thanks especially to award winning Young Adult author, Penny Joelson for her help with the text, and to children's author, Jo Franklin for help at the early stages of planning.

Thank you Ruth Grant for so graciously doing the copy editing, and thanks to David, for all that proof-reading and loving support. I couldn't have coped without you.

Thanks as well to my Survivors Voices friends for their comments on the text and for support as I tried to pull the book together. And finally, thank you Malorie Blackman, for the idea to write about what I feel passionate about.

You can contact Sue via the Survivors Voices Press
writing@survivorsvoices.org

About the author

Sue lives in South London with her husband and Westie. She used to be a primary school teacher but then went into research to explore how children could learn maths more effectively. She has lectured in maths education in the UK and internationally. She has published a range of books, from academic books for teachers to short stories for children. Some of Sue's books are listed at the start of this novel.

Sue has run 10 marathons and 3 ultras, and she likes running along the Thames Path looking for kingfishers and egrets. She also likes curling up on the sofa to read, especially children's literature. Since she was a child Sue has been a birdwatcher and she especially likes doing that in Scotland. She also likes growing and searching out wildflowers, and eating chocolate. She has two children and eight grandchildren.

About the designer

Artist Catherine E. Holbrook is a creative spirit based in the heart of Yorkshire where she plays piano, writes her own music and works on various creative community and education projects both online and in-person. Her work possesses a rare authenticity that touches the hearts and souls of those who encounter it.

You can find out more about Catherine's work by visiting her website: www.catherineholbrook.co.uk

Other projects that might be of particular interest to readers and Survivors are:

Catherine's blog **'An Artist's Response . . .'** https://anartistsresponse.wordpress.com/ which includes her creative ponderings and responses to life, faith, the world and her own journey as a Survivor.

Catherine's music for solo piano **Barefoot Piano Prayers** https://barefootpianoprayers.bandcamp.com/

About Survivors Voices Press

Survivors Voices Press (SVP) is a survivor-led independent publisher that amplifies the voice and experience of survivors, promoting understanding of trauma and ally-ship with survivors of abuse.

Our mission is to provide a trauma-informed platform for survivors' work, filling the gap in mainstream publishing and challenging the stigma associated with accounts of abuse. SVP is a project of Survivors Voices, a survivor-led organisation that turns the pain of abuse into the power to improve responses to trauma. We work with survivors of all types of abuse and are a non-profit organisation.

We run peer support groups, undertake research, promote co-production and create change through education, activism and publications. We work anywhere to engage and amplify the voice of survivors. If you are a survivor who needs support or wants to be heard, a practitioner who wants to listen, or an ally who wants to support us, we want to hear from you.

connect@survivorsvoices.org
www.survivorsvoices.org
X: @voiceofsurvivor
Facebook: survivorsvoicesuk

Instagram: survivors_voices

You are not alone

If the issues in this book have affected you or someone you know, you can find out about the help we offer and many other support organisations on our support page

https://survivorsvoices.org/support/

www.ingramcontent.com/pod-product-compliance
Ingram Content Group UK Ltd.
Pitfield, Milton Keynes, MK11 3LW, UK
UKHW020203040125
453072UK00002B/70